## Praise for the Timber Creek K-9 Mysteries:

"Mizushima gives us wonderfully drawn characters along with a cracking good plot and realistic law enforcement details . . . Highly recommended."

—Deborah Crombie, *NYT* bestselling author of *A Killing of Innocents*

"Tense and satisfying."

—J.A. Jance, New York Times bestselling author of the J. P. Beaumont series

"Thrilling . . . Will leave you wanting more."

—Amy Rivers, award-winning author of *Complicit* and *All the Broken People*

"It is a rare pleasure to discover a book in which the author's skill with her craft is so fluently meshed with her deep knowledge of the story's subject and terrain."

—Baron R. Birtcher, award-winning author of *Fistful of Rain*

"I've fallen in love with Margaret Mizushima's Timber Creek K-9 mystery series . . . Nobody weaves a tale like Mizushima."

—Saralyn Richard, award-winning author of *A Murder of Principal*

"Memorable characters, rugged setting, and a page-turning mystery. Brilliant!"

—Bruce Robert Coffin, award-winning author of the Detective Byron Mysteries

"Mizushima has a gift when it comes to crafting immersive settings."

—*Associated Press*

"It's impossible not to fall in love with Robo."

—*Publishers Weekly,* starred review

"The tension and drama of this series installment will satisfy fans of K-9 partners and solid police procedurals."

—*Library Journal,* starred review

"Will tug the heartstrings of every dog lover."

—*Booklist,* starred review

## ALSO AVAILABLE BY MARGARET MIZUSHIMA

## The Timber Creek K-9 Mysteries

# GATHERING MIST

## A Timber Creek K-9 Mystery

*Margaret Mizushima*

CROOKED
LANE

NEW YORK

Published in the United States by Crooked Lane Books, an imprint of The Quick Brown Fox & Company LLC.

Crooked Lane Books and its logo are trademarks of The Quick Brown Fox & Company LLC.

Library of Congress Catalog-in-Publication data available upon request.

ISBN (hardcover): 978-1-63910-894-7
ISBN (ebook): 978-1-63910-895-4

Cover design by Melanie Sun

Printed in the United States.

www.crookedlanebooks.com

Crooked Lane Books
34 West 27th St., 10th Floor
New York, NY 10001

First Edition: October 2024

10 9 8 7 6 5 4 3 2 1

For K-9 handlers and their dogs
in all fields of service

# ONE

Weather could make or break a search and rescue mission, and the wind would play havoc with the scent trail today.

Deputy Mattie Wray stood at the back of her K-9 unit beside her patrol partner Robo, a large German shepherd who weighed just short of a hundred pounds. Brilliant sunlight glistened off his glossy black coat while he lifted his nose and sniffed the air as if tasting it. Wind ruffled his fur.

Their mission today: find a missing child by air scenting. Mattie knew the child was somewhere in this vicinity but she didn't know exactly where, and at this point they didn't have a scent trail on the ground for Robo to find. Her dog's ground tracking skills were strong, but lately he'd been using air scent to find objects and people more often, so Mattie felt sure he would be up for this new challenge.

"Take a break," Mattie told Robo quietly, sending him off to her Explorer's tire. Nothing halted the momentum of a search mission faster than a potty stop. "Okay, let's put on your harness."

She removed his blue nylon tracking harness from the storage compartment in the back of her unit and lowered it toward Robo. He stepped up and lifted his head for her to slip it over his ears before she buckled it into place under his chest. As a team, they associated this harness with a search for a human, while his nylon collar signaled a drug or evidence search. Overlap of these skills always existed during missions, but for the most part, Robo had learned to anticipate the major emphasis for his work based on his equipment.

Mattie zipped up her Carhartt coat to protect her from the gale's icy chill. A cold front was driving in from the northwest and dipping down into southern Colorado, threatening snow for Timber Creek County tonight. She needed to hurry and get started.

Since she would ask Robo to air scent today, it was important for her to know from which direction the air flowed at all times. She snipped off three feet of orange flagging tape and tied it to her left wrist. When she raised her arm, the tape fluttered out toward the southeast in a horizontal position and snapped in the wind. She strapped on her duty belt and turned back to her dog, who eagerly awaited instruction as he watched her with uplifted eyes and danced on his front paws.

"You're a good boy, aren't you?" Mattie took out his bowl and splashed fresh water into it from the jug she always carried for him. This would moisten the membranes in his mouth and indirectly his sinuses, an important step to enhance his ability to take in scent.

While he drank, she shrugged into a backpack that contained her own equipment including extra water and food for both of them, a Mylar space blanket that could retain up to ninety percent of a person's body heat, heat packs for feet and hands, a first aid kit, a GPS unit, a compass, and a map of the wilderness area around Timber Creek.

Finally, she closed the hatch of her Explorer and began the high-pitched chatter Robo loved, meant to increase his prey drive. "Do you want to find someone? Yeah? Let's go! Let's go find someone."

Robo pranced in heel position beside her, looking up at Mattie with intelligent, adoring eyes as the wind buffeted his fur. She gave him the eye contact he wanted and leaned over to ruffle his fur, keeping up the chatter that made him so excited. The mission they were about to embark on held many new challenges for both Robo and her, but she felt confident they were ready as a team and could accomplish the job together.

At last she withdrew a plastic bag from her pocket, opened it and lowered it for Robo to whiff. The bag contained a scent article: a pink sock that she'd taken from the missing child's laundry basket earlier. The sole of the sock, darkened from being worn around the house without shoes, attested to the fact that it had not been laundered and would be laden with the child's scent.

Robo wagged his tail vigorously as he took in the smell. Mattie stroked the black fur on top of his head, giving him one last pat before she raised her arm to give him the command he'd been waiting for.

"Search!" she said, flinging her arm out to encompass the area, planning to establish a large grid pattern. Robo lowered his nose to the ground and busily tried to find the track, which didn't surprise her. Typically she directed him toward the ground at the beginning of a search to find a scent track . . . but today she knew there wouldn't be one here.

She observed him closely, letting him think it through and watching to see if he'd work out the problem by himself. She would intervene if he started to look frustrated, but she believed it important to let a dog in training learn to think through problems as much as possible. That way, when they were separated— and in the high country she often sent Robo into areas where the terrain was too treacherous for a human to follow—he would still be able to think through a problem without her directing his every move.

She continued to watch while he sniffed furiously at the ground in front of him for about a minute. When he raised his head and sampled the wind, she rejoiced inside. It was exactly what she wanted him to do.

"Good boy!" She waved toward the expanse in front of them again as she turned to walk toward her left. "Let's find someone out here."

Robo surged ahead of her with his head up, facing into the wind. Rocky ground, covered with dormant buffalo grass, surrounded them and stretched out for about a mile and a half as it ran uphill toward the foothills north of Timber Creek. Boulders and stones littered the area. Patches of rabbit brush and scrub oak grew on the hillside along with scattered groves of spruce and limber pine. A rocky outcropping lined the area to the northwest a little over a mile away.

Mattie jogged behind her dog, letting him range out in front. After he'd traveled about a hundred yards, she called him back toward her as she shifted direction and started running toward the right. She wanted to establish boundaries for them to search, working the area back and forth until Robo either found human scent or they determined no scent was present, a process referred to as clearing the area.

Robo already knew how to quarter an area for scent, characterized by sweeping back and forth with his nose either to the ground or in the air in a grid-like pattern. But today Mattie wanted to set the width of the grid, as if the territory had been assigned to them. When he'd crossed about three hundred yards, she was close behind him, dodging stones and clumps of grass as she ran.

When they hit the edge of her imaginary boundary, she reversed directions again, moving back to the left but angling ever forward into the wind. Robo immediately went with her, loping out in front. "Good boy!" she shouted, marveling at what a quick study her dog was, even though that's how he'd always been when picking up new skills.

She decided not to cue him again, wanting to see if Robo stuck loosely to the grid she'd established. She also wanted to allow him the freedom to follow his nose once he caught the child's scent in the air.

Sergeant Jim Madsen said that Robo was the best dog he'd ever trained. And while Robo was the only dog that Mattie had ever partnered with, she knew the words of the more experienced handler and trainer had to be true. Robo never failed to amaze her.

Mattie and Robo kept up the back-and-forth pattern, working the grid while moving uphill toward the rocky horizon. After they'd moved about a half mile upslope, Robo stopped short and raised his head as high as he could, sniffing the air with his lips slightly parted. He stared toward the rock formations to the northwest, his ears pricked forward and his chin raised.

Mattie recognized her dog's signal for an alert. He'd caught the child's scent on the wind. She did a quick wind check with the tape on her arm—still coming directly from the northwest. She glanced around and made a mental note of her surroundings so she could record the details of terrain, direction, and distance in her training journal once they found their subject. She noticed they were in an area where the grasses grew taller as they approached the creek that ran through the dry land.

"You smell her, don't you? Good boy. Let's go find her."

Robo ran directly toward the creek bed, his nose still in the air but occasionally dipping toward the grass. Mattie sprinted behind, working hard to observe every ear prick, every nose dip as Robo homed in on the scent. It was her job to learn how to read Robo's body language, possibly a dog handler's most important skill. It was hard to always know what your dog was telling you during the heat of a mission, and it required a lot of practice.

Robo reached the creek and lowered his nose to sniff the grasses that grew alongside the edge. He moved back and forth against the ice that had formed along the stream, its shallow water moving slowly down the center of the rocky bed. Again, Mattie made note that Robo was searching the ground thoroughly here, and she knew it was because the scent had gathered along the moist vegetation that grew on the creek's bank.

A handler needed to understand the behavior of scent, another crucial skill. Humans shed skin rafts all the time. These cells move through the air away from a person, blowing on the wind and even flowing on the water. Robo proved to her that this was the case now as he moved into the water and nipped at it, tasting the scent that had been captured there.

"Good boy!" She encouraged him to work the scent as she picked her way across the creek, jumping from stone to stone.

Robo didn't care about the water. He crossed right through it before lowering his nose to the ground to work the odors caught in the grass on the other side of the stream. Mattie could tell he was trying to find a track to follow, but again she knew there wouldn't be one. She paused to see if he could come to that conclusion by himself.

It took longer this time for him to give up, probably because the scent was so strong in the damp grass. *He just knows there must be a track here*, she thought. She prepared to redirect him but stopped short when he raised his head, faced the wind, and sniffed. He stared hard into the distance, every line in his body telling her he'd found scent in the air again. He took off in that direction.

"Good boy! You're so smart! Let's go. Let's go find her!"

Mattie knew he'd recaptured the child's scent, and it was important to let Robo work through the find by himself. He shifted back and forth, rushing uphill as he narrowed the grid on each pass.

He was working the scent cone, something Robo was especially good at. As long as their missing child stayed still, her skin rafts would spread in the wind in a cone-shaped pattern with her at the tip. Mattie had watched bird dogs exhibit this same skill when they hunted pheasant, narrowing down on the bird's scent until they came to a standstill and assumed a point position—stretched out from nose to tail, one foreleg raised, unblinking eyes focused on the bird.

She slowed and then stopped and waited so that Robo would find the child by himself. He dashed forward and disappeared into the rocky outcropping they'd been moving toward since leaving their vehicle. Mattie smiled as she heard Robo's excited bark and the child's high-pitched greeting. She could imagine the hugs Robo would be receiving right now, something more rewarding to him than the toy she would give him at the end of their training mission.

Robo reappeared at the edge of the outcropping, running Mattie's way at full tilt. She knelt and reached for him as he darted up to her, his eyes gleaming with excitement. "Did you find her? Did you find Sophie? Show me!"

He whirled and headed back among the rocks, this time with Mattie close behind. Sophie and Angela, her fiancé Cole Walker's two kids, stood side by side with blankets wrapped around them against the cold. Nine-year-old Sophie danced and jumped with Robo, throwing her blanket aside in favor of hugging him whenever she could get him to hold still long enough.

Sixteen-year-old Angela picked up Sophie's blanket and smiled down affectionately at the two youngsters before turning her smile toward Mattie. "That didn't take long."

"It went really well," Mattie said. "Thanks so much for taking the time to help." She'd asked Angela to drive Sophie to a drop-off point and stay with her so the young girl wouldn't be alone. Mattie no longer took her loved ones' safety for granted. Their quiet little town now seemed dangerous since a string of homicides had hit their mountain community.

"It was fun," Angie said. "But he didn't find the other sock, did he?"

"You're right, he didn't. Where did you plant it?"

Angie pointed off to the left. "Down there about a hundred yards under those bushes."

Mattie caught a glimpse of pink at the base of a scrub oak off to the left. She figured that by the time they reached this level upslope, Robo had been locked onto Sophie's scent cone and had made a beeline toward her where the scent was strongest. Also, Sophie had been sitting directly upwind of Robo the whole time, a strong factor that would lure Robo right to her rather than searching out clothing articles outside of her scent path.

"I guess the results are mixed," Mattie told Angie. "He found Sophie but skipped over finding the clue. Next time we'll use a bigger search area and plant the clue farther away from our search subject. Would you be up for that?"

"Sure. I could drive to a place to plant the clue and then go farther up the road to plant Sophie."

"Or maybe we'll use Hannah or Riley as a subject so Robo isn't always searching for the same person," Mattie said, referring to two of Angie's friends.

"They'd love it." Angie pointed at another outcropping of rocks off to the right. "I hid there where I could watch Robo work and still keep an eye on Sophie. It looked like he was doing a great job."

"Yep. And he matched the scent article by going to Sophie instead of you. He's so smart." The two of them shared a smile.

Robo and Sophie came running up to Mattie, both of them still jumping with pleasure. Mattie leaned down to embrace them together despite them almost knocking her down. "Whoa, you two." She laughed as she hugged them and they settled into her arms. "You guys did a great job."

"I was sure he could find me. He's a super-duper search dog!" Sophie separated from the hug so she could hop on one foot while she praised and petted Robo.

"You did a great job at sitting still, Sophie." Maybe being still for that length of time resulted in this current outburst of energy. "Some other time we'll challenge him by having you move from one place to another. We'll have to find a new area to go to, though, because knowing Robo he'll remember you were here and come search it first."

Sophie giggled.

"Let's go home and warm up with a cup of hot chocolate. Mrs. Gibbs said she'd make some for us." Mrs. Gibbs was Cole's resident housekeeper who also acted as a mother figure for the girls since his wife left them all a year ago last spring.

Sophie piped up. "Can I ride with you and Robo, Mattie?"

"Sure. Hop in Angie's car while I go get that other sock. Then she can take us back to the Explorer. It's too cold to walk that far." She turned toward Angie's used Corolla parked about fifty yards away beside a dirt track that led to this area from Lookout Mountain, a hill north of Timber Creek.

Once they arrived at the Walker home, Mattie parked under a leafless cottonwood that shaded the front yard in the summer. The wind whipped its bare branches and battered the front end of her vehicle. Her cell phone rang in her pocket and she fished it out to check the caller ID at the same time that Sophie opened the passenger side door. A cold blast of air whooshed in as Mattie's phone's screen told her that Sergeant Jim Madsen was calling.

"I need to answer the phone, Sophie, but I'll follow in just a few minutes. Go ahead and run inside."

The wind slammed the door shut and then Sophie turned to skip up the sidewalk toward the porch in front of Cole's two-story log home. Angie drove past to park inside the garage on the other side of the house.

Eager to tell Madsen about Robo's training mission that morning, Mattie answered the call. "Hi, Sarge."

"I hope you can fly to Seattle with me tonight," Madsen said, not wasting any time on chitchat. "We need Robo's nose on a search mission out there. We'll leave Denver on a redeye at twenty-three hundred hours. I've already got approval for three dogs to go with us."

Questions filled her mind. *What? Why? Eleven o'clock?* That barely gave her enough time to pack and make it to Denver in time to check in at the airport. "What's going on?"

"You ever heard of Chrystal Winter?"

"The actress?" Mattie knew her all right; the star was one of her favorites. She usually appeared in popular psychological thrillers.

"Yeah, that's the one. Her nine-year-old son wandered away from a movie set in the middle of a forest on the Olympic Peninsula and no one can find him. We need a couple dogs that can air scent large wilderness areas too rough for humans to search. And

I mean rough. This is the forest primeval, Mattie. Nothing like we've got out here in Colorado."

Mattie's gut clenched. Nine years old—Sophie's age. "Um . . . you know my wedding is about a week from now."

"Yup. We'll have either found the kid or cleared the area well before then."

A few months ago, Sarge had told her about joining a regional on-call team for search and rescue missions. They'd talked briefly about putting Mattie and Robo on call as well, although she was unaware that any formal steps had been taken. She'd been training Robo steadily, but they weren't certified for area search yet. Besides, her first duty lay with the Timber Creek County Sheriff's Department. "I'll have to talk it over with Sheriff McCoy."

"Already done. He says you're good to go."

Mattie would check in with McCoy before leaving anyway. The time off she'd scheduled for her last-minute wedding preparations and short honeymoon would begin in a few days, but her mind churned with everything she needed to accomplish before then.

"I'm not sure Robo is ready for that big a task. Results of our training today were mixed." She summarized their training mission briefly.

"He accomplished the big goal. And he's got the best nose in the business when it comes to tracking and air scenting."

"That's true." Mattie still hesitated, but one thought made all the difference . . . the boy was only nine years old. She couldn't refuse. And she hoped Cole would understand and feel the same way about her leaving him to handle the final wedding details. "Okay. I'm on board. Is there anything else I need to know before I leave?"

"Pack your unloaded service weapon in a separate case. I've made arrangements for us to clear them through TSA. You never know if we'll need to be armed or not." He paused for a second. "Oh yeah, and make sure you've got good rain gear."

# TWO

Gusts of frigid wind blasted against the northwest side of the shed while Cole stood behind a cow in a cattle chute. His arm was shoulder deep inside the black Angus mama, checking for pregnancy. The calf felt to be well on its way for a March delivery on his dad's ranch.

"This one's pregnant," Cole told his dad. At the same moment the cow pulled her tail from where he'd tucked it and flicked a manure-laden switch at its end against his cheek. *Yuck. This is dirty work. Give me a horse to work on any day,* he thought.

He withdrew his arm and gave the cow a vaccination to protect her and her calf from upper respiratory disease followed by a combination vitamin and dewormer. "Okay, move her out."

"Cherry," Cole's dad shouted, "bring her in." Samuel Walker turned on the hydraulics to the chute, filling the air with a loud hum. The gates at the front and back clanked open, and while the cow that was inside moved out, a small red border collie named Cherry ducked beneath the fencing in the alleyway. When Cherry nipped at the heels of the next cow, she snorted but stepped into the chute where Samuel captured her neatly. He used levers to catch her head and then squeeze the sides so that she stood still to be worked on without anyone getting hurt, including the cow. It was a slick operation; Cole and Samuel had been working together this way every year since Cole graduated from vet school and came back to establish his practice in Timber Creek.

They happened to have scheduled a horrible day to work cows this time, Cole thought as he noticed his dad's bright red cheeks in front of his cap's earflaps. "You want to take a break and go inside to warm up after this one?" Cole asked him.

"Nah, we're almost done. We only have about twenty head to go."

Samuel Walker was a rangy man, once built like a fullback who could lift one-hundred-pound bales all day in the field with ease. Now, since he'd arrived at the far side of sixty, his muscles had become knotted and stringy, his fingers bent from rope injuries, and his joints swollen with arthritis. Despite Samuel's reddened face being spattered with muck, his thick, graying mustache remained perfectly groomed, the ends waxed and twisted to a point. Minus the mustache, Cole supposed he would look exactly like his dad someday.

Cole's arm outside his coverall was shielded only with a long plastic sleeve, so he felt completely chilled by the time they finished. Samuel squinted at him, narrowing his eyes against the wind. "Okay, let's clean up and go inside. Your mom's got some cake and a pot of hot coffee waiting for us."

Cole admired his dad and they always got along great. Now . . . his relationship with his mother? That was a challenge.

Cole didn't have any other appointments scheduled, and the weather had turned nasty, so he would have rather taken this opportunity to drive straight home to see Mattie and the kids. She and his daughters had the day off, and because of everyone's busy schedules, moments to grab family time were few and far between. But he didn't want to disappoint his dad, who still lectured him about spending more time with his mother.

"I need to beat this storm home, but it'll be good to see Mom. And it's hard to pass up her cake."

"It surely is." Samuel grinned, making Cole happy that he'd said the right thing. "Make sure you tell her that."

"Yes, Dad."

"I'll move these cows back into their pen while you clean up." Samuel whistled to Cherry as he turned away and headed toward the far gate. "C'mon, Cherry. Bring 'em up."

Cherry darted off to circle the cows. She would fetch them and push them through the gate by herself while Samuel held it open. Cole loved to watch the little dog work, but he didn't linger in the cold today. He hustled toward the barn where he could find running water and shelter.

While he hosed off the bulk of the filth on his coveralls, Cole pondered his parents' marriage. It wasn't the first time he'd wondered about it, but since he'd be saying vows again in seven days, it wouldn't hurt to analyze a marriage that had lasted over forty years.

When he'd become old enough to notice, the thing that stood out most in his parents' relationship was how his mother bossed, complained about, and criticized his dad. His dad's typical response was to tease, cajole, or gaze at her fondly and give her a compliment, which often shut down her . . . Cole guessed he'd have to call it meanness, though he'd never say that to her face.

His father's example in the home had been to always treat his wife with respect. He displayed zero tolerance for criticism from his kids, especially any directed at their mother. Both parents had been strict, but his father had shown his love in many ways, while his mother seemed to withhold hers.

Thanks to his dad's example, Cole had grown up wanting to be just like him. But it was only after his ex-wife left him that Cole realized maybe he needed lessons in how to show his love and communicate better. So he'd turned to family counseling and hoped he'd learned a few things on how to build and keep relationships.

During his teen years, Cole had developed a thick skin, but his kid sister Jessie had taken things more to heart. As adults, he avoided his mother while Jessie, after years of therapy, had come to a sort of peace with it. Whenever Jessie took time off from her law practice in Denver to come home, she seemed to enjoy visiting Cole and the kids. But she typically stayed with their parents and made sure she spent time with their mother in particular.

By the time he turned off the spigot and laid down the hose, Cole had to grit his teeth to keep them from chattering. He stripped off his dirty coveralls that had kept his jeans clean and then slipped on a clean shirt. He took a few extra minutes to go to the back of the mobile vet unit in the bed of his pickup truck and gave his hands a good washing with soap and warm water. Only then did he shrug into a warm coat that he'd left in his truck.

His dad and Cherry returned from the pens and beat it over to the truck. Samuel climbed into the passenger side and Cherry settled on the floor at his feet while Cole took the driver's seat. Cherry put her head on Samuel's knee and used her border collie stare to gaze up at him fondly. He, in turn, placed his hand on top of her head, a position Cole had seen them assume whenever Samuel sat down to rest.

Cole smiled as he turned on his truck's engine. He supposed he'd come by his love for dogs honestly. He noticed that Cherry's fur was still spotted with cow manure and so was his dad's face. "You two are a mess," he said.

Samuel stroked the fur between Cherry's ears and she wiggled closer to his legs, neither of them deterred by their sorry state. "We'll clean up when we get home," Samuel murmured, looking down at his dog.

"Mom's not gonna like it."

"Your mother understands."

Cole wondered if that would be true as he drove them the quarter mile to the house, a sprawling single-level building with white stucco walls. Its main rooms were built using adobe at least a century ago with wings for bedrooms and bathrooms that had been added during modern times. Cole loved the old place, surrounded by cottonwood trees that kept the rooms cool in the summer and warm in winter.

He parked outside the door that led into a mudroom with an ancient linoleum floor—brown and ugly but serviceable for a rancher's needs. As they entered, he noticed that fresh clothing had already been laid out for his dad. Cherry scooted into the room and sought out a dog bed in the corner while Samuel started stripping off his clothing so he could take a shower. "You'll get yours next," he told the little dog.

"I'll go find Mom," Cole said as he made his way through to the utility room that lay beyond.

The spray hissed as Samuel turned on the water in the mudroom's shower. "She's probably in the kitchen."

His dad would be a while, especially if he planned to bathe Cherry too. Cole continued through a modernized utility room with a large, heavy-duty washer and dryer on a gray tile floor. An oversized sink used for soaking extra-dirty items along with cabinets lined one wall where Cole stored veterinary supplies for his dad to do his own doctoring when possible.

Despite working outside on the ranch almost every day, his mother kept the house spotless. She seemed to be tireless when it came to working, cooking, and cleaning. Or maybe she was a perfectionist.

His mother stood with her back to him at the kitchen sink, where she was scrubbing a pan. The delicious scent of roasting meat and freshly baked cake greeted him. He spoke to her as he crossed the kitchen to place a light kiss on her cheek. "Hi, Mom. How are you?"

Nora Walker turned an unsmiling face his way, meeting his eyes and giving her typical reply. "Oh . . . I guess I'll make it another day or two. And yourself?"

"Doing good, Mom, doing good. A little chilled from the wind. Dad said you made coffee and cake. I can't stay long, but I wouldn't want to pass up a bite of your cake."

His mother was an attractive woman with dark brown hair streaked with gray, worn long and held to the side in a thick ponytail. A pinched and downturned mouth was the only thing that might mar her beauty. Her skin still appeared tan from hours in the sunshine last summer and fall. She withdrew her browned and callused hands from the dishwater and dried them on a white dish towel.

"Well, at least you're willing to come in to sample my cooking," she said, still looking him in the eye.

Cole realized he'd put his foot in it. "I would've come in to say hi anyway," he hurried to say. "Cake and coffee are an extra perk."

"Um-hmm." Nora gave him a skeptical look before turning away to pick up a coffee mug with a bright yellow daisy on it. "You still drink yours black?"

"I do." As she handed him the coffee mug, Cole eyed the yellow cake sitting on the cabinet. Looked like one of his favorites. "Is that lemon?"

She turned to cut him a hefty slice. "Yes. I know you like your lemon cake."

Her thoughtfulness touched him. "I surely do. Thanks, Mom."

She set his plate down on an antique oak table that sat in the kitchen's dining nook. It had belonged to Cole's grandmother, and his mother had inherited it when he was a child. After setting his coffee down beside his plate, he took a seat on one of the matching oak chairs. He sipped the aromatic dark brew while he waited for his mother to join him.

Nora busied herself with the cake, cutting two more slices and putting them on plates. After setting them on the table, she turned and noticed that he hadn't tasted his cake yet. "Go ahead and eat."

"I'll wait for you."

She shrugged. If his politeness made an impression on her, she didn't show it. "Suit yourself."

He continued to wait while she poured herself a cup and laced it with cream from a small china pitcher. As she took a seat across the table from him, she used a silver spoon to stir it, clinking the sides of the cup. His mother had always liked nice things.

He took a bite of the cake and its lemony sweetness melted in his mouth. "Mmm . . . wow, Mom. This is delicious," he managed to say around the burst of flavor on his tongue.

"I thought you'd like it. It's one of Dad's favorites too."

That pretty much ended Cole's repertoire of chitchat, so he focused on the cake, hoping his mother would bring up a topic for them to discuss. He tried to hear if his dad had finished in the shower, but the spray still seemed to be going. He was probably bathing Cherry.

Nora sipped from her mug, eyeing Cole over the top. "So you still plan to do this thing?"

*This thing? What thing?* "Eat this cake? Yes, I plan to finish it and maybe have seconds."

"You know what I mean."

With a frown to show his puzzlement, Cole paused, his fork raised halfway to his mouth. "What thing, Mom?"

"Oh for Pete's sake." His mother gave him a disapproving look. "Get married next weekend. It's not too late to call it off."

Cole felt blindsided. He placed his cake-laden fork down carefully on his plate. "Of course I'm getting married next weekend. Mattie and I are excited about the wedding, and I can't wait to have her join our family." He wanted to add "whether you like it or not," but he bit his tongue.

"You just got divorced from that other one. Why would you want to jump right into another marriage that will probably head south?"

Now that comment hurt his feelings. Why would she assume he would end up with another failed marriage? He felt himself getting angry, his go-to emotion during a confrontation. But his months of counseling since his divorce had taught him to pause and try to understand the other person's point of view before going off half-cocked.

"It's been a year and a half since Olivia and I divorced," he said quietly as he leaned back in his chair and took a breath.

"I read an article in one of my magazines that said men shouldn't even date until after a year. You've no business getting married so fast. Didn't you learn anything about marrying someone you don't know all that well the first time around?"

Cole worked hard to control his temper. "Olivia and I knew each other well enough when we married. Things changed the year before she left."

"Not as far as I could tell. That little biddy never was satisfied with what you gave her. She always lorded it over the rest of us."

Cole knew that his mother's attitude toward Olivia had been one source of his wife's pain. He realized his hands had formed fists in his lap, and he spread his fingers wide on the tabletop beside his place setting. He'd like to explain about Olivia's bout with depression, but his mother had never been someone he could talk to.

Since his counseling, he even wondered if his mom might suffer from depression too, although he didn't have the type of relationship with her to mention it. "Mom, please don't call Olivia a biddy. She grew unhappy with her life here in Timber Creek, and I know I'm partially to blame. I've learned a lot from her leaving, mistakes that I won't repeat."

Nora sniffed. "Looks to me like you're making the same old mistakes again. At least Olivia had the decency to stay home and take care of her children. Until she abandoned them, that is. Is this one going to do that?"

"Mattie has a career in law enforcement, Mom, and she's trained to be a K-9 handler. She won't retire anytime soon."

"Humph, I suspected that would be the way of it. At least you're old enough that there won't be any more babies she should stay home to look after."

Cole shrugged and forked the bite of cake that had been sitting neglected on his plate into his mouth, closing his lips to chew so that he didn't have to answer. He and Mattie had discussed having more kids, and the jury was still out on that decision.

Mattie wasn't sure if she wanted to raise a baby; she preferred to wait and decide later. Cole was willing to go whichever direction she chose. He was satisfied having two daughters, but if Mattie wanted to add a baby to their family, he was all for it. Babies were a lot of fun, and despite what his mother seemed to think, he wasn't too old to become a new dad again.

He was relieved to hear Samuel say "You stay here" to Cherry before closing the door to the mudroom. When Samuel entered the kitchen, Nora rose from her chair to pour a mug of coffee for him.

Samuel clapped a hand on Cole's shoulder as he passed by to take a seat between Cole and his mother. "Is that cake good?"

Cole had taken another bite to keep his mouth full, and he chewed and swallowed quickly. "Sure is. Coffee's good too," he added, taking a drink.

Samuel twisted an end of his mustache as he looked back and forth between Cole and Nora. Cole wondered if the tension in the room hung thick enough for his dad to feel. After Nora plunked Samuel's mug of coffee down in front of him, he murmured, "Thank you, sweetheart," while still eyeing Cole as if trying to gauge his level of emotion.

"I've been telling our son what I think of him getting married again," Nora said.

*At least Mom doesn't beat around the bush*, Cole thought.

"Well, dear, I think that's Cole's business, don't you?"

"Not when it affects our grandchildren."

That took Cole by surprise since he hadn't heard his mother express this concern before. "If you're wondering how the kids feel about the wedding, I'd say they seem pretty darn happy about it," he said.

"Maybe so, for now," Nora said, retaking her seat. "But what happens after the newness wears off? What will they think about someone trying to take their mother's place?"

Samuel's eyebrows were raised and he was looking at Cole as if also interested in the answer. The concern about their grandchildren seemed legitimate. He decided to be more forthcoming.

"I've talked about that with both Mattie and the kids. Mattie doesn't want to take their mom's place, and she's on board with helping them reestablish a relationship with Olivia. She'll definitely step up in a parental role when needed, but you know that Mrs. Gibbs also helps out with that. The three of us should be able to handle the adjustment," Cole said with more confidence than he felt. They'd had their ups and downs in this area, and family counseling was always an option if things got out of hand. He decided to say as much. "You know, the kids and I have seen a family therapist occasionally to get feelings out in the open and deal with them ever since Olivia left. We can always go as a family if we need to."

"Piffle," Nora said, her brow pinched in a frown. "What good does a shrink do?"

Cole met her eyes. "Actually, a shrink has done me a lot of good. That's why I'm not afraid of getting married again."

Samuel spoke up before Nora could respond. "Now, Mother, Cole is a grown man and he can think for himself. Besides, this isn't some floozy we're talking about. It's Mattie. She saved our Sophie when she got kidnapped. You know how grateful we are for that."

Nora met Samuel's eyes while he spoke, then looked down at her plate in silence, evidently unable to argue with his point. "I just want what's best for the kids."

Cole jumped at a viewpoint on which they could unequivocally agree. "We all do, Mom. Thanks for caring about them so much."

In reality the girls had a rocky relationship with his mother as well. Perhaps it was because for much of his kids' childhood he had avoided his parents, despite living only a few miles from them. And Angie was old enough to be well aware that her grandmother's criticism had contributed to her mother's unhappiness. It was complicated, and he felt a twinge of guilt that he'd done nothing to repair what he knew needed to be fixed.

"You know, Cole, I do love them, even if I don't get to see them very often," Nora said. "First their mother kept them away from me and now it feels like you do."

Samuel jumped in. "Aww, sweetheart, you know how young families are. The kids are busy with their friends and Cole is busy with his work." He'd had years of practice trying to smooth his wife's ruffled feathers.

If Cole wasn't mistaken, his mother's eyes looked sad. "Mom, I didn't know you felt that way. We need to fix that. We'll try harder to get out here to see you guys more often."

Nora lowered her gaze. "I suppose you'll be busier than ever with a new wife. I wish you'd reconsider, Cole."

It felt like they'd come full circle and he needed to wrap things up, even if it looked like he wanted an escape. "Mom, I've considered and reconsidered already, and I know that Mattie and I are meant for each other. Besides, having a spouse in law enforcement is not so different from any other career. Both of us will be working, but Mrs. Gibbs will be there to help run the household and make sure the kids get what they need after school. Mattie and I are homebodies, so we'll be together as a family in the evenings. Maybe you can come for dinner sometime after the wedding."

"We'd love that," Samuel said with gusto. "Wouldn't we, sweetheart?"

Nora looked from Samuel to Cole. "We don't want to force ourselves on you."

Cole stood, stacked his empty dishes, and circled the table to give his mom a one-armed hug. "You're not forcing anything, Mom. I'm sorry I didn't realize you felt left out. We'd love to see you more often." He gritted his teeth as he set his dishes in the sink. "I'd better get a move on before this storm blows in some serious snowfall. I still have chores to do."

Cole slipped on his jacket, and his father followed him to the front door as Nora cleared the rest of the table. Together Cole and Samuel stepped out onto the porch.

"Thanks for that, son," Samuel said. "Your mother has a hard time adjusting to change."

Cole gave his dad a hug as the cold wind buffeted them. "Maybe we all do, Dad. Now get inside before you catch a cold. I know Mom wouldn't like that."

Samuel's chuckle followed him as Cole dashed toward his truck and climbed inside. He fired up the engine, turned up the heater, and exchanged waves with Samuel as his dad stepped back inside.

*Now, why did I go and do that?* Cole asked himself as he drove away. The girls were fine without a relationship with their grandparents, and he knew for a fact that Angie preferred it that way. Mrs. Gibbs was a pro; she wouldn't object to having his parents for dinner. But how would Mattie feel about it? He should've discussed it with her before putting his big foot in his mouth.

His phone beeped with a text, and as if conjured by his thoughts, the text was from Mattie. Driving slowly down the lane that led from his parents' house, he tapped it open. It read: I've been called on a mission in WA. Have to leave in an hour to make it to airport. Call when you can so I can explain.

*What? Going to Washington on a mission? What kind of mission? Why now, one week before our wedding?* Cole's mind filled with questions as he tapped the icon to call Mattie. The call went to voice mail after the first ring. "I'm on my way home, Mattie. What's this about Washington? What about our wedding? What's going on?"

After ending the call, he realized he'd sounded upset, even though he wasn't sure he felt that way. But after thinking for a few seconds, he decided that maybe he did feel out of sorts. He'd just explained to his mother that marrying a law enforcement officer was no different than marrying a woman with another type of career, even though he knew better. Maybe he felt a wee bit chagrinned.

Why would Mattie drop everything and rush off to the state of Washington just days before their wedding? He'd just defended her commitment to family to his mother, and now this.

Scattered snowflakes splattered his windshield as he headed homeward into the wind. *And Mattie plans to drive to Denver in this storm?* Cole's emotions roiled as he told himself to slow down and not lose his temper when he had a chance to talk to her.

# THREE

Mattie disconnected the call with Sheriff McCoy. He'd been all for his one and only K-9 team joining Sergeant Madsen on the trip to Washington. He'd said he thought it would be good for the department to help out in another jurisdiction and perhaps gain regional recognition for their great teamwork. She guessed it was meant to be this way, and she hoped that she and Robo could make a difference in rescuing this lost child.

She'd have to trust that Cole could handle last-minute arrangements for the wedding, a job that wasn't her strong suit anyway. Besides, she'd already decided to keep things simple. She felt mild concern that she still hadn't bought a dress, but she'd have to worry about that later.

Mrs. Gibbs removed a pencil from above her ear, absently patted her gray curls back into place, and flipped a page on the stenographer's notebook she'd been using to keep track of wedding details. "Have you added anyone to the guest list since we last spoke, Mattie?" she asked, her words colored with the lilt of her Irish brogue.

Mattie zipped the insulated bag that Mrs. Gibbs had provided to pack the supper they'd quickly thrown together out of sandwich fixings, fruit, and homemade chocolate chip cookies. Robo sat on the floor watching every move along with the Walkers' Bernese mountain dog, Belle, and Doberman pinscher, Bruno.

Mrs. Gibbs glanced up from her lists. "Oh, and grab a couple cans of soda or flavored water too."

Mattie returned to the refrigerator to retrieve a can of cola and a lime-flavored sparkling water. "I haven't added anyone new to the list. On my side, only my family and the crew from the sheriff's department are coming, although Rainbow might be bringing a friend. She's been dating Ned Dempsey from the Watering Hole. Do you know him?"

Mrs. Gibbs nodded. "He seems like a nice young man."

Mattie smiled at the old-fashioned euphemism, thinking that Ned, who tended bar at the local grill, might cringe at being called a "nice young man." But she agreed with Mrs. Gibbs that he was definitely a good guy. "I'm glad Rainbow finally admitted she likes him. He's been trying to get her to go on a date for months."

Mrs. Gibbs penciled Ned's name onto the list. "Rainbow is cautious about these things."

Mattie nodded, although the whole story was complicated. As a dispatcher at the sheriff's station, Rainbow typically came across as everybody's friend and was first to welcome newcomers to the community. But she'd shared with Mattie that she thought Ned might not be looking for a serious relationship, and Rainbow was done with guys who couldn't commit. Mattie tried to stay out of it but had encouraged Rainbow to follow her heart.

Rainbow had suffered a scare the month before that left her afraid of further trauma, but evidently her heart had told her that Ned might be a contender for a serious relationship after all. Mattie hoped Rainbow's decision wasn't caused by fear of being alone after she'd been abducted from her own front yard, although Ned seemed very willing to be Rainbow's protector. Mattie just wanted her friend to be happy and for her to make decisions for the right reasons.

Mattie added the drinks to her supper bag and joined Angie and Sophie where they were sitting at the kitchen table. "I'm so grateful you girls will help with flowers. There isn't much left to do since we already decorated the great room for Christmas."

A week earlier, Mattie had helped Cole and the kids trim a Christmas tree that stood at least ten feet tall, reaching toward the log rafters at the top of the cathedral ceiling in the family room. They'd strewn swaths of evergreen boughs woven with red bows and pine cones on the mantel above the fireplace, beautiful against the rock wall that lined the chimney all the way to the ceiling. The same evergreen garland graced the staircase railing.

"All we have left to do is set out some poinsettias and make a few fresh bouquets," Angie said, absently petting Hilde, their buff-colored Siamese kitten that lay purring in her lap. "It'll be fun."

"And I think I'll be home in time to help arrange flowers anyway," Mattie added.

"If you're not, I'll pick up your order," Mrs. Gibbs said, jotting a note on her to-do list.

"Or remind Cole to do it," Mattie said.

"Are we going to have cake?" Sophie asked, leaning both elbows on the table, her mug of hot chocolate centered between them.

"Yes, we are, little miss sweet tooth," Mrs. Gibbs said, smiling at the child. "I'm making three cakes—one chocolate, one white with vanilla frosting, and one strawberry."

Sophie's brown eyes twinkled. "Mmm . . . how do we decide which kind we want? Maybe I'll have a piece of all of them."

"Tsk, tsk." Mrs. Gibbs shook her head with a mock frown. "Only one piece on wedding day, young miss. But don't worry, I'll make you the cake of your choice while your dad and Mattie are away for their honeymoon."

"I can't wait!"

Mattie exchanged smiles with Mrs. Gibbs as she said, "Thank you." She knew the kind lady planned to make it as fun as possible for the girls while their dad was away, something to help ease Mattie into the family. They'd already had their tussles with Angie about Cole marrying again, though thank goodness it had worked out well. Sophie, on the other hand, had always accepted Cole's new relationship, evidently loving the idea of a different mother figure in the home that would also bring another dog into the family. The kids loved Robo.

Mattie remembered she'd received a voice message from Cole while she'd been talking to the sheriff. She wanted to listen to it but time was getting away from her and she needed desperately to get home to pack her things so she could get on the road. "I'm going to have to go now, girls. Please call or text if you have any questions or if you want to talk, okay?"

Sophie jumped up from her chair to give her a hug. "Stay safe, Mattie. Don't get lost in the woods."

The scent of sweet chocolate on Sophie's breath wafted toward Mattie as they exchanged cheek kisses and hugs. "Robo and I will be fine," she said as she squeezed the child, touching the back of her curly brown hair, the same color as Cole's. "And you don't get lost either. Save that for when Robo and I get home and can search for you, okay?"

Sophie's cheeks bunched in a grin. "Yeah, we'll wait for you," she said, leaving Mattie's arms to embrace Robo.

Mattie approached Angie and the two gave each other a quick hug. "Thank you again for helping with the flowers, Angie," Mattie told her as she brushed the teen's long blond hair with her fingertips. "I appreciate you so much."

Angie smiled. "You'll probably be here to help anyway."

Mattie nodded and gave Mrs. Gibbs a quick squeeze, saying, "Call me if you need anything." She then turned to leave, forcing Sophie to release Robo.

"Safe journey," Mrs. Gibbs called from the kitchen as Mattie passed into the great room to retrieve her coat and hat.

She donned her warm outerwear and let herself and Robo out the front door onto the wooden deck at the front of the Walkers' home. A wind gust struck her face, bringing with it damp sprinkles. Robo dashed down the sidewalk toward the Explorer that had been modified into a fully equipped K-9 unit perfect for traveling the wilderness area that surrounded Timber Creek.

As she pulled out into the lane that led to the highway, Mattie finally listened to Cole's message. Then she listened to it again. *Hmm . . . he sounds peeved*, she thought. She felt herself stiffen in her seat, a preprogrammed response to get ready for a fight. *Take a breath*, she told herself, wanting to quash the fight or flight response her body had been conditioned for during childhood. The deep breath helped, but she didn't know how successful she'd be in maintaining her equilibrium if Cole was mad at her.

She paused at the highway and sent a quick text to him: I'm headed home now to pack. Come there or call if you want to talk.

As she pulled out onto the highway to drive the mile into town, snowflakes pelted her windshield and her vehicle rocked in the steady wind. *Geez, this is just what I need.* She thought of the four-hour drive that lay ahead of her, over several mountain ranges and high-elevation passes. Sheriff McCoy had approved her taking her unit, equipped with snow tires and chains if she should need them, to the Denver airport where one of Sarge's officers would drive it to park at their station while she was away.

She'd argued with Cole over performing her duties in the past, but she thought they had resolved all that. His focus was always on her safety, and she understood his concern. But she also knew that her life as a LEO could lead her into danger every day of the week and he needed to come to terms with that. But this time, he sounded miffed that she was leaving before their wedding, so it felt different.

*Maybe I should have consulted him before agreeing to go.* But a second thought immediately chased that one out of her head. *No, this is my job, my duty, and a child's life is at stake. If Cole can't understand that, then maybe we're not right for each other after all.*

Mattie tried to ignore the hollow feeling that formed in her chest as she drove to her home. She didn't want to fight with Cole before leaving town. That wouldn't be right.

On the west side of town, Mattie pulled up to her small home, an ancient one-bedroom adobe covered with stucco and painted tan with brown trim. She loved this little place and swallowed against the growing lump in her throat when she thought about leaving it. After their brief honeymoon in Steamboat Springs she would move into Cole's place with his family. *Only one more week here, and I'll be away for at least half of it.*

Or maybe the tightness in her throat was caused by the thought that she and Cole shouldn't be together. Things seemed complicated, and she felt loss either way. She tried to reframe her thoughts into moving forward to something great instead of focusing on losing the comfort of her own home.

Mattie opened the door on the steel mesh partition that separated Robo's compartment from the front, and he bailed out into the passenger seat while she opened her car door and exited. After jumping out behind her, he ran toward the front porch. *Change is going to be hard for both of us,* Mattie thought as she approached their little oasis.

She made Robo wait at the door so she could enter first, a nod to alpha training. These large male police dogs could challenge a handler, sometimes with serious results, including bites. Sarge had warned Mattie when she and Robo became a team that she should stay on top of their training at all times so Robo would respect her role as boss. So far, he'd only challenged her once when she'd become depressed and depleted of energy. Brody, chief deputy at their department, had helped her realize what was wrong. After she corrected her own behavior, Robo fell right in line and never backslid again. Consistency was key with dog training.

The front door opened into the living room, and a hallway beyond that led to a kitchen on the right, bathroom in the middle, and bedroom on the left. Mattie's furnishings were meager compared to Cole's: one chair, a couch, a coffee table, and a chest to hold her small television. But this was her home, her shelter when things got too tough in the world. She tried to shake off a feeling of being overwhelmed and headed back toward her bedroom to pack as Robo trotted ahead.

Her cell phone rang in her pocket. Thinking this would be Cole, she reached for it to check caller ID. Chief Brody. She answered the call. "Hey, Brody."

"I hear you're headed to Washington."

"Yep. As soon as I can get packed, I'll be on my way to Denver."

"I've been tracking the storm on our weather channel here at the station," Brody said. "This is a southern Colorado storm, so once you clear the first pass, things should smooth out. But leave as soon as you can. They're predicting twelve inches or more around here."

"I will. Thanks for the info. I was worried about what lay ahead on the passes."

"And watch your back out there in the forest. I have a creepy feeling about this. I called the county sheriff out there and talked to one of the deputies. He said that the area is rugged and there was another missing child they never found about a year ago. No telling what you're getting into. This might not be a case of a kid wandering away from home."

Mattie frowned as she considered this news. Sarge hadn't told her about this other child. "Good to know. Thanks, Brody."

"Okay . . . be careful out there. Check back in when you can."

After saying goodbye, Mattie disconnected the call and put her phone back in her pocket. Brody had become a friend in the past few months and he always seemed to be watching out for her. She appreciated him more than she could say, even though she was happy to be partnered with Robo instead. Brody had a temper that he worked hard to control, whereas Robo . . . well, Robo was steady and reliable and just about perfect in every way.

Her dog had launched himself at his bed under the window and was digging at the fabric with both paws, scuffing up the canvas covering.

Maybe not perfect in *every* way. Robo could be a little intense at times too. "Whoa, buddy. Settle down there before you dig a hole and ruin your bed."

Robo kept his focus on the bed while he continued to dig.

"Robo!" Mattie used her disciplinarian voice. "That's enough!"

He glanced at her before circling to lie down. She shook her head, smiled to herself, and went to the closet to pull out a large, internal frame backpack that she used when hiking and camping. It had a rain cover as well as being waterproof, so it would be perfect for the climate where she was headed.

She placed it on the bed and started pulling out clothing and equipment to lay beside it. She took off her duty belt and removed her Glock from its holster to drop the magazine from its grip. Then she packed the unloaded gun into a foam-lined case used for transporting and laid it on the bed. She would carry ammo and magazine separately. She stuffed everything into her backpack before going into the bathroom to pack her toiletries into a small carrying case.

A knock at the door made Robo bark a warning and skitter across the wooden floor toward the sound. Having experienced enough danger even in her own home during the past several months, Mattie no longer left her doors unlocked when she was inside. She followed Robo, who was bouncing at the entryway, and heard Cole's voice on the other side of the door while his key worked the lock.

"It's me, Robo," Cole called from the porch. "No need to get in an uproar. Settle down."

By the time Mattie reached the door, Cole had opened it and stepped inside. He spread his arms, and she walked into his embrace. He hugged her tightly while Robo gamboled around their legs trying to nose them apart. Mattie turned her head to place her ear against Cole's chest.

His voice rumbled against her ear as he spoke. "What's this about Washington? Tell me what's going on."

Remembering Cole's reaction to her first text, Mattie pulled apart far enough to see his face, though their forearms remained clasped. If he was upset with her, she wanted to know so she could stand up for herself. She told him about Sergeant Madsen's call, Chrystal Winter's lost son, and the need for air-scenting dogs. "The boy is nine years old, Cole. Sophie's age. I have to go help find him."

Cole's face had registered surprise when she told him it was Chrystal's child who had disappeared. "Could it be a kidnapping for ransom?"

"There's always that possibility, especially in a high-profile case like this. But Sarge didn't mention a ransom call, and it sounds like they think the boy wandered off from the movie set. I should be briefed as soon as we get together at the airport."

"Do you know when you'll return home? We're not going to have to postpone the wedding, are we?"

"Sarge says we'll have either found the child or cleared the area before then. The local jurisdiction is in charge; we're just helping out. He thinks I'll be home in plenty of time." Mattie continued to search Cole's face. "You sounded upset on the phone. I hope you understand that I need to do this."

Cole grimaced. "Yeah, I was upset at first, but I talked real hard to myself while I drove here. Maybe I was still upset about an argument I had with my mother. Anyway . . . after thinking about it, I decided you wouldn't agree to leave right now unless it was important."

Relieved, Mattie merely nodded. "I hesitated, but the child's age got to me."

"I suppose this is to be expected with the reputation that you and Robo have developed. Can I help you pack? Make some food for the road?"

Mattie squeezed his arms before stepping back from his embrace. This was the Cole she was used to, and it felt good to know that he was so supportive. "Mrs. Gibbs and I took care of supper and I think I'm all packed. Sarge says to be prepared for rain."

"We'll take care of everything while you're gone."

"The girls and Mrs. Gibbs have notes on what's left to do. There's not much."

"Let's get a rain slicker for Robo from my clinic on your way out of town. I also just received some dog goggles I ordered that you might want to try. They're made for UV protection from the sun's reflection off snow, but they might also shield Robo's eyes from the rain. You'll have to decide if it helps or hinders his vision with rainfall."

"Sounds good. I have a go bag ready for him, but I need to add more food and his favorite Kong toy," she said.

Cole and Robo followed Mattie into the kitchen where she kept the dog food.

"I've been thinking about this being a celebrity's child," Cole said. "I have trouble imagining he could wander off from a movie set surrounded by forest. This just doesn't seem right. Could it be a ploy for Chrystal to get media attention?"

"I don't know. We're used to my focus being criminal investigation rather than search and rescue. I guess I'll just have to play it by ear."

But as she finished up, her mind swirled with criminal possibilities. She hoped that's all they would be—possibilities, and not facts.

# FOUR

A TSA agent escorted their small group into a private waiting room that Sarge had requested at Denver International Airport. Although the room was sparsely furnished, with one green plastic-covered couch and a few uncomfortable black chairs, Mattie was glad they didn't have to wait out in general boarding. They would be first to board and sit in the front row of the plane where the extended legroom would accommodate three dogs. It had been much cheaper for their crew to fly commercial rather than by private jet, but at least a few concessions had been made for them.

Sarge, a tall, burly man with a shaved scalp and an image of a police badge tattooed above his ear, shrugged off his backpack and set it on the floor by the couch. Leading Robo at heel, Mattie chose one of the chairs and followed suit. Her dog had lifted his nose and was sniffing the air in the room. She could tell he'd like nothing better than to do a sweep of the whole place, but she decided that to allow it would be inappropriate.

"I'll go get us some coffee," Sarge said.

"I'll do that, sir," said the dark haired, powerfully built man in his twenties who'd been introduced to Mattie as Officer Drake Hill. He looked at Mattie. "Do you want coffee, Deputy?"

"Yes, thanks. Black, no sugar. And call me Mattie."

He nodded. "And I'm Drake. I'll leave Fritz with you," he said, handing the bloodhound's leash to Sarge before letting himself out the door.

Sarge owned Fritz anyway, although Drake had been assigned to accompany them as the young bloodhound's handler. Fritz had been trained in human remains detection. His inclusion on the team surprised Mattie at first, but then she decided it made sense to bring a cadaver dog along—just in case.

Though the child had only been missing for a short time, the forest was a dangerous place, filled with unforgiving terrain and wild animals. Mattie knew of at least one Colorado-based search and rescue mission in which the remains of a toddler weren't found until years later. The boy had been killed by a cougar shortly after being separated from his family and then carried off to its den, a place where for some reason the SAR canines couldn't track to find the child sooner. Maybe the cougar's odor combined with fresh human decomposition turned away the dogs that were used to finding live humans. The true reason for the failed search was still unknown, but maybe Sarge had decided to double their chances for success by including a human remains detection dog.

Sarge lowered himself to the couch with a sigh, and the true star of the show settled to lie at his right foot. Banjo was Fritz's sire as well as an experienced K-9 officer with years of duty under his collar. The elder bloodhound's burnished red coat glowed in the overhead light and, like Robo, he lifted his black nose to sniff the air of the room, tasting the residual odors left from countless previous customers. Fritz sat on Sarge's other side and yawned. Banjo yawned too and placed his head on his paws. Clearly the two bloodhounds were used to being asleep at this hour of the night.

Sarge pulled a slim file from his backpack, unzipped it, and took out some papers. "Drake has seen these already, so I'll brief you before we get on the plane."

Mattie scooted to the edge of her chair while Sarge rifled through the papers and then handed her a photocopy of the missing child's picture.

"River Allen," Sarge said, "nine-year-old son of Chrystal Winter and Roger Allen. First noticed to be missing at eleven o'clock this morning, now missing an estimated ten hours. His nanny-slash-tutor, Sally Kessler, left their trailer at approximately ten thirty on an errand for Ms. Winter while the boy was supposed to be on the computer doing a downloaded lesson. When she returned thirty minutes later, River was gone. Private security searched the movie set and the immediate area for about an hour before contacting local authorities. And you know how that goes.

"The county's human volunteer SAR crew combed the area. They didn't find the kid, but they sure contaminated the scene for the dogs. A local canine SAR team has also been called in and they've started working, but most of their dogs track on the ground. I guess one of them can be used for air scenting, but the area is large, rugged, and they need more help. None of the ground-tracking dogs have been able to follow a scent beyond the beginning of a trail into the forest where it gets dense. And to complicate matters, it's been raining all day. They believe the kid is out there, but they haven't been able to follow the track. That's where we come in. And by the way, the sheriff running incident command is Don Piper, an old friend of mine."

Mattie studied the photo while Sarge spoke. River Allen posed beside a boulder surrounded by a green meadow filled with yellow and white daisies. He was slender, with elfin features similar to those of his mother's—golden hair worn long and down around his shoulders, and pale blue eyes. The words "beautiful boy" came to Mattie's mind while she memorized the child's appearance. "What kind of errand did Ms. Winter send the nanny on?"

"I'm not certain, but it involved driving ten minutes to the local grocery store and back. I guess it's common for her to leave River alone for thirty minutes. The kid's trailer is surrounded by other trailers and people, so he was believed to be safe enough. But evidently there was a disturbance on the other side of the set, a fire in a work area. Everyone drifted over that way to see what was going on and no one paid attention to the boy."

"Sounds suspicious."

A frown crinkled Sarge's forehead. "Agreed. But so far there's been no ransom contact and the boy has been known to wander away from the set by himself before. The fire seemed to be related to oily rags thrown away carelessly near a space heater. They're assuming the child's lost rather than taken."

Mattie considered the information, not liking what she'd heard. Mom sends caregiver on errand, fire starts in trash can, child disappears. She'd be handling this as a crime scene if she were in charge.

Sarge offered her two other sheets of paper. "Here's a satellite view and a topo map of the surrounding forest," he said, referring to a topographical map.

The satellite view showed a thick forest canopy stretching out endlessly, with very few openings that displayed the ground. The topo gave her a better idea of the rise and fall in elevation of the land and the location of a stream that ran through a valley choked with trees. There were a few narrow roads into the area, but according to the satellite view, trails appeared to be nonexistent. "Is the forest this dense, or are there trails we can pick up to take the dogs through?"

"It's that dense. Wait'll you see it."

Drake returned to the room, a cardboard tray in hand containing three cups topped with plastic covers and a bag tucked under his arm. He raised his eyebrows. "Anyone want maple scones?"

"You bet!" Sarge replied.

Mattie arose from her seat to give the papers back to Sarge and help Drake with the coffee, which made Robo stand to watch. "Lay back down," she murmured.

"Eat fast," Sarge said. "Only twenty minutes before we board."

★ ★ ★

## Early Friday Morning

The flight took a little less than three hours and was uneventful. Despite it being Robo's first time flying on a commercial airline, he settled at Mattie's feet and slept most of the way. Mattie had trained him to accept the basket muzzle required for all dogs trained in apprehension, so it didn't seem to bother him. Caffeine buzz and a less than comfortable seat kept Mattie from sleeping soundly, but she did try to nap.

Once they landed in Seattle and deplaned, an officer escorted them to another concourse where they descended stairs to the tarmac. The airport smelled damp, and rain splattered Mattie's coat as they stepped outside to board a helicopter that would whisk them across Puget Sound toward the Olympic Peninsula. Outside the bell-shaped windows, the sky was soupy with fog that blocked her view of the water beneath them. Robo sat against her, strapped to the seat with a harness made especially for K-9s and his muzzle still in place. She leaned back and stroked his silky head, thinking it was probably better that she didn't have a view of the water below.

After a short flight, they landed on a grassy strip within a small village near the water. After unloading, they ducked down to hurry away from the buffeting wash of the helicopter blades. Rain pelted them as they threw their backpacks into the back compartment of a Humvee with a sheriff's department insignia on the door. Mattie and Drake crowded into the back seat with all three dogs, while Sarge stepped up into the front passenger seat.

"I'm Deputy Gage Casey," the driver said, his windshield wipers beating a rhythm back and forth. "We'll have you there in about ten minutes. Strap in and hang on."

Droplets streamed from Mattie's coat as she buckled her seat belt. She already felt damp and chilled, and she welcomed the heated interior of the vehicle. The driver accelerated quickly down the street, which after a few fast turns became a bumpy, muddy track leading into the forest. From what little Mattie could see in the beam from the headlights, towering evergreen trees pressed in on both sides of the vehicle, immediately setting off her sensation of claustrophobia. She sucked in a few breaths, trying to smooth out and extend her exhalations as she struggled to relax her shoulders.

Drake was holding onto Fritz as he looked out his window. "Oh, man," he muttered to his dog. "With the density of this forest and the rain, you'd better get your nose ready, bud."

Mattie couldn't agree more. No wonder they'd called for air-scenting dogs. Moisture helped the ground and foliage retain skin rafts shed from humans, making it easier for a dog to track. But heavy rain would wash those same skin rafts off plants and send them downhill, shifting the scent trail in all directions and ultimately splashing it into the drainage system—streams, rivers, and lakes.

An air-scenting dog would search for the human's scent in the air, locking onto it when the dog came close enough to narrow down to the origin of the scent, thus finding the subject, like Robo had done in their training yesterday. But again, heavy rain could play havoc there too. She hoped the rain would ease up soon or even stop by sunrise.

The driver responded to Sarge's questions with noncommittal grunts, and the whir from the heater soon shut down all attempts at conversation. Mattie studied Deputy Casey's gray hair that grazed his collar, so different from Brody's buzz cut, and figured he might be in his early sixties.

They drove through the tunnel of trees until it opened up in a clearing illuminated with countless lights, revealing tents, trailers, vans, and campers set up and parked all over the place. She realized that klieg lights, probably used for filming, had been converted into spotlights in various parts of what she guessed had once been the movie set, now turned into an incident command center.

Deputy Casey pulled up to a fifth-wheel trailer attached to a green dually truck, its stout frame and double rear wheels looking powerful enough to pull the twenty-five-foot travel trailer. A gust of wind dashed heavy rain onto the windshield, obscuring the view out front for a few seconds while the wipers beat furiously to clear the glass pane.

Mattie rubbed Robo between his ears and exchanged glances with Drake, who shrugged, his eyebrows raised and one hand lifted in a gesture of submission. She interpreted it as a complaint about the terrain and weather and nodded her agreement.

"Okay, guys and gal, here we are," Casey said. "Leave your gear in the truck and go on inside to meet Sheriff Piper. He's been anxiously awaiting your arrival."

"Since we don't have a separate cage for the dogs, let's take 'em with us," Sarge said, confirming Mattie's inclination. She doubted that Robo would wait patiently out here in the Humvee and feared for the safety of its upholstery.

She opened the door and climbed down into the rain, inviting Robo to join her. As a wave of driving rain hit her, she wondered how in the heck they were going to search for a missing child in this mess.

# FIVE

Warm air washed over Mattie as she followed Sarge inside the trailer. Mud and pools of water smeared the floor at the entryway. Leading Robo, she scooted into the interior behind Sarge to make room for Drake and Fritz to enter.

"Watch out, that floor is slippery!" a male voice boomed from beyond Sarge. Mattie peered from behind to locate the speaker.

A tall, lean man who resembled a stork arose from a chair at a table that was littered with maps, laptop computers, disposable coffee cups, and papers. His long legs and beaklike nose had given Mattie her first impression, but she also noticed intense gray eyes surrounded by squint lines and a once clean-shaven face now darkened by five o'clock shadow. A shock of brown hair turned smoky with gray covered his head.

He came forward with his hand extended toward Sarge. "Jim, thanks for your quick response."

"Certainly, Pipe. Hope we can help," Sarge said, pumping the man's hand. He turned to Drake and Mattie. "This is Don Piper, sheriff of Baker County and incident commander for this mission."

Piper offered a firm handshake to each of them as they introduced themselves. "We appreciate you coming out to help us try to locate this young'un. Our volunteers are just about wiped out from a rough day."

"I can imagine," Sarge said. "Has it been raining like this all day?"

"Not exactly as hard as this, but the rain started about the time the child went missing, and it's gained momentum ever since. Conditions have become more and more difficult."

"How many people do you have to work with here?" Sarge asked.

"We've got a team of eleven volunteers from this county, and I've reached out for help through Washington's Emergency Management Division. We expect thirty more people to arrive from adjacent counties by six AM. We've got three K-9 search teams, so with you, that makes six. I'll be able to deploy more teams sometime tomorrow when help comes in from other counties, but I don't know how many yet."

"And what's the current status of the search?" Sarge asked.

Piper looked discouraged as he shook his head. "I pulled everyone back in for the night around eleven o'clock. It's too dark and rainy to make progress, and one of our volunteers broke a leg in some deadfall directly west of here. I couldn't afford for anyone else to get hurt, so I called a halt until morning."

Mattie did not like the sound of that—deadfall so thick that someone suffered a severe injury.

"That's too bad," Sarge said with a note of sympathy in his voice. "Still no ransom contact made?"

"None."

"Have you eliminated the possibility of foul play?" Sarge asked.

"Not at all. That's why it's useful to have you three cops join our team." One corner of Piper's mouth tightened upward in a grimace. "But we've found no evidence of kidnapping, and when the dogs could still track, they went directly into the forest west of here. Until we find evidence the boy's been taken, I have to continue looking for him out there." He swept his hand outward in the general direction of the outdoors.

Sarge nodded. "What are your plans for us?"

Piper checked his watch. "We're going to reconvene at six o'clock, so you could get a few hours of sleep before then. We've commandeered a couple of trailers and have set up tents to shelter volunteers. I can put you folks up in a camper tonight if you're okay with sleeping co-ed."

He looked at Mattie when he spoke, raising one eyebrow, and she quickly nodded to signal her agreement. In fact, she doubted she would sleep but preferred trying to rest among people she knew. "I'll bunk with these guys as long as that's okay with them."

"We have male and female quarters set up, but folks are already sleeping there. Tonight's shelter will probably be temporary," Piper said.

"Wherever you put us will be fine," Sarge said. "What's the plan for tomorrow morning?"

Mattie thought Sarge was as eager to get to work as she was, and he wasn't interested in sleeping arrangements. He wanted to know when they were going to start and what they were going to do.

"I've assigned three local volunteers who are familiar with this area to team up with each of you, so the volunteer can act as guide and field assistant while you work your dogs." Piper turned away toward his desk. "I've assigned each of you search grids on these maps here. Do you want to look at all this now, or are you ready to get some shuteye?"

Mattie echoed Sarge and Drake as they all said, "Now." She figured that even though her energy had started to flag, she was still too wired to sleep.

Piper picked up three sheets with topographical maps on them and spread them out on the tabletop. They all huddled while he pointed out features on the top one. "These are all the same, but I've marked a different grid on each one. This top one is the master, showing all four areas marked with different colors. We have one other air-scenting dog and I plan to deploy that team along with you three as early as possible."

The map showed the typical elevation contour lines that indicated hills, mountains, and valleys, but it also included black lines for roads and highways. Mattie noticed the blue area that indicated a large body of water only a few miles to the east and blue lakes dotted the land that stretched off to the west.

"Is that Puget Sound?" Mattie asked Piper, tapping the large blue area.

"Actually, it's a bay off Hood Canal, a natural finger of water that reaches southward from the Sound. This water system includes fjords and straits to make up the Salish Sea."

Though the name wasn't familiar, Mattie nodded anyway. The contour lines indicated a general rise toward mountains in the west. "Where are we in relationship to Olympic National Park?" she asked.

Piper tapped a green area that lay west of where he'd marked off rectangles with colored ink. In fact, the map was mostly green, indicating the land around them was covered in forest. "Right here to the far west. The terrain is rough between here and there, and there's no road to access the park from here. I don't see any way that child could make it that far."

"So we won't be searching the park itself?" Sarge asked.

"Not in the plan at this time unless we determine the boy actually did go that far. Very unlikely though." Piper rubbed his finger over the search grid again. "This is where we think the boy could be."

"Does the child have medical issues or any physical or emotional issues we should know about?" Mattie asked, still worried about the delay in getting out there to search, despite the conditions that inhibited them.

"No, he's evidently healthy and as well-adjusted as a kid with a famous parent can be. River Allen, age nine, long blond hair and blue eyes. Have you seen a photo yet?"

"I shared the one you sent me," Sarge said. "You told me earlier that River has a history of wandering off."

Piper raised his eyebrows. "Yes, he does. This is the second time he's gone missing, but the parent didn't call our department the first time. Evidently he went off to explore and after a short search, he came back when his nanny and mom called him. They gave him a lecture about the danger of getting lost in the woods.

"But this time they thought he'd just gone off on his own again, and it kept them from calling us until after the rain started. By the time we activated the search volunteers and the first dog team arrived, the rain had settled in good and steady."

Since the child had a history of wandering, Mattie thought it odd that his mother was comfortable leaving him alone, even if for only a short time. "You said you haven't ruled out foul play yet. Has Ms. Winter received any threats to herself or her family?" she asked.

Piper nodded. "Apparently she received death threats after her last movie release about a year ago. That's when she hired bodyguards and set up a better security system at her home."

"Has anyone threatened her son?" Mattie asked.

"She denies it, but it's always a concern with these high-profile celebrities," Piper said.

"It seems suspicious that Ms. Winter sent the nanny on an errand and then there was a fire that distracted the remaining people on the set. Have you cleared Ms. Winter of any involvement in her son's disappearance?" Mattie asked.

"Not yet. I've interviewed her and am checking out her background. But my initial impression is that she's appropriately distraught over the situation and is trying to help as much as she can."

Mattie had to wonder about Chrystal Winter's emotional response since she was such a good actress. "How about the child's father? Is there a custody issue? Could this be a parental kidnapping?"

"I don't think so, but it's too early to tell. The dad, Roger Allen, is supposed to arrive soon. We'll be able to get a better handle on relationships tomorrow . . . well, I guess I mean later today." Piper scanned their faces. "Any other questions or is it time for you to get some sleep?"

"One more thing," Mattie said. "I hear that another child disappeared from this area and has never been found."

"Two other kids to be exact." Piper's eyes narrowed. "A teenager named Troy Alexander about a year ago and another boy several years before that. Both were investigated and presumed lost. I'm afraid it's hard to find and recover people in this territory."

Sarge spoke up. "It's important we get into these grids to search with dogs before any more contamination. I hope you plan to deploy us ahead of the other volunteers."

"I hear ya. Sunrise here is shortly before eight o'clock. The weather forecast is for rain to continue tomorrow, so it'll be fairly dark until then. I imagine we'll send the dog teams out around seven at first light if we can. I plan to use human eyes after the dog teams search, so I'll orient the new people and get them organized and ready to go out once you've been able to clear the first two hundred yards or so. Is that enough of a cushion?"

"That should work," Sarge said.

"We'll have coffee and some sort of breakfast here for you around six then."

The three of them shuffled out of the trailer, leading their dogs carefully down the portable metal stairway that was slick with rain.

Once on the ground, they scurried to the Humvee where Casey waited, sipping from a Yeti mug. Mattie could tell it contained coffee when they opened the door and the delicious aroma swirled out of the vehicle. She wondered where hot coffee had come from.

"Where'd you get that?" Drake asked as he helped Fritz up onto the floor of the back seat and climbed in after him.

Casey pointed toward a large tent with an awning flap that extended about ten feet in front of the opening. "In there. That's the mess tent. You can get drinks, cold and hot, and snacks there any time. Breakfast will be served at about six. Do you want coffee now?"

"Nah, I'll wait," Drake said.

Casey started the engine and pulled away from incident command into a muddy alley that wove between tents, trailers, and small house-like buildings. He turned on the wipers to dash rain from the windshield. "Here's the showers and latrines," he said, pointing out two portable trailers that sat side by side. "Men on the right, women on the left. They were already here for the movie folks."

He parked in front of a pull-behind camper trailer set up on leveling jacks and stabilizers. An awning covered the steps that led into the trailer. Mattie unloaded Robo and told him to sit under the awning while she joined the others at the back of the Humvee to get her gear.

Instead of following the two men into the unlocked camper, Mattie set her bags just inside. "I'm gonna take Robo for a potty break. Do you want me to take all the dogs?"

"No, I'll take the bloodhounds," Drake said as he came back down the camper steps with Banjo and Fritz in tow, leaving Sarge inside to get settled.

Mattie led Robo off to the side under some huge evergreens that gave off an incredible scent. They looked like giant pines, with shorter needles and boughs that began far enough up the trunk that she could stand below for shelter. Their massive trunks, covered with moss, looked to be two to three feet in diameter. The air around this grove smelled like a cross between citrus and an intense, almost antiseptic, aroma of pine.

"These trees are amazing," she said to Drake as she leaned back to try to see how tall the tree was. Even though she couldn't see clear to the top, she felt its towering presence above her.

"Old growth Douglas fir, common in the Pacific Northwest woods, along with western red cedar, hemlock, white pine, and others. I used to live near Seattle."

"Moss on the trunk. You won't find that in Colorado."

Drake chuckled. "No, you won't. Not in our drought-ridden forests."

She stayed beneath the cover of the trees and encouraged Robo to hurry up while Drake did the same with his pair. Lights came on inside the camper and, after Robo took care of his business, Mattie clambered up the steps with him at her heels. Sarge had placed her pack on a narrow sofa that ran along the wall and had a cushion for a mattress. His and Drake's backpacks were on the floor next to a double bed made from what had once been the table and its benches. Folded blankets had been placed on each of the beds.

Sarge pointed to the bed that held her pack. "Mattie, you take that one and Drake and I can bunk here. We have about three hours before six, so we'd better crash while we can."

Feeling chilled to the bone, Mattie sank down on her mattress. The camper had a radiant heater that felt like it couldn't keep up with the damp cold seeping in through the windowpanes and cracks. Robo sidled up close, looking at her with mournful eyes.

Sarge would probably pitch a fit if she invited Robo up to share her bunk, something forbidden in alpha training. But they'd slept together on his dog cushion at the station when they were on a case, so what the heck was the difference? Robo deserved better than sleeping on the hard, cold floor. And even though his fur was still damp, she could certainly benefit from his body heat.

She took off her boots, but before she could swing her legs up to lie down, her right foot came into contact with a wet spot, saturating her sock. *Damn,* she thought as she settled under her blanket onto the bed. She slipped off the sock and left it draped from the edge of her mattress, hoping it would dry by the time she woke up.

Robo stood and placed his nose on the bed beside her pillow. That was enough to tip the balance between what Mattie thought was best for her dog and what she thought his trainer would say about her decision. She scooted to the inside of her narrow space, turned on her side, and patted the mattress beside her.

Robo crept up beside her one leg at a time, as if he knew he needed to be stealthy. She smiled as she signaled for him to lie down. After he sank down beside her, she pulled him in close to spoon him. Seeking comfort from his warm body, she put her face against the damp fur on his head and kissed him. His tongue swiped her face one time, something else that was forbidden, and he turned his face away before she could correct him. "That's right, no licking. Now let's try to get some sleep while we can," she whispered before laying her head on the pillow.

Though she thought she wouldn't sleep at all, she dozed fitfully, dreaming of wolves in a forest of huge, moss-covered trees that closed in on her on all sides. The wolves snarled and growled and she crouched beside Robo ready to defend him with her life, only to startle awake to the sound of the two men snoring in the bunk nearby. She'd fallen back asleep when the gentle sounds of chimes and singing birds awakened her, coming from Drake's cell phone alarm.

Sarge sat straight up in bed while Drake untangled himself from his blanket and sat on the edge. Mattie was easing Robo off her bunk when Sarge spoke. "I see that, Deputy. Do you let your dog sleep with you as a general rule?"

A glance told her Sarge was frowning. "No, sir. At home he sleeps in his own bed, but I needed his body heat to try to warm up. I didn't have a bed partner like you two did."

Sarge laughed, indicating he'd faked his original disapproval. "For the record, my bed partner was a whole lot noisier than yours."

Drake had tied his boots and stood to allow Sarge to scoot to the edge of the bed to reach his. "What?" he said. "Did I snore? I thought that was you."

"I'm pretty sure you both did. At one point I woke up thinking I was in the middle of a pack of wolves," Mattie said, getting a quiet snort from both men as she retrieved dry socks from her pack. Robo was getting excited and he pranced in place, beating a trail back and forth between Mattie and the door. "I see you. Just a minute and I'll feed you."

The two bloodhounds had pushed up into a sitting position and were yawning, their eyes droopy with sleep. Mattie fed Robo while Drake and Sarge took care of the other two dogs. She opened Robo's go bag and transferred to her backpack small bags of food and treats needed to replenish his energy throughout the day, as well as his collapsible water bowl, his leashes and equipment, and his reward toys. Her own supply of energy bars and trail mix were already packed in the outside pocket. She planned to fill their water supply when she got to the mess tent.

"Make sure you have your rain gear today, team," Sarge said. "We've got some serious business out there to take care of, and I have a feeling it's gonna be wet."

From the sound of the rain on the roof, that would be an understatement. It was going to be a rough day in unfamiliar conditions. If only it would pay off at the end with finding a child, alive and safe.

# SIX

After the dogs ate, the team left the camper to go find the mess tent. Darkness cloaked the area, but spotlights lit the way as they trekked through the mud. Raindrops pattered the hood of Mattie's jacket and drizzled off the yellow slicker she'd placed on Robo before they'd exited the camper. He trotted on leash by her side, prancing to keep up with her long strides in order to match the pace Sarge set. Both bloodhounds wore slickers too, and they stayed close to their handlers without prompting. Sarge was a hard taskmaster when it came to dog training, and he expected his trainees to be obedient at the very least.

The tent flap was open and the aroma of the coffee that Mattie yearned for greeted her when she went inside. She spotted the hot drinks station first, but seeing Robo lift his nose to sample the air made her sniff too, and her eyes sought the source of the delectable scent of sausage and bacon. Across the way from the drinks sat a long table with the burners and ovens of a portable kitchen set up behind. It looked like a hot breakfast, made up of scrambled eggs, meat, potatoes, and different choices of breads, was being served. People milled around the food filling plates, and some had taken seats on folding chairs at long tables that stretched down the middle of the tent. The murmur of quiet conversation was punctuated by the clang from chefs striking metal lids and spatulas against pots and pans.

"Mm-mmm," Sarge said, heading toward the food. "Let's fuel up, team."

Mattie went with the others to fill her plate and then followed along to find a spot at the end of a table where the dogs would have room beside their chairs. Then she and Drake, with their respective dogs beside them, went to fill coffee cups while Sarge held their seats.

The floorless tent had been pitched on a once grassy area that was now trampled into a matted layer of thatch beneath Mattie's boots. As she took her seat back at the table, she decided to let Robo choose whether he wanted to sit, lie down, or stand on the wet ground. Having chosen to stand, he remained beside her, gazing around his surroundings while she tucked into her breakfast. The first sip of coffee burned her tongue and the back of her throat as she gulped more than she should have.

Robo pricked his ears and stared at the doorway. Mattie followed his gaze to see Sheriff Piper enter the tent with Chrystal Winter. Because Mattie was a fan, she recognized Chrystal immediately, although granted, she'd never seen the actress look so haggard. Chrystal's blond hair was piled into a messy bun atop her head and her eyes were red-rimmed and swollen, ashen circles and smeared mascara darkening the fragile skin beneath them. She wore a burgundy raincoat over what might be dark, tight-fitting yoga pants.

Piper and Chrystal paused in the doorway, his eyes searching the tables until they landed on Sarge. Piper pointed their way before taking Chrystal's elbow and steering her over to their table. Two men in camouflage rain gear followed them, and Sarge and Drake stood as the foursome approached. Torn between standing and sitting, Mattie decided to stand as well, primarily so that Robo would realize she was in charge and she didn't need protecting. Robo had been trained to accept handshaking, but it never hurt to be cautious. It was best to quash the mistaken need for protection before the notion surfaced in her dog's brain.

"Ms. Winter wanted to meet you," Piper said before introducing Sarge, who in turn introduced Chrystal to Mattie and Drake.

Mattie tried not to act like the fan she was as she shook hands. Chrystal's dark blue eyes met hers as she murmured, "Pleased to meet you."

Mattie was taken by surprise at the firmness of Chrystal's handshake, although she wasn't sure why. Perhaps because the actress looked soft and vulnerable. "I'm sorry this has happened," Mattie said quietly. "I hope we find your son today."

Tears brimmed in Chrystal's eyes and she dashed them away with slender fingers. "I can't stand the thought of him out in those woods in this rain," she said in a choked voice.

"He's probably found shelter," Mattie said, wanting to offer hope but fearing her words could be false.

Chrystal reached out and squeezed her hand again before turning her gaze to include all of them. "Thank you so much for coming to help look for River." She gave a downward glance at the dogs that clustered around their legs. "And for bringing your dogs. I hear they're considered the best of the best, and I'm grateful beyond words that you're here."

"I hope there's enough scent out there so they can do their job, Ms. Winter," Sarge said. "I understand you've already given scent articles to the volunteers, but if you don't mind, we need to retrieve and bag some for ourselves just to make sure we have good samples that haven't been contaminated by handling yesterday. We'd like to go to your quarters and get those here in a bit."

"Of course. Anything you need."

"Tell us about River," Mattie said. "Is he athletic? Does he like to explore the woods? Is he experienced with handling situations alone or is he usually with someone?"

"River is more intellectual than athletic," Chrystal said before looking even more crestfallen. "Oh, I don't mean that athletes can't be intellectual. I just mean that he likes reading and computers and playing with technology more than he likes sports. I hope I haven't offended anyone."

Chrystal's eyes searched their faces, and Mattie realized they probably looked like an athletic threesome, which they were. "No offense taken," she said. "How about his experience in the woods or handling situations by himself?"

Chrystal shook her head slightly, glancing downward once more. "He's always with someone." She turned slightly to gesture toward the two men still standing behind her. "This is Buck and Gunner. I employ them to keep us safe, and when River isn't with Sally, his nanny, he's usually with one of these guys. Just not yesterday." She looked away, biting her lower lip as she shook her head.

Mattie recognized regret when she saw it. Both bodyguards stood about six feet tall, and though their rain gear hid their exact body types, she could tell they were heavily muscled. Buck appeared to be the younger of the two, his black hair cut short, while Gunner wore his graying dark hair pulled back away from his face.

Mattie didn't want to push this obviously upset mother, but she decided that she had to. "And River wasn't with either of your men because . . . ?"

Chrystal made eye contact again as a tear leaked from each eye and trickled down her cheeks. This time, the actress didn't wipe them away. "Because River was with Sally and he was supposed to be working on a lesson when she left. He's old enough to be left unsupervised for short periods of time, and I had no idea he would wander off on his own."

"But he had before, right?" Mattie said.

Chrystal's eyes widened. "But when we talked to him about it, he promised he wouldn't do it again."

Mattie could tell she'd jabbed a bit hard, but she wasn't willing to stop yet. "And Sally left because . . . ?"

A pained expression crossed Chrystal's face and she raised her hand to place her fingertips against her cheek. "Because I sent her to the store to get some supplies I ordered. Some of the items were personal and I needed her to make sure the order was complete. I preferred she do it, but now I regret that selfish decision."

Tears continued to stream from Chrystal's eyes, but Mattie noted that she didn't seem to choke up or stumble while she spoke. In her experience, people who were stressed enough to cry had trouble controlling their voice, but Chrystal's remained smooth and clear. Odd.

Piper took Chrystal's elbow and spoke to Mattie. "Excuse us now. Ms. Winter and I want to address the volunteers. I'll send over the three people I've assigned to you and you can coordinate with them when you want to get started. You can meet the other dog handlers out front as soon as we finish speaking to the group."

Mattie nodded but said to the actress, "We'll work hard to locate your son, Ms. Winter."

"Call me Chrystal . . . please." She pressed Mattie's hand before turning to leave.

Mattie sat to finish her coffee and noticed that Sarge was looking at her with raised eyebrows. "What?" she asked.

Sarge tilted his head. "Damn if you didn't jump right in with the questions, Deputy."

She felt her cheeks flush, but she shrugged. "I guess I did. But I gotta say, this isn't sitting right with me. Did you notice how her tears flowed but she didn't get choked up? It was like a disconnect between her face and her emotions."

Drake nodded, but Sarge lifted his hand, his fingers spread in a "stop it" gesture. "Right now we're here to search, not investigate. But I can tell you this—I did notice, and I don't blame you for asking questions. Things don't smell as clean as a pine forest around here, do they? This mother is used to acting, so I'm not sure how that plays out when things get real. We'll leave that up to Piper to explore. We have a different job to do."

Mattie nodded, although she still wasn't sure about the situation. If the child had been taken, every minute spent now was a minute lost when a crime should be investigated. But Sarge had left her a way to see the child's living quarters. "I can go get the scent articles."

"I see what you're doing there, Mattie. We'll go together. I want to take a look too." Sarge glanced at Drake. "Bring Fritz. Let's run a quick sweep to make sure there's no scent of blood in the child's living area."

Piper called out from in front of the serving table. "Could I have your attention?"

The conversational murmur in the room trickled off to stillness.

Piper gestured toward Chrystal, who stood beside him looking brave. "Ms. Winter and I want to share a few words with you before we hand out assignments and get organized. First, thank you all for your time. I know you're volunteers, and we want you to know how much we appreciate you dropping everything in your own lives to come help us. Second, I want to thank Mr. Merc Foster, the owner of our local grocery store, Bigfoot Market, for organizing and cooking our breakfast this morning."

Piper held out a palms-up hand toward a man with steely gray hair brushed back and held under a hairnet, which accentuated his square face and large jaw. He paused, spatula in hand as he raised it to salute the crowd. Piper went on. "Without Merc, we'd be eating doughnuts and fruit this morning. Let's give him a round of applause to say thank you."

The applause swelled into whistles and whoops of appreciation as Foster tipped his head in acknowledgment and smiled. He then went back to flipping pancakes and the group settled into silence as they returned their attention to Piper.

"Most important, we're here to find a little boy named River Allen, and he's our top priority today."

Piper gestured toward a group of people in uniform that Mattie assumed were deputies from his jurisdiction or officers from local towns. Upon his indication, they began passing out flyers with River's photo and description on them. "Here's the boy we're looking for. He's the son of this lady here, Ms. Chrystal Winter."

There was a stir in the room as those who weren't already in the know realized the celebrity status of the missing child's parent.

Piper used both hands in a few short downward gestures to suppress the buzz. "River is nine years old and not used to our forests and climate. We're going to deploy the dog teams at first light and then the rest of you shortly afterward to do a visual and auditory search of whatever terrain you can get into.

"So far we've been able to keep the media out of this, and I kindly request that none of you notify anyone about the identity of this child. The last thing we need is a bunch of yahoos that we have to deal with. But in case members of the media show up, please don't speak to anyone and direct them to me."

He pointed to the table at the end of the room. "I'll be at that table right over there to give out assignments and maps in just a few minutes. I'll also assign a local guide to head up each group and you can study your map with your guide. But before we get to that, Ms. Winter wants to say a few words."

Mattie watched the actress closely when she took the floor. Chrystal's shoulders rounded and she huddled next to Piper with her arms crossed over her midsection. Her sapphire-colored eyes brimmed with tears, and despite the darkened circles below them, she still looked beautiful.

"I want each and every one of you to know how much I appreciate your help finding my baby boy." Her voice caught and she paused, making an apparent effort to control her emotion as tears coursed down her cheeks. "River is the light of my life, and I just know he's out there somewhere cold and frightened. Please . . . please help bring him home today. Please . . ."

Her voice trailed off as she bit her lip and lowered her face. Piper took over with directions for the group, but Mattie couldn't help but wonder if those had been the words of a distressed parent—or was it a performance for a captive audience? She glanced at Drake as she began to gather her things. He met her eyes and nodded. She could tell he was wondering the same thing, but when she glanced at Sarge, the veteran had on his cop face and she couldn't tell what he was thinking.

"Let's go meet our guides and the other teams out front," Sarge said. "Then we'll go take a look at the child's room."

Mattie shrugged on her backpack, bused her tray, and with Robo at heel headed to the front entrance of the tent. As they went, four people came from different parts of the tent to meet them, as if they'd been watching and waiting for the Colorado party to make a move. Two men—one with a gorgeous German shepherd—and two women, all looking fit and dressed in rain gear, joined them outside under the awning at the tent's entryway.

"I'm Ken, incident commander for K-9 teams," the man with the shepherd said, extending his hand. He wore his black hair tucked behind his ears. "Ken Russell. And this is my partner Knoxville."

The shepherd raised his intelligent brown eyes to his handler's face when Ken said his name. His tan chest and legs contrasted beautifully with the black fur on his muzzle and body.

Ken went on to introduce the humans. "This is Rena Powell, Jessica Whiteside, and Hunter Bailey. Jessica lives in this neck of the woods and is a volunteer who's provided field assistance for search dogs before. Hunter's a forest ranger with Washington state parks, and Rena is a handler on one of our volunteer teams."

Everyone shook hands as they introduced themselves. While Ken, Jessica, and Hunter seemed to welcome them, Mattie noticed that Rena appeared hesitant if not downright unhappy. She decided to withhold judgment in case she was reading the woman wrong. Maybe it wasn't so much unhappiness as a feel for the seriousness of the situation.

"I understand that one of your dogs is trained in HRD," Ken said, referring to human remains detection.

Sarge pointed at Fritz, who was gazing upward with his soulful eyes and drooping face. Mattie had met the bloodhounds previously when Sarge had brought them to Timber Creek to work a case. She loved their steadfast personalities.

Ken seemed to have been taken with Fritz too. "Can I pet him?" he asked Drake.

"Sure can. Fritz, make friends." Although in general bloodhound personalities weren't as volatile as the shepherds Sarge worked with, he always established a "make friends" command for his trainees so they would know in advance that this person reaching toward them had a friendly agenda.

Fritz wagged his tail gently as Ken stroked his ears.

"So soft," he murmured. "And who's this?" he asked, looking at Banjo.

"His name's Banjo, one of the best tracking and trailing dogs in the state of Colorado," Sarge said, his voice colored with pride. "Make friends, Banjo."

Ken smiled and patted Banjo while the others looked on. Mattie thought Rena looked even more disgruntled than before.

Ken turned toward Robo. "And this must be Robo," he said, glancing up at Mattie and then down at her dog again. Robo's tail waved as Mattie told him to make friends, and he lifted his face to be petted.

"Your reputation precedes you," Ken murmured as he stroked Robo's head and patted his shoulders. "You're a handsome fellow. Yes, you are."

Robo stood, his tail wagging. He looked like he was on the edge of getting excited by the attention, so Mattie tightened his leash slightly to restrain him. He'd evidently had enough rest during the past few hours to be ready to work. "Robo, sit," she said quietly and then patted the soft fur on top of his head when he did what she asked.

Ken pointed to his own dog. "Knoxville is one of our air-scenting dogs. I'll be out in the field with you guys today."

"He's beautiful," Mattie said, knowing how much a compliment pleased a handler.

Ken smiled his appreciation and ran his hand down Knoxville's head and neck to rub his shoulders. "We had a hard day yesterday, but he's ready to go again."

Four other dog teams had gathered and now clustered around them trying to get under the awning. Rain still pattered on the tarp above, although it had slowed since they'd entered the tent. Ken made introductions, but Mattie was distracted by the dogs and didn't even try to remember handler names. She would reintroduce herself one by one as they worked together. There were two black Labs, both with male handlers, and a tricolored Australian shepherd and what looked like a shepherd mix, both with female handlers.

"You've all got your assignments," Ken said to the others. "Try to stay in your grid as much as you can, although we'll need to cross territory occasionally to access trails. We have enough light to get started now."

The four local teams dispersed as Ken continued to line out instructions to Mattie and her teammates. "Jessica will pair up with Sergeant Madsen for the morning, Hunter goes with Officer Hill, and Rena will go with Deputy Wray and Robo."

Mattie glanced at Rena Powell and saw her frown deepen. What was that about? Did she disapprove of being assigned to them?

"We go by Jim, Drake, and Mattie," Sarge said, gesturing toward each of them in turn. "And we need to go to River's quarters to get fresh scent articles before we head out to the woods."

"Okay," Ken said, "first name basis all around. I'll take you to the trailer, and then we'll split up. The forecast is for this storm to lighten, and it looks like the rain is letting up. Let's pray the weather gods favor us today. They certainly didn't yesterday."

Ken pulled up the hood on his raincoat and started to move out from under the shelter into the alley that led through camp. Mattie glanced again at Rena, but the woman avoided eye contact and didn't speak. She turned to leave and Mattie followed, wondering how this day would go with someone as surly as her guide in the lead.

# SEVEN

Ken led their small group to a thirty-foot-long trailer, its charcoal exterior accented by silver chrome and black trim. A metal deck with three short steps leading up to it had been attached in front of the main door. Ken climbed the stairway and knocked.

After a brief pause, a young woman with red hair opened the door. Reddened, puffy eyelids marred her pale but pretty face, and the skin around her nostrils had grown pink as if irritated by the repeated use of tissues. "Yes?" she said as she opened the door a few inches.

"Sally, these are the officers from Colorado who've brought dogs to look for River," Ken said. "They want scent articles from his laundry basket."

"Okay," Sally said, her voice tentative as she widened the door's opening. "Come in."

"This is Sally Kessler, River's nanny," Ken said as he came back down the steps and spoke to Sarge. "Our boots are muddy, so we should limit the number of us who go inside."

Sarge nodded as he held out Banjo's leash to Drake. "Would you take Banjo while I take Fritz inside?"

"Yes, sir," Drake said, looking not at all upset at being told to wait instead of working the cadaver dog.

"Mattie, you and Robo come with me." Sarge entered the trailer with Fritz at heel. "Is it all right if we do a quick search with our dogs?"

Sally looked confused for a moment. "I guess it's okay. Chrystal said you'd be coming over and for me to let you in."

That was evidently good enough for Sarge. He led Fritz deeper into the room as Mattie and Robo followed him inside.

A quick scan revealed what looked like luxury accommodations: leather furniture in the sitting area with a full-size kitchen that held a shining walnut table and chairs with brass trim, cherry wood floors that gleamed and would have to be cleaned again after they left with the dogs.

"River's room is back this way," Sally said, leading them into a narrow hall and stopping at the first door on the left.

"Thank you," Sarge said. "Mattie, you sweep it first."

Robo had been trained to search for gunpowder and narcotics as well as people, which Mattie assumed was what Sarge wanted them to look for. She paused at the doorway to the room to take Robo's blue nylon collar used for this type of search out of a pocket on her duty belt. She snapped the quick release buckle onto her dog's neck and took a few seconds to give him the chatter that signaled time to work. Robo raised his eyes to hers and pranced into the room, letting her know he was ready.

The room was tidy, with a desk, computer, and study lamp in place. A small bookshelf with reinforced glass covers stood next to the bed. Astronauts and rocket ships adorned the curtains and bedspread, and a small bathroom lay beyond the far wall. "Okay, Robo. Let's find something," Mattie said as she swept her hand out to encompass the room.

Robo moved forward eagerly, sniffing high and low as Mattie gestured along the walls and furniture. She opened a tidy closet and asked Robo to whiff the floor and then the clothing. He followed her lead and they quickly cleared the room.

"Nothing, Sarge," she murmured as she left the room.

Sarge led Fritz inside and, using similar hand gestures, they searched high and low for the scent of blood or early decomposition that might be retained on the carpet and tile. When Fritz reached the bed, he nudged the bedcovers aside until he could press his nose under the pillow. His tail wagged, a low-level show of excitement compared to what Mattie was used to with Robo. Fritz then sat and stared at the spot he'd been sniffing.

"Oh boy," Sarge muttered, throwing a look over his shoulder at Mattie.

Mattie's gut contracted; she knew how Sarge felt. This was a hit, and it either meant blood or decomp. And with Fritz, the odor had to come from a human. This dog didn't make mistakes.

Sarge stroked Fritz's ears and told him he'd done a good job. Then he pressed on his radio and contacted Sheriff Piper. "Pipe, come over to Ms. Winter's trailer, please."

"Be right there," Piper replied.

Sarge ruffled the fur at Fritz's neck and used as high-pitched a voice as a man his size could manage to increase his laid-back dog's excitement. "Good boy. He's a good boy, yes he is. Let's find more, Fritz. Find something."

He directed Fritz in a search of the rest of the room, with no further hits. They finished with a quick search of the bathroom just as Piper entered the trailer. Mattie stayed in the living room to keep an eye on Sally while Sarge and Piper conferred in the bedroom. Both looking stern, the two of them came out of the room together, Fritz at Sarge's heel.

Piper didn't hesitate to address his concerns with Sally. "We have a hit on River's bed that could indicate blood. I've called in a forensics team, and they'll be here shortly. If you have any information about what might have happened to this child, you'd better tell me now."

Sally looked shocked, all color drained from her already pale face. "I . . . I don't know. I mean, River was fine when I left him. I'm sure he's all right. I mean . . . he's lost but . . ." She appeared to be thinking hard.

Her eyes widened. "River had a nosebleed the other night. I changed out his pillow and cleaned the mattress, but . . . Could that be what the dog smells?"

Mattie felt some of the tension release from her shoulders. If true, a nosebleed certainly could leave enough scent for a dog like Fritz to find, even if the mattress had been cleaned with a strong disinfectant.

Piper looked at Sarge.

"It could be the reason Fritz hit on the mattress," Sarge told Piper. "It still needs to be investigated."

"Agreed," Piper said before turning back to Sally. "Ms. Kessler, I need you to stay here with me while we wait for the techs to arrive. Then we'll go to incident command and talk before I have a chat with Ms. Winter. Sergeant Madsen and Deputy Wray can get on with their work if they're finished in here."

Sarge nodded and went back to the bedroom. Mattie and Robo followed, finding Sarge at the laundry basket retrieving a scent article, his hand inside a plastic bag so he wouldn't touch it directly.

"Maybe it's only a nosebleed," Sarge murmured.

"Yeah. I hope that's all it is." Mattie chose a dirty sock and bagged it the same way Sarge had bagged his. Tucking it into her duty belt, Mattie and Robo followed Sarge back into the combination living room/kitchen where Sally waited with Piper. The nanny looked like her stress had doubled.

Mattie had some unanswered questions. "I heard that River wandered from the set earlier. Did he show any sign that he might leave the trailer before you left?"

"No! If he had I would've taken him with me like I sometimes do. He's a smart little guy, and we've talked about staying safe time and time again. He loves our virtual units, and he was eager to work on it."

"Did he complete it before you got back?"

"No, and that's so unlike him. He was only about a quarter of the way through the lesson when he stopped."

Mattie continued to press. "Was there any indication why he quit? Was the lesson too hard or something like that?"

Sally dabbed her eyes with a tissue. "He got everything right, like he usually does. I saw no reason why he might've quit."

"Did you find any evidence that someone else came into the trailer while you were gone?"

Sally shook her head. "No, but it wouldn't be unusual for someone to check on him. Buck and Gunner were around. But when I asked them, they said they didn't stop in because they were involved with securing Chrystal's safety and helping put out the fire."

Mattie decided to go ahead and express what she was thinking to get Sally's reaction to it. "I'm surprised Buck or Gunner didn't come check on him."

"I know it! I was surprised too."

Her answer made Mattie feel like she had to ask, "Do you have any reason to suspect that River might have been taken or lured from this trailer?"

Sally dissolved into tears, putting her hands to her eyes as she struggled to control her emotion. "No, no, nothing. There have been no threats, no indication that he was in any kind of danger."

Piper had been quietly observing the conversation, but now he spoke up. "Is his father content with the visitation schedule? Could he have taken River?"

"I don't think so. I mean, his divorce from Chrystal was anything but amicable, but he's tied up with his business. They always fight over the dates for visitation. Sometimes I think Chrystal just likes to yank his chain, you know? But he doesn't seem to want more time with River than he gets."

"Do you go with River when he visits his dad?" Piper asked.

"Sometimes, not always. The older River gets, the less I'm needed when he goes to San Francisco. That's usually when I take my vacation." Sally paused as if thinking. "I don't think I've seen Roger for a year."

"And when you're not on set like this, where do you live?" Mattie asked.

"Hollywood, at Chrystal's house. I guess you could describe it as a mansion."

Sarge made a move toward the door, signaling he was ready to get started.

"Thank you for answering our questions," Mattie said. "It gives us a better sense of the big picture."

"Sheriff Piper already asked most of them," Sally said, glancing at Piper. "Roger is coming in this morning if you want to talk to him in person."

Mattie nodded, thanked Sally again, and followed Sarge out the door and down the steps where he was trading leashes with Drake and reclaiming Banjo.

Ken stepped forward, looking curious. "What's going on?"

"Just giving the sheriff more work to do," Sarge said, scanning the sky. "Looks like the rain stopped."

"Yeah," Ken said. "At least for now."

"Let's go then," Sarge said. "We need all the breaks we can get."

They moved to the edge of camp, where Ken stopped. "Here's where we split up."

They paired up with their guides and went their separate ways. Knowing they had assigned her a section that stretched away from the trailer where River had last been seen, Mattie followed Rena to the edge of the forest. The rain might have stopped but heavy mist hung in the air, eerily floating through the trees. It felt like stepping into a spray of water as they walked, and beads of moisture clung to Robo's slicker.

Rena turned to face her. "I checked this area yesterday, but evidently Piper wants you to sweep it again."

This might explain the disapproval Mattie had been sensing. "It's always good to get a second take on an area. Were you using a dog or doing a visual search?"

"I have a Lab I use for SAR work. We're not certified, but we know what we're doing. I cleared this area."

Mattie nodded. "Like I said, it never hurts to go over an area with a different dog the next day, especially an area where the missing person is most likely to be. Why aren't you out with the other teams today?"

Rena glowered. "Our SAR team leader decided that Dozer and I didn't have enough experience, and he and Piper decided they needed me as a guide."

"I see." Mattie didn't really understand why they would choose to have one less dog team. But it wasn't up to her to decide. She drew the map she'd been given out of an inside pocket of her raincoat. "Let's review the boundaries of my territory."

Rena leaned forward, pointing at the map to indicate landmarks. "This strip is about a quarter mile wide. There's a rough trail into the forest here on the right. It's not wide enough for a vehicle. The left is bordered by Mills Creek. It's usually pretty shallow, but I noticed this morning that the rain has swollen its banks."

Mattie felt a twinge of alarm. "Did you go into this area this morning?"

Rena's scowl deepened. "No, I came from home and drove over the bridge down south where the creek flows into the canal."

Mattie realized her question had annoyed her guide, but she couldn't help it if the woman was overly sensitive. "Okay. Let's get started."

She turned her attention to Robo. He'd been standing quietly at heel while she'd studied the map, and now as she folded it to put it into her pocket, he observed her.

She eased off her backpack to get his collapsible bowl and water, a necessary part of their warm-up before starting a search. He appeared excited and ready to work.

"You don't need to carry water for him," Rena said in a disapproving tone. "There are plenty of puddles and streams he can drink from around here."

"Yep, I see that. I know that your streams and standing water might not be as stagnant here as they can get in Colorado, but I always carry water to keep Robo hydrated and to avoid contamination. Giving him a drink before we search is a part of our routine. It lets him know what we're doing."

Rena still had a look of disdain on her face. "I'd think you'd want to avoid carrying the extra weight."

"I carry it for me too, so it's not a problem. Sometimes I can't keep him from drinking from streams in the forest, but for the most part, I encourage him to take water breaks with me." Mattie didn't want the woman's attitude to distract her, so she turned her back on her, hoping to discourage further comment while Robo emptied his bowl. She returned the bowl to her backpack, shrugged it on, and took his tracking harness out of a large pocket on her duty belt. "You ready to work, buddy?"

Robo danced in place, pausing to stand still while she removed his rain slicker so that he could run unencumbered through the brush. After she buckled on his search harness, he rose beside her in a pirouette, his tail wagging.

"You're ready, aren't you? You're ready to find someone. Let's go find someone." Mattie took the scent article from her duty belt pocket and lowered it for Robo to smell. His tail beat back and forth while he dipped his nose into the bag and sniffed the sock. After giving him plenty of time to catalogue the scent in his memory, Mattie sealed the bag and replaced it in her pocket. "Okay, buddy, let's go. Let's go find someone."

She unclipped his leash and waved her arm to the right, casting him out toward the trail that Rena had mentioned. Mattie started to jog after Robo, her boots slipping on the muddy foliage at the edge of the movie set. Once Robo reached the trail, he turned to follow it, with Mattie close behind.

Muddy footing hampered Mattie's speed. The woods to the left were choked with underbrush as tall as her head, creating a serious obstacle to casting Robo back toward the creek. He trotted up the trail ahead of her, his nose to the air, doing exactly what she needed him to. But how could they quarter their area if they couldn't leave the trail?

*My guide should be able to answer that question*, Mattie thought. "Robo, wait." He stopped and looked back over his shoulder, his brow raised as if asking her what's up. "Rena, how do we get through this wall of shrubs to quarter back toward the creek?"

"You probably can't without chopping it down with a machete," she said, sounding somewhat smug. "This area is filled with salal, currants, roses, and berry bushes. They all spread and take over. You just have to look for places to penetrate into the woods where you can. Once you're beneath the forest canopy, this type of growth isn't quite as thick."

"How did you clear this area yesterday?"

Rena frowned. "My dog searches on leash, so I had to look for places where I could go in. I went at least a half mile up this trail, but there really aren't many places to go into from here. I was able to get to the creek a few times."

Mattie started to understand part of Rena's frustration. She probably thought that if she couldn't search this area, someone from out of state wouldn't be able to either. And apparently Robo's good reputation didn't add to her confidence in the newcomers.

Rena added another thought. "I figure that if I can't get off the trail, the kid couldn't either."

"That's possible. And yet he's smaller than we are and who knows what his intention was when he left the set. Maybe he wanted to explore the deep woods."

Robo had been sniffing the air during their short conversation, and Mattie wanted to get back to work before they lost any more momentum. "Let's see what we can do with Robo," she said, gesturing toward her dog. "Maybe we can find someplace where he can go in."

Rena shrugged and Mattie turned to focus on Robo. "Okay, boy. Let's find someone."

He trotted up the trail with Mattie close behind looking for holes in the base of the shrubs. About twenty-five yards uphill, she spotted the first one. Robo was a short distance ahead of her, so she called him back. "Right here, buddy. Go in here. Search!"

She held back the branches of a plant with long stems and thick, waxy leaves that dripped with moisture. Robo lowered his nose as if burrowing his way in and soon disappeared within the shrubbery.

"I don't think this is going to work," Rena muttered.

"It won't work if we don't try." Mattie continued to kneel near the opening, waiting to see if Robo turned around to come right back or if he would find another route to search. She trusted her dog to do the job whether she was right beside him or not.

# EIGHT

Mattie waited five minutes, listening hard for Robo's bark. Though it wasn't raining, moisture hung in the air, creating a heavy fog that seeped down the trail from uphill, covering the forest like a damp white blanket. The mist felt otherworldly and gave her the creeps.

It also seemed to put a damper on the ability for sound to travel through the air, and she began to wonder if she would even hear Robo if he barked. Besides, she was freezing while she huddled here on the trail; she needed to get moving again. She called for him to come before pulling on her water-resistant runner's gloves and starting to walk slowly up the trail.

"Giving up on that?" Though the question was innocent enough, Rena's tone reflected pure goading.

"Nope, just sampling to see how he comes back."

"If he does come back."

Despite trying to keep an even keel, Mattie felt her brow lower. "Why wouldn't he?"

Rena shrugged.

*Passive aggressive.* Mattie knew the type. She decided the best response would be no response. Within minutes, Robo popped out of the shrubbery about twenty yards farther up the trail, his coat thoroughly drenched. He gave a mighty shake of his whole body, ending with his tail, and then looked her way, dancing on his front feet and wagging. No sign of a hit, but Mattie knew he'd been searching while traversing whatever pathway he could find through the forest.

She jogged uphill, praising her dog for coming when called. A glance told her that Rena was trailing behind, a sour look on her face. Mattie squatted beside Robo with one arm over him, drawing him close for a hug. She noticed drops of blood from scratches on Robo's head and worried about his eyes. *He must've had to press through thorn bushes.*

"What did you find in there, buddy? Is there a trail?" She opened her backpack and withdrew the doggy goggles that Cole had given her. She thought Robo wouldn't need them for rain, but they should protect his eyes from thorn injury.

She adjusted the straps and made sure Robo was going to tolerate the new equipment before taking out the bag that contained the scent article and refreshing his memory with a quick whiff. She placed it back in her belt pocket for safekeeping and then directed him up the trail. "Okay, buddy. Let's go. Let's search!"

Determined to go with him this time, Mattie followed him uphill, searching for another opening in the bushes. At a hole that looked promising, she squatted to gaze into it past stems and branches that appeared to open into less congested territory. Robo nosed his way in, helping make her decision. "Okay, buddy. Let's go search."

Robo went first and she followed on hands and knees as raindrops and condensation on the leaves dripped onto her coat and hood.

"You're not going to be able to go far," Rena called after her. "Do I have to go in there too?"

Mattie paused and strained to look backwards in the small tunnel. Rena had crouched down to watch and Mattie felt happy to leave her frowning face behind. "No, I've got my bearings. We'll come back to the trail farther uphill."

Robo's tail was disappearing out the other end of the tunnel by the time Mattie turned back, and she hurried to catch up. She crawled about fifteen feet into a gauntlet of limbs that slapped and scratched her face, forcing her to lower it and lead with the crown of her head, using her hood for protection. Though these bushes had wider leaves that held the moisture, it wasn't too different from crawling through willows at the edge of a creek back home.

By the time she reached the tunnel's end, it opened into a whole different world. She stood and straightened to look around. Giant evergreen trees towered over her, creating a canopy in the dim light of dawn. Douglas fir grew tall and thick, interspersed with a tree that looked like a colossal cedar, both having branches that started high on their moss-covered trunks. Other trees with drooping boughs near the ground filled the lower space. Deadfall covered the ground, a stick puzzle of logs and branches covered in grasses and a light green mossy film.

Mattie remembered that a volunteer suffered a broken leg in this stuff the night before. She took a tentative step upward onto a massive felled branch, and her boot skated sideways on the wet, slippery moss. Catching her balance while she looked ahead, she spotted Robo hopping delicately across the deadfall, his nose in the air. But then he disappeared into the mist.

Forest and fog pressed upon her, triggering claustrophobia that she'd battled since childhood. She paused to take a deep breath and slowly exhale, attempting to stave off panic as she remembered words from Sarge during a training session. "Don't worry if you lose sight of your dog when he goes into ravines or places you can't follow. He'll do his job and he'll always know where you are. Remember that his sense of smell tells him exactly where to go."

Taking cautious steps, she ventured into the forest. Back home she would be running, dodging rocks, boulders, tree roots, and clumps of buffalo grass as she followed Robo across country. But here . . . a rotten branch emitted a muffled snap under her boot as she took another step. Gingerly, she made her way through the deadfall, going in the direction where she'd last spotted her dog.

She realized that Rena might have been right when she'd said the child wouldn't go off trail into this particular area. After all, her guide did know this country better than she did. Maybe searching this part of the forest on foot wasn't worth the risk. But as she made her way through the enormous trees in the dampened quiet of early morning, the vastness of the forest spoke to her in many ways.

Taking in another deep breath of the moist air soothed her soul as well as her emotions. Yes, the cop side of her recognized that someone could hide a body that would never be found in this place, even while her spiritual side felt a connection to this lush earth where plants were nurtured by the fertile soil and plentiful rain. As the early morning light brightened, it was like entering an emerald cathedral.

She continued on, picking her way while learning how to traverse the area without stumbling. She wondered if Robo had traveled as far as the creek that marked the edge of their grid. She figured at his rate of speed, he'd probably come close. He would continue to sample the air and the ground as he went and would let her know if he found River's scent or something outside the environmental norm. He'd once caught the odor of a dead child from close to a mile away, and even though the wind conditions had to be just right for that kind of distance, she felt sure that he would be well within scenting range in their narrow territorial slot.

Today the air was damp, heavy, and with a slight breeze that flowed downhill. While the rain might have washed a track away, conditions for air scenting should be good. Mattie worked her way through the deadfall to the top of a ravine, its edge glittering with ice crystals. Looking for Robo, she scanned toward the bottom, placed her foot wrong on an icy spot, and lost her balance. In the blink of an eye, she was tumbling down the ravine wall, crashing into tree branches and rocks as she went. She stopped when she butted up against a fallen tree trunk.

She moaned as she struggled to sit, taking stock of her shaky limbs. Nothing broken. The mist had begun to thin, and she caught sight of Robo coming toward her, his dark shape taking form as he moved silently through nearby trees. He trotted up to her and nosed her carefully, as if to check why she was sitting on the ground.

Relieved to see his bright eyes and smiling face, she planted a kiss on the top of his head and hugged him. "Good boy. I'm okay. Just one of my klutzy moments."

She picked herself up and brushed off leaves and mud that clung to her clothing. Thinking she would be stiff and sore, she rubbed a few tender spots on her legs. The creek burbled from nearby, shifting her attention from herself to her dog. "Is it time for some more water?"

Again, she thought of Rena's disapproval of her carrying her own water, and again she admitted that the guide might be right. There would be plenty of places for Robo to hydrate here, and it might be unnecessary to carry his water with her. But it was part of their routine, and it had always seemed like the safest thing to do for Robo.

Dogs weren't as susceptible to giardia and other waterborne pathogens as humans, but they could still succumb if exposed to virulent strains. And Cole had told her about a dog that contracted lead poisoning from contaminated water, something that caused seizures and organ damage. She watched while Robo slurped up the water she'd poured into his bowl. He was used to her providing it for him, so she would continue to do so.

The radio on her shoulder crackled to life and she heard Rena's voice through the speaker asking her to reply. She pressed the switch to activate her mic. "This is Mattie."

"Are you coming out to the trail? Over." She sounded impatient.

"We've found a corridor in the interior that we can search. I think we'll stay here and range uphill." Mattie preferred straight talk on radio channels.

"Do you need my help with your grid?"

"No. I have a handle on my boundaries now."

"I'm going back to incident command to see if I can pick up a grid with Dozer. Over."

Mattie remembered that Dozer was Rena's dog. She could understand Rena wanting to get back out there with her dog, although it felt wrong for a field assistant to leave a K-9 team alone. But Mattie had to admit she was happy to see Rena go. "Good. Sounds like a plan. Your skills are wasted standing around waiting for me."

When Rena answered, she sounded appeased and maybe even somewhat surprised. "Thanks. I'll see you later. We're all expected to check back in around noon for rebriefing and lunch. Over."

"Ten four. See you at noon."

Robo had been watching her expectantly. "You want the scent again, big guy?"

She continued to chatter as she offered the open bag again. He buried his nose in it, waving his tail gently. "Okay, let's go find someone, bud. Search!"

When Robo angled off to the right this time, Mattie trailed after him. He hit the boundary marked by thick brush and shifted back to the left on his own, continuing uphill, lifting his nose to sample the air. The dense fog had lifted, and Mattie stayed close enough to observe him. She stayed in the middle of their territory while he traversed back and forth, and they worked their way uphill for what she judged to be at least a couple of hours. It was slow going.

When they were near the trail, Robo stopped and nosed the ground. Lifting a front paw and then pausing before taking a step, he appeared to concentrate as he approached an opening in the bushes. When he opened his mouth to touch something in the grass and then sat and stared at it, Mattie's heart rate kicked up a few notches. She hurried as fast as she could to get near him.

"Have you found something, buddy? What did you find?" she said as she leaned over him, ruffling the fur at his neck and peering down into the grass.

A paper wrapper lay nestled in the long, green stems, partially covered. It didn't look very degraded, so considering the rain and wet conditions, it must have been left fairly recently.

Mattie reached for the toy that she used for rewarding him with one hand while patting her dog with the other. "Good boy! Good job, Robo." She tossed him the squeaky ball on a rope, which he snapped up neatly in his powerful jaws. He began to chomp while a rather dreamy expression filled his eyes.

She pulled off her gloves so she could use her cell phone to photograph Robo's find in place. It was the brown wrapper from a small bag of M&M's. No telling if it had been left here by River or not, but Mattie intended to treat it like evidence anyway.

As a patrol dog, Robo had been trained to indicate anything that didn't fit the environmental norm regardless of the scent left on that object, a skill that not all working dogs had been taught. Mattie wondered if this wrapper bore River's scent or if her dog had found it simply because it didn't belong out here in the forest. When Robo had homed in on Sophie during their training session, he'd missed finding her planted sock, and yet here he'd found something even less scent-laden than an article of clothing. Not for the first time, she wished her dog could talk.

She put on her gloves to bag the wrapper in case fingerprints could be found on the waxy paper. "Stay here, Robo." While he continued to chomp on his toy, she squeezed her way through the opening in the trees and bushes, following a tunnel for about fifteen feet until she came out on the narrow trail. She tore a two-foot strip of orange flagging tape from her supply and tied it to a branch of one of the bushes to mark the spot.

On her way back through the opening, a thorn snagged her rain jacket and then pricked her hand through her gloves as she tried to brush it away. She stopped to search visually in case the same thing had happened to the person who'd dropped the wrapper, causing them to leave behind further evidence. But she couldn't see anything.

Robo hadn't budged and was still chewing his toy when she came back out on his side. "Good boy," she said, reaching for the toy's rope. "Drop."

He took one last chomp and then released, his ears pricked and his eyes pinned to the toy while she put it away. He shifted back and forth on his feet, obviously hoping for a game of tug or fetch. "We'll play with your ball later," she told him as she reached again for River's scent article. "We still have work to do."

She planned to search this area thoroughly for River's scent before the boots on the ground volunteers came in to search. At least the terrain was more open here, and others should be able to enter by squeezing through the same way she did.

She used her radio to report in to Sheriff Piper about the candy wrapper and how she'd marked the trail by it.

"Any sign of the boy's scent in the area?" Piper asked.

"Not sure yet. Robo and I need about a half hour to search. Then you can send volunteers in to follow up."

"Ten four. I'll send a group in thirty minutes. Will you be there?"

"No. I'll keep moving uphill if I don't get a hit from Robo here. The spot is well marked with orange tape. They can't miss it."

"All right. Over."

Mattie put away her radio, chatted Robo up with the scent article, and directed his nose to the ground where he'd found the wrapper. "Search!"

He seemed to know what she was asking as he swept his head side to side, sniffing the grass. He acted interested in the area and started slowly walking uphill toward the center of their grid. By the time he wound through trees and reached more open land, he was alternating nose to the ground with nose to the air. He circled several times, stopping to sniff a grassy patch here and there, but not seeming to pick up a track that he could follow. Mattie sensed his frustration but stayed silent and let him do his work.

In a ragged start-stop pattern, Robo continued to work his way uphill until he came to a faint game trail through the underbrush. He stayed on the trail, working both sides of it as he sniffed grass and bushes. Mattie thought the heavy rain during the evening and night was inhibiting his ability to find a solid track. She couldn't help but think that Robo's slow and careful work was a result of finding patches of scent here and there but then losing the track again because scent cells had been washed away.

She wondered if River had come this way. Why else would Robo be so interested in this game trail that he stayed with it? And he seemed to be working the ground more than the air, a different pattern than when they'd begun earlier this morning.

She was relieved that the game trail allowed her to stay with him, and she told him he was a good boy to encourage him to keep working. Together they toiled uphill through the dense forest.

★   ★   ★

Hours later Mattie felt exhausted and she could tell Robo did too. His tail drooped and he'd lost his enthusiasm, although he'd hung in there like a trouper as he swept their grid. At times he'd left the game trail, moving back and forth with his nose up as if searching for a scent and then going back to the game trail to sniff the foliage at its edge.

Mattie kept him engaged with praise, water breaks, hugs, and pats, but she could tell that without the reward of finding someone, his interest had begun to flag. They had reached what she thought was the top part of their grid, and she decided that it was time she gave her dog a much-deserved break and time to play, eat, and rest before taking on more territory.

She called Robo to come to her and then knelt beside him to give him a hug and a kiss. She offered him some water and he slurped greedily. "You're a good boy, you know that? Good job. It's time to go eat."

The air had grown heavy with moisture so that droplets gathered on her face despite her hood. Rain began to patter, although they could stay relatively dry if they huddled beneath one of the huge evergreens.

She led the way to the right, crossing over deadfall and mossy logs as she slowly picked a pathway toward the trail. She squeezed through bushes, got snagged on brambles, and finally came out onto the main trail, where she set a course downhill. Robo seemed happier and more refreshed as he trotted in front of her, his step jaunty. The freedom of moving downhill on the relatively clear trail gave Mattie an added boost as well.

When they reached the branch marked with orange tape, the forest ranger guy who'd been paired with Drake earlier was standing there. Mattie searched her memory for his name and came up with Hunter. Hunter Bailey.

He raised a hand in greeting. "Hey."

Tail wagging, Robo trotted up to Hunter, who bent to pet him. Robo sniffed Hunter's pants from the knees down as his tail continued to beat a rhythm side to side.

*He probably smells Fritz*, Mattie thought as she drew up beside the two of them. "Hey, Hunter."

Robo was pressing his nose hard against Hunter's calves as he gave the man's trousers a thorough going over, and she leaned down to grasp the nylon handle on top of his search harness to pull him back a few inches.

"Robo, that's enough." Still bending over her dog while she patted him, Mattie looked up at Hunter. "I think he smells one of his buddies from Colorado on you."

Hunter smiled. "That would be the sad-eyed Fritz. I was with him most of the morning."

She nodded, tipping her head toward the interior of the territory she'd cleared. "Find anything else in there?"

"No, I'm afraid not." Hunter touched the broad-leafed branch of the bush she had marked. "You found a wrapper on the other side of this patch of salal?"

"Right." She withdrew the evidence bag that held the candy wrapper and showed it to him. "It's in pretty good shape, so in weather like this I can't imagine it's been out here very long."

Frowning, he looked at the wrapper and then at her. "This is a strange spot for it to have ended up. I can't imagine someone squeezing through here and dropping it. Maybe it blew in with the storm."

"It was in a sheltered spot under the bush, but I suppose anything's possible." Mattie secured the bag back in her backpack. "I'm going to head on down and check this in with the sheriff."

"Okay, there's food in the mess tent too. Don't miss out."

Mattie nodded and headed down the trail. She found Piper in the trailer used for incident command and checked her evidence in with him. She couldn't resist asking, "What's the status of the hit on River's mattress?"

A muscle clenched on Piper's jaw before he spoke. "Chrystal Winter told the same story that Sally Kessler did, and I know they didn't collaborate before I questioned them separately. I still took the mattress as potential evidence even though we're probably looking at a simple nosebleed. I'm sending it to the state lab to be examined in case they find blood that's more widespread. I'll have my people take a look at this wrapper, though."

Mattie felt relieved that Piper took Fritz's hit seriously. "Sounds like a good plan. We're headed to the mess tent now, but we'll be ready to go back out this afternoon."

"I've prepared assignments. I'll meet you over there in a bit."

Mattie followed the muddy alley to the tent. When she reached the entrance, she met Sally Kessler coming out carrying three Styrofoam clamshells.

Sally had her head down, watching her footing, and appeared startled when she glanced up. "Oh, hello."

Mattie greeted her, pleased to have a chance to ask her more questions. "My dog found an M&M wrapper at the base of a bush near the trail we were searching," she said. "Is that one of River's favorites?"

"He loves plain M&M's." Sally's eyebrows were raised as if in surprise. "Is the wrapper brown?"

"It is. Brown and small. Did he have a bag of the candy yesterday before he went missing?"

"No, I'm sure he didn't." Sally looked discouraged as she shook her head. "Chrystal doesn't like for him to have sweets, so we don't keep them around, especially candy. He loves it so much and would overeat if we allowed him to."

Mattie recalled River's photo and his slender, almost waiflike body build. "He's a thin child, right?"

"He is. I think a little sweetness wouldn't hurt him a bit, but it isn't my call to make." Sally looked down at the boxed lunches she carried. "I suppose I should get these to Chrystal and the guys. They'll be waiting."

Mattie said goodbye and watched Sally trudge off through the mud. Was there a deeper meaning to her statement that a little sweetness wouldn't hurt River? Did the child lack sweetness in his life?

She led Robo into the mess tent and sought out the table where the box lunches were stacked. The same person who'd cooked and served breakfast was manning the table. The local grocer, if she remembered right, but she couldn't recall his name.

"Right here, ma'am," he said, offering her a smile as he pushed one of the boxes toward her at the table's edge.

"Thank you. I'm starved." Mattie took the box from him. "I know you were introduced this morning, but I can't remember your name."

"Merc. Merc Foster. Merc is short for Mercury. My dad was a weather buff," he said, grinning and offering a handshake. "I own Bigfoot Market."

She juggled her lunch and Robo's leash to shake his hand. "It's nice of you to help out with the food."

The grin dropped from his face. "I'm too old and out of shape to be out searching the woods. It feels like this is the best I can do to help with the effort. A lost child is a tragedy for any community, and search and rescue is our responsibility."

*The word tragedy seems premature*, Mattie thought. "Well, let's hope the community effort ends with a good outcome." She lifted her lunch box. "Thank you for this."

"Drinks and dessert are on down the table," he said, waving in that direction while turning his attention to the next person in line.

Mattie snagged a canned soda from a cooler even as her eyes traveled down the table to a couple of large baskets filled with a variety of different candy bars wrapped in individual sized servings. Snickers, Milky Ways, Kit-Kat bars, and yes, bags of both plain and peanut M&M's. Her first thought: *These must have come from his store.*

She took a bag of the plain M&M's and a candy bar for later. She turned back to the grocer at the other end of the table. "Mr. Foster," she called and waited for him to look her way. She held up both servings of candy. "Did these come from your store?"

He flashed his big, open grin. "Sure did, miss. Everything here came from my store."

"Thanks again," she said, turning to scout out a table where she could sit and feed Robo. He needed fuel too. She had to wonder if there was a connection between the store and the wrapper she'd found, but if so, it would be hard to trace. Anyone could buy a bag of candy.

She had placed her food at the end of a table and was stripping off her backpack when a commotion at the doorway caught her attention. Exclamations of concern came from a group of people who'd gathered outside near the tent's opening. When the word "help" filtered through the murmuring of the crowd, she told Robo to heel and hurried out to see what was wrong.

Under the awning she found Rena down on her knees by a black Labrador retriever who was in the throes of a seizure. The dog had vomited and remained crouched on his belly while he shuddered rhythmically, his front legs stretched forward while his lips were pulled back from his teeth and his eyes half closed in a tight facial grimace.

After telling Robo to sit and stay, Mattie rushed forward to see if she could help.

# NINE

Six inches of snow blanketed Cole's yard as he drove his truck into his driveway. It had snowed through the night, and when he'd made his morning rounds, roads had been treacherous. Most of his routine appointments had been canceled that morning as folks called in one after the other to reschedule, which had been a good thing since it had opened up his day for the emergencies that bad weather always brought. Horse colics, premature calves and foals, pneumonia. *And even though no one wants to brave the slick highways, I'm expected to,* he thought, feeling sorry for himself.

But on second thought, he decided it was rightfully so. *This is what I signed up for when I became a large animal vet.* He thought of Mattie, wondering what type of weather she was facing today in the Pacific Northwest. He wished she would call.

As he pulled into the garage, snowflakes spattered the windshield, the wipers scraping against a thin layer of ice at the top of the glass. He turned off the engine and relaxed a moment against the headrest of his seat while the door rumbled closed. He was late for lunch, but when he'd checked in with Mrs. Gibbs earlier, she'd been making chicken noodle soup, something to look forward to on a day like today.

After exiting his truck, he stripped off his coveralls, dampened from knee to ankle by melting snow, and hung it on a hook near the door to the kitchen. Slipping off his boots to leave on the tray, he tiptoed in his wool socks over the cold concrete to the doorway.

As he entered the kitchen, the aroma of chicken soup mingled with that of freshly baked bread, immediately making his taste buds vibrate with anticipation. Mrs. Gibbs stood at the stove using a wooden spoon to stir her delicious concoction in a large pot.

She turned toward him, saying, "Ooch, get yerself in here and warm up. If you want to take a seat at the table, I'll dish up a hearty serving of this hot soup for you."

Cole counted his lucky stars that this woman had come into his life to run his household and help him raise his kids. "Thank you, Mrs. Gibbs. You don't know how much I've been looking forward to this ever since we talked. Let me wash my hands and I'll be right there."

She chuckled. "I have an idea how much you've been wantin' your soup. And I baked fresh sourdough to go with it."

"I can smell it," he said as he stepped into the utility room to wash up in the sink. "Delicious!"

Hilde scampered in around the corner, sliding to a halt before jumping up on the counter where her food bowls were kept out of reach of the dogs. But instead of going right to her kibble, she arched against his arm, rubbing back and forth. With his hands still in the water, Cole lowered his face so that she could put her nose up against his to greet him. After drying his hands, he stroked her soft fur before she turned away to hunker down to crunch a few tidbits.

"You're a beauty," he murmured as he gave her one last rub behind the ears. Going back into the kitchen, he spotted soup and a plateful of sliced bread at his place at the table. "Thank you, thank you. What a wild morning it's been."

"How are the roads?" Mrs. Gibbs asked.

"Terrible." He sampled his first bite of the soup, the rich broth savory on his tongue, the warmth spreading into his throat, chest, and stomach as he swallowed. "Mmm . . . this is perfect."

"Do you want something hot to drink?"

"Coffee if you have it, but I can get it myself."

"Keep yer seat." She filled two cups of the hot brew and brought them both to the table, taking her seat across from him. "Do you have to go back out?"

"Not right away. I do need to get to the clinic to make sure the chickens and Mountaineer have water and feed."

"Sophie took care of the chickens, so they're okay. Angie checked the horse and said he had water, so the tank heater must be perkin' away like it's supposed to."

Surprised, Cole looked at her and raised a brow. "That's great! I thought they might have conveniently forgotten their outdoor chores on a day like today."

Mrs. Gibbs smiled gently. "Ooh, they needed a bit of a reminder, but they went willingly enough."

Cole returned her smile before tucking back into his soup. "Where *are* the girls, anyway?"

"Angie's in her room and Sophie's watching television. They just finished their lunch after doing chores, so I figured they'd earned some downtime."

Cole nodded as he buttered a slice of warm bread.

"The weather report says this storm should clear out by late afternoon," she said. "We're in for a bit of a cold snap but no more snow for a few days. Have you heard from Miss Mattie?"

"Not since her text saying she arrived in Seattle during the night. I hope she calls soon." His first bite of bread transported him to his childhood when his mother made sourdough like this. Which reminded him that he wanted to talk to Mrs. Gibbs alone about his parents before involving his daughters in the conversation.

"When I saw Mom and Dad yesterday I found out that my mom is feeling left out." Remembering his mother's criticism made Cole's shoulders tighten. He looked up to meet his house-keeper's unemotional gaze and grimaced to show how he felt about his next statement. "I ended up asking them to come over for dinner sometime."

Her bland expression shifted toward a frown.

Cole felt like he'd made a mistake. "I'm sorry I spoke out of turn. I should've asked you about having guests for dinner before I invited them. I can do the cooking—I've gotten real good at grilling burgers."

"Ah no, it's not that. I'm happy to cook a good meal for yer folks, but I'm thinking of Miss Angela. She won't be pleased."

"I know. I'm afraid of that too. But I'll have to explain to her, and I think she'll come around. She's still defensive of her mother, even though she's been on the outs with her."

Angie's voice came from behind Cole. "What's this you have to explain to me? What's Mom done now?"

Cole turned to see his oldest paused in the doorway to the kitchen. She padded forward on her teal sock-slippers, her stride lithe and graceful. She wore black yoga pants and a teal-colored tee with a charcoal hooded sweater, her pale blond hair loose about her shoulders. It struck Cole that she'd grown into a young lady, and she looked more like her mother every day. And like her mother, she was frowning at him as she approached.

He took a breath and decided he might as well tackle the subject head on. He pushed out the chair next to him. "Come join us. I was at your grandparents' house yesterday. That's what we're talking about." He thought a hospitable approach might serve him well. "Do you want something warm to drink?"

She gave him a suspicious look as she settled onto the chair, one leg bent under her. "No thanks. What about Grandpa and Grandma?"

*How to start?* "Well, we were talking about the wedding—"

She interrupted him. "And Grandma is opposed to it, right?"

*How did she know?* He felt it best not to share too many details. "Kind of. She's just concerned that it's too soon for Mattie and me to get married, but after we talked about it, I think it's more because she feels left out."

"After she drove Mom away, keeping her at a distance from Mattie is probably a good thing." Angie bent a lock of her hair upward to study the ends, picking at them gently.

"First of all, I'm not so sure Grandma drove your mother away. You know how Mom's mental health affected her decision to leave . . . we've been over that many times." Cole felt himself getting defensive, and he paused to take a breath. "Besides, Mattie is a completely different person."

Mrs. Gibbs edged out of her chair. "I'm going to leave you two to discuss this," she said as she turned to leave.

Cole understood that she was giving them privacy, but he felt abandoned all the same. A little reinforcement when dealing with his daughter might have been nice. He started over. "Both of your grandparents wish they could see us more often, and I think it would be nice for them to get to know Mattie better too. Grandpa seems to really miss being with you guys, actually both of them do. I think they were sad, and well . . . I decided we should have them over for dinner once in a while. We don't have to do it all the time, you know, just now and then."

He paused, feeling like he'd started to backpedal even before he needed to. Although his daughter continued to fiddle with the ends of her hair, her intense blue eyes had remained on him while he talked. "You and Mattie can have dinner with them."

"But it's you kids they say they miss."

"Then they can see Sophie. Grandma loves Sophie."

Cole felt perplexed. "She loves you too. They'll want to see both of you girls."

Angie gathered a different lock of hair for inspection. "Um, Dad . . . you know how you can just *feel* things? Well, maybe you don't. Anyway, I can *feel* that Sophie is Grandma's favorite. And that's okay, you know. It really is, 'cause Sophie's a great kid, and I don't want to be around Grandma anyway. She'll be just as happy spending time with Sophie."

"Angel, I don't think that's true." Cole tried to search her face, but she kept it downturned, making a show of studying her hair.

"It's true, Dad." She glanced up at him and he thought he saw hurt feelings in her eyes. "Sometimes you've got to face the truth. You've told me that before."

"Well . . ." He started to protest but realized he couldn't argue her feelings away. And who knew? With his mother, it was quite possible she *would* choose favorites. Angie looked like Olivia, someone his mother never did like, while Sophie resembled him. And even though he'd never felt like his mother's chosen child, he thought she at least liked him better than Liv.

"You know, Angel, I can't tell you what Grandma thinks. And if she does show favorites, all I can say is that's not the way I think a grandparent should act. But I can tell you that both of them said yesterday that they wish they could spend more time with you kids, and they seemed sincere about it. Maybe we should give Grandma another chance."

She squinted at him through her frown. "I'm not so sure about that."

Cole decided to quit while he still had a chance of influencing her later. "I'm glad you told me how you feel. Why don't we think about this and talk about it again later. I'm not planning a get together until sometime after the wedding anyway, so we'll have plenty of time to discuss it."

"I don't think I'll change my mind. I could go hang out with Ben or you could always say I'm upstairs sick in my room."

Cole shook his head as he gave her a thin smile. He didn't want to set a precedent of either of his daughters hanging out with a boyfriend to avoid family events. "I'm not sure either of those options would be a good solution. Let's table this for now, okay?"

She gave him a dubious look, lips pressed together. "Ooo-kay. But I'm not going to change my mind."

He could tell he wouldn't make any more headway today. "Just try to keep your mind open, okay? Now, change of subject. I appreciate you girls agreeing to help us get things ready for the wedding. Has anything come up that you need me to do before I go get the flowers later in the week?"

Angie sat straighter and quit fiddling with her hair. "Not really. Maybe Mrs. Gibbs knows of something."

"The storm should clear out today and I'll get groceries tomorrow. I'm done with calls now until Monday unless another emergency comes in, so I can hang out tonight."

"Oh." She raised a thin eyebrow. "I already made plans with Ben."

He felt his own eyebrows lift. "You aren't planning to go out on a night like this, are you? The roads are horrible out there."

"We're going to a movie. We'll just drive between here and town."

It felt like Angie's previous concern that he was never around to spend time with his kids had come full circle and landed on her own doorstep, but he decided it would be counterproductive to point that out. "I think you should reconsider. Invite Ben over here if you want to, and maybe we could have game night or something. Or watch a movie in the great room in front of a fire."

She squirmed in her seat, perhaps realizing that the shoe was now on the other foot. "I'll call Ben and see what he says. I'll get back to you on that."

It had become hard to negotiate such things as dates now that Angie was approaching seventeen. Cole wasn't sure if this was one of those times to put his foot down or not. Ben drove a four-wheel-drive Jeep, and he seemed to be a responsible kid, so maybe Cole should let this one play out with an early curfew. It was hard to know. "If you decide to go out, maybe you should get home early so we don't have to worry. The temperature's going to plunge after the clouds clear out."

Angie shrugged and stood, clearly ending the conversation. "I'll let you know," she said before leaving him alone at the table. He was about to reply, but his cell phone jingled in his pocket, so he reached for it instead. It was Mattie.

He connected the call. "Hey, sweetheart. I'm glad you called."

Mattie released an audible breath as if she'd been holding it. "I'm so glad you answered."

It felt like something was wrong. "Is there a problem?"

"There is. We have a dog here that's very sick."

Alarm shot through him. "Robo?"

"No, he's fine. Someone else's dog."

"What's going on?"

"Intermittent seizures, vomiting, diarrhea."

"Is he seizing now?"

"No, he's lying stretched out on his side at the moment. He tried to walk, but he sort of staggered around and then lay down like he just couldn't stand anymore."

"Any history of seizures?"

Cole could hear Mattie pass the question on to someone else, presumably the dog's owner.

She came back on the phone. "No, no previous seizures. Healthy until just about a half hour ago."

"Did the dog eat or drink something it shouldn't have? Did it get ahold of any meds, anything like that?"

There was another pause as Mattie referred the question to the person standing by. "Not that she's aware of. She didn't see the dog eat anything but his food earlier. Here, I'm putting you on speaker phone."

Cole waited until Mattie gave him the okay. "Standing water? Anything that could've leached out lead-based paint, like an old paint tray or something like that?"

Another woman's voice came through the speaker. "I didn't see him drink anything like that. He drank from the stream but not any standing water that I saw. Although there are plenty of puddles in the woods."

"Okay, I think you need to get him to a vet as soon as you can. It's hard to say without examining him, but in the absence of a seizure disorder, this is probably something your dog ingested."

"The nearest vet is about an hour away." The woman's voice was tight with stress. "Should I do anything or give him anything to try to make him vomit more?"

"No. He's already done that on his own." Cole was thinking poison of some kind, and there were some poisons that did more damage coming up the esophagus than going down. But he didn't want to say that at the moment. "Get a clean paper cup or some kind of container and take a sample of what he expelled into the vet with him. And if you can, get a baggie with a stool sample too. Can you do that?"

"I'll get that for her, Cole." This time it was Mattie on the line. "We can find a volunteer to drive her to the vet."

"I've got my car," the other woman said. "Maybe I can find someone to drive it so I can hold him."

"If you have a crate in the car, that's a good place for him," Cole told her. "Or keep him on the floor. Anything to keep him from falling if he should seize again."

"Okay," the woman said, sounding close to tears. "Thank you."

"Sure thing. Get him to a vet as soon as possible."

"I will."

Mattie came back on the line. "You're off speaker. Thanks, Cole. I'd better help her get those samples and find someone to go with her."

"Is it snowing there?"

"No, just rain."

"And both you and Robo are okay?"

"We are. I'll call you back as soon as she gets on the road."

"Okay. I love you."

"Same here." She disconnected the call.

He could tell Mattie was in her business mode and would handle things as efficiently as she always did in these matters. Even when they first met, she had assisted him with caring for Belle's injuries, needing only a minimum of coaching. And when it came to Robo, she could manage him with a glance, a word, or a gentle hand, even when he was injured.

While he waited for her to call back, Cole pondered conditions that could lead to an accidental dog poisoning. The most common would be the dog getting into medication for treating parasites and ingesting enough for an overdose, but poisons of various types could also be found in fuels, herbicides, and pesticides. Nowadays it would be less common for a dog to contract lead poisoning from lead-based paints, but it still could happen if the dog was kept in an older building.

Then his mind went to a darker place and considered the possibility of someone poisoning a search and rescue dog on purpose. This would be even less likely. But what if this child had been kidnapped instead of lost in the woods? Wouldn't that increase the likelihood of search and rescue dogs and personnel being threatened or in danger? And with that thought, he became worried about Mattie and Robo.

Mrs. Gibbs drifted back into the kitchen. "You look upset. Did it not go well with Miss Angela?"

He'd momentarily forgotten all about his previous discussion with his daughter. "We're both thinking things over and we'll talk about it later. Probably after the wedding. But I just heard from Mattie. One of the search and rescue dogs is sick, and it sounds like it might be from poison."

"Ooch, that's serious."

"Yeah, it is. I can't help but worry about Robo and Mattie. I'm waiting for her to call me back." Cole stood and began to clear the table.

Mrs. Gibbs began putting away the extra food. "You're a long ways away to help them if yer needed."

She'd summed up exactly how he felt. "Yes. I guess the closest vet out there is about an hour away. That hour could make a big difference in survival for an animal that's ingested poison."

"You could go, you know. That is, if you could get to the airport." She gave him a speculative look.

He truly hadn't considered it. He set his dishes in the sink and leaned on the counter as he studied her face. "There's still work to do for the wedding, groceries to get tomorrow, animals to care for. I think I could make it to the airport. Once I get out of this valley, the roads will be more passable."

She paused in her work and faced him. "Everything's status quo for the wedding over the next few days. I can manage getting to the grocery store, and I'm sure Miss Sophie would help me with the shopping. We can take care of the horse and chickens if you can get Garrett to be on call in case we need him."

Garrett Hartman, Cole's long-term friend and best man for the wedding, would be glad to help out if it meant assuring Robo and Mattie's safety. They were both near and dear to Garrett's heart as well as to his wife Leslie's. Cole began to get excited about joining Mattie and standing by to take care of Robo or any of the other dogs if needed. "I'm sure Garrett would agree to be on call. And my schedule's clear at the clinic over the weekend. Tess could reschedule Monday appointments and even Tuesday if I need another day to get back."

"Why don't you go, then? You could get to Denver before dark if you leave right away."

He remembered Angie's plan for tonight. "I asked Angie to stay home tonight instead of going on a date. We sort of left it up in the air depending on the roads and weather."

Mrs. Gibbs paused as if to think. "That young man of hers drives that Jeep in all kinds of weather. I think he's very capable. How about you let me help her decide by late afternoon. He can always come over here for the evening and we can make popcorn. I can let them have the television to themselves to watch movies."

Warm feelings for this lady swept through him. No one could ask for a better helpmate. "Are you sure this all sounds okay to you? I'd be leaving you with a lot of responsibility on your hands."

"We'll be fine. I can always call Miss Stella for help," she said, referring to the Timber Creek County detective and one of Mattie's attendants for the wedding. "Or even the sheriff for that matter. I couldn't stand it if anything happened to our Mattie and her sweet dog."

# TEN

Cole was coming. As Mattie disconnected the call with him, a wave of gratitude swept over her that made her almost weak with relief. Or maybe it was the loss of adrenaline from her system that left her feeling the fatigue from a short night, a hard morning's work, and lack of fuel to energize her system.

By the time she and Rena had arranged transport for Dozer, he had become lethargic and difficult to arouse. Maybe it was the onset of a seizure disorder, or maybe something he ate. She hoped the samples she'd sent with Rena would be helpful in diagnosing the problem.

Robo had sat watching Mattie, staying in place until she told him to lie down. Now, as she released him from his down-stay, she crouched beside him and hugged him, patting his chest and rubbing his fur. He nestled into her embrace and stole a few kisses, which she returned on his soft cheek. She decided to keep an extra watchful eye on him just in case Dozer had consumed something he shouldn't.

Ranger Hunter Bailey came out of the mess tent to join her. He'd returned along with several volunteers during Dozer's incident and had helped assign someone to drive Rena's SUV while she sat and held her dog in the back compartment. After sending Dozer on his way, everyone else had gone inside the tent to grab lunch.

"Did you get lunch yet, Mattie?" Hunter asked.

She gave Robo one last hug before standing. "I had a lunch but left it on the table when I heard Rena call for help."

"Let's go eat," he said, directing her inside ahead of him.

Robo followed at heel. Mattie spotted her backpack still sitting on the table where she'd left it, but the lunch was gone. "My backpack's right there," she said, pointing to it, "but looks like I need to get another lunch."

"Okay if I join you? I can go get us a couple of lunches."

"Sure. I need to feed Robo. I'll set him up here beside us." It took only a moment to remove his supply of kibble from her backpack and set some down in a collapsible bowl as well as a bowlful of fresh water. The murmur of conversation returned as people milled around the tent, getting their meals and taking seats at various tables.

She'd sat down to clean her hands with a sanitary wipe when Hunter came back with their lunches.

"That was intense," he said on a heavy sigh as he settled back in his chair.

"Agreed. I talked to my fiancé—he's a vet back in Colorado— and he thinks Dozer might have ingested something poisonous."

Hunter frowned. "I think that's pretty much impossible. I don't think anyone would poison him."

That surprised Mattie. She hadn't said anything about a purposeful poisoning. "That's not what he was thinking. It's entirely possible for a dog to eat or drink something poisonous accidentally. Plants, chemicals, even some medications that are supposed to be used sparingly can result in a toxic response if the dog gets into it by accident."

"Oh. You'd think a dog would know better."

Maybe he'd never had a dog. "Some dogs will eat pretty much anything, whether it's good for them or not. Especially a Lab."

Mattie unwrapped her sandwich filled with a thick mixture of tuna, chopped celery, pickle relish, and mayonnaise. Her first bite made her wonder how something so simple could taste so delicious. But then being starved after the kind of morning she'd had helped enhance the flavor of everything.

"I'm paired up with you this afternoon," Hunter said, pausing before taking another bite of his sandwich. "We're going higher into the forest. There's a two-track jeep trail that leads to some private holdings back in the woods that we'll be heading toward as we search."

"I thought this was state forest all the way to the national park." She popped a potato chip into her mouth.

"Yeah, it pretty much is, but there are some old homesteads and private property located here and there. I'll be able to point them out as we go."

Mattie nodded as she chewed. She still felt tired, but the food helped. An apple and a brownie rounded out the boxed meal, promising an additional burst of energy. She also had some energy bars in her backpack to give her an extra boost if needed later in the day.

Sarge brought his lunch to the table and sat across from Hunter. "I heard we had an incident with one of the SAR dogs," he said as he retrieved a collapsible bowl for Banjo and filled it with a portion of kibble.

Robo acted interested in Banjo's food, but a word from Mattie and a side-eyed look from Banjo stopped him in his tracks. He sat beside Mattie's chair and watched while the other dog gobbled every chunk. Robo then shared his water bowl while she massaged behind his ears and filled Sarge in on what had happened with Dozer.

When Mattie returned her attention to her own meal, Robo circled and lay down beside her, resting his head on his paws. "Cole thinks the dog might have accidentally ingested something poisonous in the area. That and the fact that it takes so long to get to a vet here made him worry about the other dogs, so he's going to come out. He should be able to get here by tomorrow morning."

Sarge raised his eyebrows. "So he can't let his bride out of his sight for long, huh?"

Mattie's cheeks warmed. "He's worried about Robo."

Sarge grinned. "Uh-huh."

Hunter smiled along with Sarge's infectious grin. "When's the wedding?"

"Our Mattie is due to marry in just a few days. Didn't she tell you?"

"The subject didn't come up," Mattie murmured, wanting to redirect the conversation. "Cole is bringing vet supplies for emergency first aid in case something happens to one of the other dogs."

"Sounds like congratulations are in order for the bride and groom," Hunter said. "It's good of you both to take the time to come help us."

Mattie glanced at Sarge, who was still smiling around a large bite of his sandwich. "I was easily persuaded once I learned we were talking about a nine-year-old kid."

Merc Foster came over to their table with another box lunch in hand. "Anyone want seconds?"

His mouth filled with food, Sarge raised his hand, but then pantomimed deferment to Mattie or Hunter as he chewed.

Merc chuckled and handed the box across the table to Sarge. "There's plenty more where this came from. Do you two want another one?" he asked, glancing between Hunter and Mattie.

"No, thanks," Mattie said while Hunter nodded.

"I'll be right back." Merc left but returned within seconds with another meal. He placed the box on the table near Hunter and took a nearby seat, looking at Mattie. "That was good of you to help Rena with Dozer."

"I wish we could've done more. Thanks for getting clean containers for the samples we needed." Merc had come outside to help but hurried back to the kitchen to retrieve baggies and plastic cups with lids for samples. "So do you know Rena and Dozer?"

Merc brightened. "Absolutely. I know most everybody who lives in this neck of the woods. Most folks support my store so I can keep it open." He placed his hand on one of Hunter's shoulders. "This guy even stops in to get candy pretty often. I have to make sure I keep the M&M's well stocked."

Hunter shrugged as he unwrapped one of his brownies. "What can I say? I've got a sweet tooth."

The name of Hunter's favorite candy caught Mattie's attention. She searched his face for a reaction that might signal his connection to the wrapper that Robo had found, but if he had one, he didn't show it.

She turned back to Merc to ask a question. It still bothered her that River disappeared when his mother sent his nanny on an errand. "Sally Kessler said she was at your store yesterday. Did you see her there?"

"I was stocking shelves most of the afternoon, but I do remember her coming in. The influx of folks associated with this movie set has been good for business. I'm just sorry the boy wandered away from the set. I hope we get him back soon."

Mattie nodded. "Did you happen to see what Sally bought?"

Merc shook his head. "Like I said, I was stocking shelves. I can ask my employee if you want me to. She was running the cash register."

"I'd appreciate that if you get a chance."

Merc smiled, his face creased and wrinkled, as he stood to leave. "Sally comes in often to pick up things that Ms. Winter has ordered, and she usually buys a little bag of candy or two. But Sally asks us to keep it secret from Ms. Winter. Evidently she doesn't approve of her son having candy."

As he walked back to the kitchen, Mattie watched him, thinking it strange that he would mention Sally's secret. Did he have a hidden agenda such as suspecting Sally had something to do with River's disappearance? Did he know she'd found a candy wrapper in today's search? Was she letting her cop senses see red flags instead of innocent conversation?

Sarge spoke in a low voice meant for only Hunter and her to hear. "I talked to Sheriff Piper about treating this case as a kidnapping even as we search to make sure River isn't lost. He said he's had his investigators comb through the family's housing and other nearby trailers. He's interviewed the bodyguards, River's nanny, and others. As time passes, he's becoming more concerned River might have been taken."

His eyes downcast, Hunter opened his second lunch. "There are too many people around for the kid to be taken against his will. I think he saw his opportunity to go off exploring again, like he did when they first moved in here."

Mattie made eye contact with Sarge. "Or he could've been taken by someone he knows. Lured away somehow."

Hunter stood and gathered his things. "There's Ken over there," he said, indicating Ken Russell, the SAR K-9 team commander, with a nod of his head. "I've got to talk to him before we move out again. Mattie, I'll meet you out front in about a half hour. Will that work for you?"

"You bet. I'll be there." Mattie gazed after him, making sure he joined Ken. She then glanced back at Sarge. "That conversation about candy seemed strange. Did you know Robo found an M&M wrapper in our area this morning?"

Sarge nodded, looking thoughtful. "Piper told me. He sent it to the lab to see if prints are on it."

"Right."

"So you're thinking the child was lured and then kidnapped."

"Robo seemed very interested in places as we headed uphill. There just didn't seem to be enough scent to follow a trail. The rain could've taken care of that."

Sarge nodded. "We still have to search and make sure he's not in this area. Determining where he *isn't* is important until we know more."

"True. I'm relieved that Piper is considering both scenarios."

"Yep." Sarge was digging into his second dessert. "How did Robo perform in these conditions?"

Mattie noticed her dog was sound asleep, his body curved into a ball with his nose buried, and he didn't acknowledge if he'd heard his name. Banjo seemed to have checked out too. She was glad that both dogs were getting some good rest during their short break. "He works like a champ. He ranges out pretty far, forges into the brush and skirts around it. He's using his nose on the ground and in the air. It's all I can do to keep up with him."

There was a commotion over at the tent opening again, and both Mattie and Sarge turned to see what was happening. A good-looking man—thirty-something, dark hair cut short on the sides with the longer hair on top bleached blond—stood in the tent's doorway with a petite brunette holding a microphone up to his face. A guy with a camera on his shoulder had also edged into the tent and started filming.

"Yes, our son, River, has disappeared and we're all here look-ing for him." With spotless clothing and a leather bomber jacket, his face dark with the three-day stubble of a scruff look, River's dad didn't look at all like he'd been out in the forest searching. Instead, he looked like a model in a fashion magazine. "He was supposed to be in Chrystal's safekeeping, but apparently that didn't work."

Mattie was surprised by both his appearance and his state-ment. She remembered that Piper had instructed everyone to send members of the media to him rather than talking to them. Sarge rose from the table and headed toward the fiasco at the doorway. Robo and Banjo raised their heads, eyes blinking, so she stayed with the dogs, murmuring reassurance that all was well and they should stay put.

Sarge got to the reporter and her cameraman just as Piper entered the tent. Both men stepped in between Roger Allen and the news crew.

"Here is Sheriff Piper, incident commander for the search effort for River Allen, son of Hollywood star Chrystal Winter," the brunette said, shifting the handheld mic into Piper's face. "Sheriff, what can you tell us about the search? We've learned you have both human and K-9 volunteers looking for River in the forest around this area."

Piper looked bleary-eyed, tired, and mad as a bear wakened from hibernation, but he stepped up to the microphone in what Mattie recognized as an attempt to keep Allen away from it. "County search and rescue teams have been deployed to search for a child. We've got boots on the ground covering this area, including teams from Colorado that have flown in to help cover our rugged terrain."

Roger Allen leaned in as if making an attempt to regain the spotlight, but Sarge blocked him, lightly taking his elbow. Mattie saw Sarge murmur something in his ear, which Allen responded to by nodding and then stepping away with him toward the table where Mattie was still sitting.

In the meantime, the reporter had asked another question. "So you can confirm that River Allen, Chrystal Winter's child, is missing?"

Piper had regained control of his temper and now wore a neutral mask that Mattie thought of as a cop face. "We have a minor child who is presumed lost in the woods around this campsite and we've got plenty of volunteers who are familiar with this area out searching. No other volunteers will be allowed in camp at this time, so if anyone is inclined to come here, please stay at home unless we call for more help. This is the type of country that only skilled search and rescue volunteers should be out in. We don't want anyone else getting lost. I'll hold a press conference two hours from now, but until then, we have no further comment."

The brunette waved the microphone under her own chin briefly. "Can you confirm that this is Chrystal Winter's son?"

"We're not making any public statements at this time," Piper said, putting up both hands palms out. "No more questions for now. I'll take questions in approximately two hours. Until then, this tent and the entire campsite are off limits for all media personnel. You may wait outside our perimeter."

The brunette eyed him as if measuring his determination, but evidently decided he was done for now. She took the mic and posed for the cameraman, who focused the lens solely on her. "I'm Abby Day, reporting for KHIP, your number one choice for local news. You've heard this breaking news here first, and we'll have updates for you as they come in. Once again, although not confirmed by local law authority, we have word from the child's father that Chrystal Winter's son has become lost in the Washington state forest near Olympic National Park. Stay tuned—"

"Please leave the mess tent so you don't interfere with search efforts," Piper said, gesturing toward two deputies who had appeared at the doorway. He had situated himself between the reporter and her cameraman, his back successfully blocking their filming. "These two officers will show you where the camp perimeter is."

Sarge had successfully diverted Roger Allen's attention by bringing him to the table. "This is Deputy Mattie Wray, handler for this German shepherd named Robo, and the bloodhound is my dog. His name is Banjo."

Roger was looking back and forth between Mattie and the dogs while he offered a handshake, his grip brief and firm.

Sarge seemed to be using the strategy of continuous talking to keep Roger occupied until Piper could free himself to take over. He briefed Roger thoroughly on which jurisdictions in Colorado they were from, including Drake and Fritz, even though they were absent, and their experience with tracking and area searches. He had begun to launch into descriptions of the skills that Robo and Banjo brought to the search effort when Piper joined their small circle.

"I'm sorry, Mr. Allen," Piper said, his face drawn and serious. "We can't allow the media full access or we're going to have a circus here that will interfere with us doing our jobs. Our priority is finding River."

"I'd think the more people involved the better," Roger said, belligerence on his face. "It's important to have more eyes out there looking for my son."

Mattie thought the father had seemed more interested in placing blame on Chrystal than asking people for help.

"Not in these woods. Not yet anyway," Piper said. "We need to allow the dogs time to search the area before people come in and disturb any scent trail River might have left."

Roger frowned. "So why haven't the dogs found him yet? I heard they started searching yesterday."

As Piper paused, Mattie decided to enter the conversation. "Although sometimes moisture enhances a scent trail, there was a deluge here yesterday, which can wash the trail away. Some of the dogs have indicated interest in certain areas, which can mean River might have gone through that way, but so far none of them have picked up a trail they can follow."

"Even these hot shot dogs from Colorado?" Roger asked.

Mattie kept her expression neutral, though she had developed a dislike for this man's attitude. "There are a couple ways dogs can find people. One is tracking them on the ground, not necessarily following footstep by footstep but by smelling the skin rafts that people shed onto the surface of the trail. The other way is by smelling a person's scent through the air, especially if there's a good breeze a dog can work."

Mattie gestured toward Robo and Banjo, who were now sitting side by side. Banjo yawned and lay back down even as she spoke. "These two dogs can do both. They've been taught to track scent on the ground, but they're also good at catching a person's scent through the air. So that's what we're combing the area for today. If River is out there, and if we have a breeze so we can work downwind, one of these dogs will be able to find him. A lot depends on the weather conditions."

Roger seemed unimpressed. "So what are you doing in here? Why aren't you out there searching?"

Sarge spoke up. "These dogs have been working for six hours already today. They need to rest every few hours, and they need to be fed so they have fuel to keep going. We were just about ready to get started again." He looked at Piper. "Unless you have anything further, we'll go now."

Mattie thought Sarge was probably as turned off by Roger Allen as she was. She was ready to go and leave the man with Piper.

"I'll have an update for you when you come back in, but for now you're free to go." Piper turned back to Roger. "I'm incident commander here, Mr. Allen. I wasn't aware that you'd arrived until my deputy informed me. Come with me, and I'll get you some food. Then we'll go to the command center so I can brief you on our mission and our plan."

"Have you considered that Chrystal has staged this for publicity's sake?" Roger asked.

This caught Mattie's attention, and she took her time gathering her things so she could hear Piper's answer.

"Ms. Winter appears distraught and has provided what assistance she can," Piper said.

Roger scoffed. "Chrystal's an actress. She's good at distraught. Besides, they're out here filming a movie about a woman lost in the woods. *Into Darkness*, they call it. What better way to get some prerelease publicity than to claim your child is lost in the same woods. *Into Darkness*." He spat out the film's title as if the words gave him a bad taste in his mouth.

Mattie glanced at Sarge; he was listening too.

Roger continued. "One thing I learned early on with that woman is that she loves her drama, whether it's on the set or at home. I'd love nothing better than to expose that side of her to the world."

The conversation faded as Piper guided Roger over to the food table.

Sarge and Mattie exchanged glances. "What do you think of that?" she asked him.

"I'd already thought of it. Hope we're not out there bustin' our butts over some publicity stunt."

Mattie nodded as she cleared the table, but privately she was thinking that she'd rather imagine the nine-year-old boy hidden away safely somewhere than out in the dark, wet forest facing wild animals at night.

# ELEVEN

Riding in the back seat, Mattie clutched Robo to keep him from falling as Hunter Bailey downshifted his Jeep to tackle the muddy, uphill two-track. The engine growled as the gear caught, jerking and bumping up the rugged trail deeper into the woods. Evergreen trees—cedar, pine, and fir—crowded both sides of the route, their boughs brushing against the edges of the vehicle.

Raindrops spattered the windshield and cold air filtered through the canvas topper, making Mattie shiver despite the heater working hard to produce what little warmth it could. A breeze had picked up, flowing downhill as the cold air settled into the valley. They were driving to the lower side of her newly assigned grid so they could work into the wind heading uphill, a perfect situation for air scenting.

"This is one of those private holdings I told you about," Hunter said, throwing the words over his shoulder as he braked to slow down. An even narrower trail than the one they were on branched off to the left.

"How far in is the household?"

"Not far, maybe a quarter mile."

"We should go in there and talk to whoever we can find. Ask if they've heard anything."

"All right." Hunter made the turn into the lane, steering past posted signs that said PRIVATE PROPERTY, KEEP OUT. "It's one guy living here off the grid. Has a cabin and a couple of sheds. Makes a living cutting out wooden statues with a chainsaw."

A man-sized wooden statue of Bigfoot holding another KEEP OUT sign appeared on the driver's side of the Jeep. Evidently an example of the man's artwork.

"Apparently doesn't like visitors," Mattie said, thinking there were plenty of those folks living off grid in the Colorado mountains as well.

"That's right. Guy's name is Edward Campbell. He's been here for years, a lot longer than I have."

The Jeep jolted up the track until they came to a clearing that held a small, boxy log cabin and two lean-to type sheds, all made from rough-cut logs, their bark in various stages of peeling off. A giant of a man holding a chainsaw stood bent over a partially carved statue of a bear that stood about four feet tall. The saw buzzed and squealed as he made another pass at the wood.

Hunter pulled the Jeep up where it might catch the man's eye, although he had his back turned partially toward them. A gray pit bull terrier with a white chest struggled to its feet on the short plank landing outside the front door of the cabin. It hobbled a few steps, demonstrating the arthritic gait of an old dog, and then it barked a few deep yips of warning without much enthusiasm.

The dog's movement was enough to catch the man's eye, and when he turned to see what the commotion was about, he straightened and turned off the saw's motor. He bent to place the saw on the ground but not before Mattie could see that he stood at least six feet six inches, his face swathed in an untrimmed, bushy red beard streaked with gray. His bare head bore an unkempt mop of hair, slightly more gray than his beard, and a patch of the same sprouted from the V-neck of the red and black plaid flannel shirt he wore beneath an olive-green open slicker.

The skin above his beard and around his eyes bore grime that went beyond that of a day's work, and his graying bushy brows lowered into a frown as he approached the Jeep. He stopped about ten feet away while Hunter and Mattie exited the vehicle.

"Mr. Campbell," Hunter greeted him. "Could we talk to you for a few minutes?"

"Do I have a choice?" His voice was deep and grumbly.

"Of course, but we won't take up much of your time." Hunter gestured toward Mattie and hurried on without pause. "This is Deputy Mattie Wray. She's a search and rescue dog handler who's helping us look for a missing boy."

Hunter hadn't offered a handshake, so Mattie followed his lead and didn't offer one either. "Pleased to meet you," she murmured.

"Speak up. I don't hear too good anymore."

Mattie repeated herself louder, and then Hunter took back the lead in the conversation.

"Mr. Campbell, we're searching for a young boy who's been missing from the movie set down below since yesterday. Have you seen or heard anything that might give us a lead? Something to indicate the boy passed through here?"

Campbell scratched the skin beneath his scraggly beard. "You say there's a movie set down below? I didn't know that."

An elderly model Ford Bronco sat beside the cabin with its hood up, and Mattie wondered if the man even had transportation.

"Yes," Hunter said. "Been there for a few weeks. Have you seen anyone go by this way, Mr. Campbell?"

"Haven't seen anybody. No one comes back in here."

Hunter persisted. "Well, like I said, we're trying to find a missing boy. Nine years old, long blond hair, slender build. Have you heard anyone calling for help from the woods?"

"Say what?" Campbell said, raising his voice and cupping his ear with his hand.

Hunter repeated the question.

"Like I said, I don't hear too well. I haven't heard anything from the woods one way or another. But I can hear Spike bark, and he hasn't been carrying on about anything lately."

Mattie pointed to the disabled Bronco. "Are you having car trouble, Mr. Campbell?"

He turned and looked at the old vehicle. "Wouldn't start this morning. I'll tinker with it and get it going again."

"Were you planning on going for supplies? Do you need anything?" Mattie asked.

He shook his head and gave her another frown. "I'm all right on my own. I don't need any help."

Although there was nothing she could put her finger on to suspect this man of foul play related to River's disappearance, the cop in her wanted to use Robo to sweep the premises for River's scent. But she needed to get this man's permission, because she really didn't have probable cause to ask for a search warrant.

"We'll need to search through these trees around here for the child before we go if that's okay with you." Mattie turned to Hunter. "Is the private property fenced off from state forest land?"

Hunter shook his head. "Not this particular holding. But I know approximately where the boundaries are. Mr. Campbell has about ten acres here."

"I don't want you tromping through my land," Campbell said, scowling.

Mattie wasn't too surprised at his response since he lived a remote life for a reason—but she wanted to make sure that kidnapping and concealing children wasn't a part of it. She raised her face to the air and felt the quickening wind on her cheeks. As long as she could get Robo downwind, it shouldn't require crossing close to the house unless River's scent drew her dog toward it. "We can search the outskirts of your land for the most part, Mr. Campbell. My dog will come close to your house only if he smells the child's scent there."

"No child has passed this way." Campbell poked a finger toward his lane. "There's a road right out there. No reason why a kid would bushwhack through the forest."

Mattie met his gaze, not willing to back down and wondering why he was unmoved by the idea of a child lost in the woods. Had he no empathy for others? "A child would wander around if he was lost and didn't know where the road was. Wouldn't it be a terrible thing if the boy was lying injured in the woods right here on your property and we didn't even know it? It's important we look. We'll move quickly and be out of your way in just a few minutes."

He toed the ground, grousing for a moment. "Oh, all right. But don't mess with anything out there. I've got some logs piled that I use for my carving. Stay away from them."

She couldn't imagine any reason why she would mess with his property in any way. "We'll barely leave a footprint and we'll avoid your stockpile," she said, at the same time thinking, *as long as Robo doesn't lead me into it.* But she didn't want to get into that and muddy the issue. "Thank you for your cooperation. It's nice to have met you."

Mattie turned toward the Jeep and walked away while Hunter said his goodbyes. The squeal of the chainsaw resumed, indicating Campbell was done with them. She climbed into the back seat, where Robo was happy to greet her, standing and wagging, and she waited for Hunter to get in and settle in front.

"The noise from that chainsaw must have damaged his hearing," Hunter said as he climbed into the driver's seat. His eyes met hers in the rearview mirror. "How do you want to work this?"

"Let's start back downhill in forest land at the edge of his property. Then Robo and I can work our way up. You could show me side boundaries for our new grid."

"That's easy on this side. It's the road. There's a creek that runs downhill about a half mile into the forest. That's your southern boundary."

"Mills Creek, same as this morning?"

"Yes."

"Okay, let's get to work."

After Hunter drove a half mile down the road, he found a pullout where he could park, and they all exited into the grassy area where, with the usual routine, Mattie prepared Robo to work. When he showed her he was excited to get started, she led him out into the tall trees.

Hunter followed. "I'll come along behind you," he said. "Tell me if you need me to do anything to help."

It felt refreshing to have a field assistant whose attitude was so different from Rena's standoffishness. "Let me know if we get too far out from our territory."

The forest floor was more open and less choked with underbrush here, making the moss-covered tree trunks appear stark and massive as Mattie and Robo wove their way into them. She refreshed his memory with the scent article, unclipped his leash, and cast him out on his own. With a last wave of his tail, he trotted into the woods, leaving her to follow by picking her way across treacherous footing created by dead branches and tree trunks that lay rotting on the moist ground. Still attached to toppled trees, towering root balls stood ten feet tall.

Robo headed southward, going toward the creek. Mattie struggled to keep up as best she could, while sensing that Hunter traveled at least twenty feet behind her. She caught sight of the creek right before Robo reached it and called him back as she headed uphill, creating the diagonal crisscross pattern she suspected Robo would continue on his own unless the child's scent drew him away.

After taking their time to sweep back and forth uphill about a quarter of a mile, Hunter called out to her. "This is about where Campbell's property begins."

"Okay, thanks," she called back, stepping up her pace to get closer to Robo. She didn't want to stop the momentum of his search, but she felt she should keep the promise she'd made to the curmudgeon about disturbing his land as little as possible.

Robo trotted into a small clearing, his nose in the air. Many of the trees had been felled here, trunks and large branches cut into chunks of various lengths and then sorted by size into stacks. Sawdust and small wood pieces littered the ground. One large statue overlooked the area—an eagle perched on a branch with a fish in its beak—that made Mattie realize the carver was actually quite talented. And to think most of this was done with a chain-saw. Under different circumstances, she would've liked to stay and watch him, although she doubted he would allow it.

She followed Robo across the clearing and entered the forest on the north side until they reached their boundary and headed back again. When Robo came close to the cabin, she observed him closely, watching for any sign that he was in scent—a head raise, a quickening of his pace, that intensity he showed when he was trailing odor through the air or on the ground. But there was nothing that might indicate a find.

When there was still no indication at the downhill edge of the cabin's clearing, Mattie guided Robo around the back side, continuing to watch for an alert. Nothing. She allowed Robo to head toward the creek, figuring they would make one more swing through the property before exiting on the uphill side.

When Mattie guessed she'd reached the end of a ten-acre strip, Hunter called to her again. She stopped to look back, and he was pointing uphill. "We're leaving Campbell's property and moving toward another private holding. It's about the same size and lies due west a half mile from here."

"Is it fenced?"

"I don't think so."

Mattie had reached a point where she felt confident about her bearings. "I can work this area and then come out on the road near the boundary of the private land. Do you want to get the

Jeep and meet me there? Then we can drive in and get permission to search."

"Sounds good."

Although her energy was starting to flag and her legs felt heavy, she turned back to follow Robo. They'd kept up this criss-cross pattern of searching for hours today, and the up and down climb across deadfall had her reaching the edge of her endurance. Her lack of sleep last night was also taking its toll. A break riding uphill in the Jeep would feel good.

Mattie needed to push through as long as Robo appeared energetic enough to continue. She observed him carefully for signs of burnout or fatigue, but he still had a spring in his step as he hopped over logs and trotted across felled timber. Robo's step was always a lot springier than hers.

They completed one more sweep toward the creek and were coming back toward the road when Mattie heard the Jeep grumbling uphill off to her right. Since Robo still didn't indicate signs of finding scent, she called him in and veered toward the two-track. By the time they reached it, Hunter had already passed and Mattie had to hike fast to catch up. She waved both arms above her head, hoping he would see her in his rearview mirror. Red brake lights appeared at the rear of the Jeep, and she and Robo hurried to load into the back seat.

"Still nothing, I take it," Hunter said, as he shifted into low and started uphill.

"Nothing seems to even interest him this afternoon."

"Maybe he's tired."

"Not yet. I've kept an eye out for that." Mattie had removed Robo's water bowl and was filling it to give him all the water he wanted. "He's still engaged and working. I'm sure we can clear the area we've covered so far. River isn't out there, and he might not have even passed through this way."

"All right." Hunter turned off the road onto another narrow lane with trees crowding both sides. "We're about halfway through the territory we've been assigned."

Mattie realized that even though she'd been traveling uphill this entire day, working back and forth, she'd not seen any mountains. In fact, the only view she'd had so far was of trees, deadfall, and underbrush in her immediate vicinity—sort of a "not able to see the forest for the trees" effect.

With one arm around her dog, she and Robo leaned on each other in the back seat. Her body ached from her fall that morning and from overuse, climbing up and over fallen tree trunks and sliding down muddy gullies and moss-covered terrain. And to top it off, the little light that filtered through the clouds and the forest canopy was beginning to wane. Even though it was only four o'clock, nightfall must come early this far north. She doubted they'd have more than two hours left to search before it became too dark to see.

The image from River's photo had begun to haunt her. He looked like a thin, vulnerable waif leaning against that boulder in the meadow. Worry about him having to spend another night alone in the woods kept her from relaxing against the back of her seat. She bit her tongue to keep from urging Hunter to hurry.

# TWELVE

Mattie continued to hold on to Robo as the Jeep rocked and bumped uphill.

Hunter projected his voice above the growl of the engine as he met her eyes in the rearview. "This next acreage is owned by Cecil Moore, and we won't be asking him if he's seen anything unusual—because he's blind."

"Blind?" Mattie's mind flooded with all the activities required for survival in a remote location like this, things she thought would require eyesight to accomplish. "Does he have a partner or family helping him?"

Hunter passed her a smile via the mirror. "Nope. He lives here by himself."

"How does he manage?"

"I actually don't know everything it takes, but I do know he has a shortwave radio set up to communicate with authorities in an emergency. I think he also talks to other folks in his network. He orders groceries and supplies at Bigfoot Market and Merc either brings them up or arranges someone to deliver them. He buys his firewood and can hire transportation or connect with a volunteer whenever he needs to go into town for something."

Mattie thought of how easily a person could get lost in these woods, where there were limited landmarks even for a sighted person. "Otherwise does he stay in his cabin or clearing?"

"You'd be surprised at how well he gets around. Or maybe you wouldn't. He has a seeing eye dog."

That bit of info set off her imagination, and she settled back into her seat, her arm around Robo, and thought of how a dog could lead a person through this type of terrain. She loved envisioning it.

"We'll get his permission to search his property and then move on uphill back into state forest." Hunter steered the four-wheel-drive vehicle over a rough patch and into a clearing that was much more tidy than the wood carver's had been.

The cabin looked fairly new, made with peeled logs and a fresh coat of sealant. There was a broad plank deck out front, with a couple of chairs and a table made from rough-hewn lumber. Even though the cabin was small, it looked inviting, with red plaid curtains showing through the windowpanes on each side of the doorway. Open shutters painted dark brown graced the windows and a huge pile of firewood was stacked neatly against the side of the cabin just off the porch to the right. A clear pathway off to the left led to an outhouse that sat about thirty yards away.

Hunter pulled into a flat area out front that provided a natural parking space and turned off the engine.

"Nice place," Mattie murmured.

"It is, isn't it?" The door hinge squeaked as Hunter opened it to step outside.

"You're going to stay here," Mattie told Robo before exiting the Jeep to join Hunter. As they moved toward the cabin, she could hear Robo scrambling around in back and turned to see him standing at the window watching her every move. *No, my dog isn't too tired to work yet*, she thought.

Before they got to the deck, a man and a German shepherd tricked out in full guide dog harness came through the doorway to stand outside to wait for them. "I didn't expect you to get here so fast. So you got my message," he called out as they approached.

"Cecil, hello," Hunter called to him. "It's Hunter Bailey here. No, I'm sorry but we're not responding to a message you sent. Can I help?"

"Oh . . . hi, Hunter. I didn't call the Forest Service, but maybe I should have. I left a message for Oscar's vet."

After the incident with Dozer, Mattie felt immediate concern. But the gorgeous black and tan shepherd standing beside his human looked healthy and fit, albeit a bit protective since his intelligent brown eyes didn't blink as he watched their approach. The fact that he cast a wary eye toward the Jeep now and then told

Mattie that he was fully aware of Robo's presence too, although he didn't bark.

"Is Oscar sick?" Hunter asked. "I've got a SAR K-9 handler with me here today, Deputy Mattie Wray from Timber Creek, Colorado. She's engaged to a vet and a wizard when it comes to dog care."

"No, Oscar is fine." A soft smile enhanced Cecil's handsome features under a thatch of dark brown hair. Darkly tinted sunglasses covered his eyes. "Hi, Mattie. Is it okay if I call you Mattie instead of Deputy Mattie Wray?"

"Sure," Mattie said, matching his contagious smile. "I have a German shepherd too, although I left him in the Jeep. Oscar is gorgeous."

Cecil's smile deepened into a proud grin. "So they say. I can also tell you that his fur is soft and he's loyal, reliable, and brave. He's a special dog."

"I've got one of those too."

"Well, we ought to have a drink sometime and trade dog stories." He became serious as he turned his head slightly toward Hunter. "Oscar's okay, but we took a walk to the upper part of the property after lunch and he acted squirrelly, so I sort of explored the best I could and found a couple of dead animals. I didn't want to lean down and touch them with my hands, but I used my cane to get a feel for the size. I think it's a deer and a fawn. If it is, that's strange. I might expect one or the other but not both. I thought Doc Harper should take a look to make sure there's not something out there that's dangerous for Oscar."

It *would* be strange for a doe and a fawn to die together. "Are the carcasses old enough to smell bad?" Mattie asked.

"Not to me, but Oscar might disagree. That's the other strange thing. They would've had to die recently because I was up there just a couple of days ago, before the rain. They're very close to my trail."

Hunter looked at Mattie. "Maybe I should go up there and take a look." Then he turned back to Cecil. "We're actually here on a search and rescue mission, looking for a missing child. We need your permission to search your property to make sure the boy didn't cross through here. Would that be okay?"

"Of course. In the future, know that if you're searching for a missing person, you definitely have my permission to look here. Don't delay."

In light of the fact that Dozer looked like he could've ingested poison, Mattie was worried the same thing had happened to the two animals Cecil described. For Robo's safety, she needed to look into it before taking him there to search. "I'll go with you," she told Hunter. "Is it far, Cecil?"

"Oscar and I can take you right to it. It should take five minutes, seven minutes tops."

She didn't want to delay the search for River, but in lieu of not knowing exactly where Dozer and Rena had been this morning, she needed to see if she could determine what killed those deer. Maybe stray bullets? "Did you hear any gunfire around here the past couple of days?"

Cecil shook his head. "No, although that does happen occasionally. Rarely, I should say, and not close by."

Mattie realized that even though this man's eyesight might be impaired, his hearing might be better than that of most people. "So . . . thinking back to yesterday, did you hear anything strange, like a person yelling?"

"Like that child you're looking for calling for help? Nothing like that. But . . ." He trailed off as if thinking.

"But?" Mattie prompted him.

"Months ago I was uphill on the property when I thought I heard a shout. Maybe a cry for help, but I couldn't be certain. Too far away. I radioed the sheriff's department and someone came up to check it out but they found nothing."

Mattie's pulse quickened. She wondered if the shout could've come from Troy Alexander, one of the missing persons who'd never been found. She tried to catch Hunter's eye, but he was scanning the woods uphill, a frown on his face.

"Could it have been a year ago?" she asked.

Cecil frowned. "Possibly. It was definitely a while back."

"What did the voice sound like? Male or female?"

"High-pitched. Probably a girl or a woman, but maybe a young boy. Honestly, it was one shout and it might have even been hikers or campers playing around. The sheriff's deputy told me not to worry about it. I kinda felt like he thought I'd wasted his time."

"Maybe he was just having a busy day. Any time someone hears a cry for help, they should call it in. You did the right thing."

Mattie turned to Hunter. "We'd better go find those deer so we can get back to our search."

"I'll take you," Cecil said.

Mattie was afraid that might slow down the process. "That won't be necessary. If you could just point out the trail?"

"It'll be quicker if I lead the way," he said, picking up the handle on Oscar's harness and taking a moment to organize his hold on both it and the dog's leash. "Oscar, forward. Let's go for a walk."

It took only seconds for Oscar and Cecil to get to a trail that led uphill. Mattie had decided to waylay any upholstery damage on Robo's part by swinging back to the Jeep to tell him to wait, so she had to jog to catch up with the two men and the dog. Cecil kept a brisk pace on an uneven trail that had been cleared, over which Oscar guided him flawlessly. Both of them appeared familiar with the muddy pathway, and Cecil remained confident and sure-footed.

Like the state forest, this hillside was heavily wooded. Cecil spoke, tossing words over his shoulder. "I had this path cleared when I moved here a few years ago. It makes a loop through the upper part of my property, so I can hike whenever I want to. By now, Oscar and I know this path like the backs of our hands, or paws if you will."

Mattie loved this guy's sense of humor, and under different circumstances she felt she would enjoy sitting down with him over a cup of coffee to share dog tales. But there was no time for that now. Mist crept through the trees and soon it would obscure what little sunlight was left here at the end of the day. It even felt like it seeped through her rain gear, dampening the layers she had on underneath. She suppressed a shiver.

As the mist thickened, Mattie sensed her world shrinking to the backs of the two men trudging ahead of her. This was Hunter's second day of searching, and she figured he was as beat as she was. After what might have been the predicted five minutes but what actually felt like much longer, Cecil told Oscar to slow down, and the shepherd cut his pace in half.

"It was somewhere near here," Cecil said, after asking Oscar to stop. "Only about ten feet off the path on the right side."

"We'll look for it if you want to wait here," Hunter told him.

"No, I'll come along and follow you guys." Taking out a retractable cane, Cecil stood to the side as Hunter and Mattie passed him.

It didn't take long. Although the forest was still thick in this area, there was little undergrowth, and the two deer were visible from the pathway even in the dim light. The doe was small, much smaller than the mule deer of Colorado, and the fawn seemed tiny, although it had to be at least several months old.

"We've found them, Cecil," she told him. "We're going off the path now."

"Okay, good. I'll wait here."

Mattie left Cecil and Oscar to follow Hunter the ten feet that Cecil had estimated into the forest. The deer lay on their sides, the ground and foliage around their hooves churned up as if they'd flailed about in their last hours or minutes of life. Mattie hated that for this mother and baby. And she thought instantly of Dozer.

Hunter leaned forward with his hands braced above his knees as he studied the site. "I don't see any blood, do you?"

"No."

"These deer don't have wounds that I can see, so a predator didn't get to them." He swept his hand around the area. "I don't see any sign of attack."

"Me neither. But they didn't die quietly. In light of what happened with Dozer, I've got to wonder about poison. Where did these animals get their water?"

Hunter straightened and met her gaze before looking around. "After this rain, just about anywhere, but my guess would be the creek. Let's do a quick scout to see if we find anything else. It's unlikely this doe and her fawn were foraging by themselves." He called back toward the trail. "Cecil, we're going to take a quick look around for a few minutes."

"I hear you. I'll wait right here."

Mattie and Hunter fanned out, forging farther into the woods. Mattie made her way into a gully where ferns and berry bushes grew and a narrow stream flowed toward an ice-lined creek. A brown lump on the forest floor on the other side of the stream materialized into another deer carcass as she approached, this one apparently another female and a size halfway between the other two. Last year's weanling? The implication of what they were finding sickened her.

She called to Hunter. "One more deer over here by this narrow stream."

He called back. "And a large raccoon over here."

They closed the gap between them, and Mattie felt certain that the concern on Hunter's face matched her own. She was thinking about Robo, Fritz, Banjo, and all the other SAR dogs that were out in this area. "We need to call this in ASAP," she said. "We've got to let everyone know to get their dogs on a leash and to keep them from drinking the water in the streams. I don't know what's going on, but I'd bet money that this water source has been poisoned somehow."

Hunter pulled out his radio and pressed the mic. It crackled to life as he called in to incident command. The mist swirled down into the gully as Mattie stood by, thankful that Robo was safely secured in the Jeep while at the same time saddened by the death of these animals. And what about Dozer? Had he ingested the same pollutant that these deer had?

Moisture hung in the air, creating droplets that drizzled off the hood of her raincoat to the ground. Fog enveloped them, making it hard to breathe as it dampened sound and isolated them. It felt like she and Hunter had been dropped into a postapocalyptic world filled with the heaviness of death and dying.

As she thought of River Allen, she couldn't suppress her shiver.

# THIRTEEN

By the time they made it back to Cecil's cabin, Mattie was almost done in. But it was important to finish the search through their new grid. An image of River dying out here alone in the woods after drinking polluted water had lodged itself in her mind and she couldn't shake it loose. She couldn't end the day's search until it was too dark to see, and the increased mist guaranteed there would be no moonlight to work with tonight.

Robo greeted her with a happy grin, his nose smudging the Jeep's rear window.

As she let him out of the vehicle, he bounced beside her, fully rested.

"Are you ready to work again, buddy?" she asked as she snugged up his search harness. After giving him a fresh ration of water, she stowed his bowl in her backpack thinking she would offer him water every fifteen minutes or so.

She snapped a short leash onto the ring at the top of his harness and gestured toward the Jeep's tire as she told him to take a break. The leash would seriously interfere with their ability to search since they could only go into places where she could follow, but she wasn't about to let him go off on his own after seeing the danger that lurked somewhere in the mist.

When she'd finished preparing Robo to resume the search, Hunter approached, followed by Oscar guiding Cecil.

Hunter was looking at his wristwatch. "Daylight is fading fast. Can you do without a field assistant for the next half hour?"

"Sure. I've got the north and south boundaries in mind. If you can give me a description of the upper western limit, I can finish up. Will you be able to meet me there or should I hike back down on the road?"

"I think I can meet you," Hunter said. "I've got to call this in to Washington Department of Fish and Wildlife and get an investigation started. I'll need to go back up there and scout around a little bit before nightfall to see if there are more animals down."

"What am I going to do with these dead animals?" Cecil asked, tilting his head back uphill toward the site.

"Don't worry. We have to remove anything we find to take in for necropsy. If you find others, give me a call and I'll arrange removal."

Cecil looked relieved. "That's good."

"I'd better get started," Mattie said, turning away.

"Radio me if you need me, or if you get lost," Hunter said.

"Will do." She thought of Cecil and Oscar navigating these woods with and without a pathway to follow, and how Cecil depended on his dog instead of his sight. Darkness wouldn't matter to them.

Mattie hiked downhill on the road until she found the spot where she'd left the woods to join Hunter in the Jeep. As she wove her way past ferns and underbrush that grew almost as tall as she was, she started the chatter that signaled to Robo that it was time to resume the search. After she let him smell the scent article, he took a few steps and then looked back at her as if to ask "What gives?"

"We have to leave your leash on so I can make sure you don't eat or drink anything that could hurt you," she explained to Robo, thinking that if Hunter were around to overhear her, he'd probably think she was weird. "Let's go, Robo. Let's find River. Search!"

He led her off into the semidarkness with her trailing only six feet behind. The footing was treacherous, and she could barely see twenty feet ahead at this point. But if Robo could get within a half mile of the boy, she had no doubt that her dog would pick up a scent through the air. He would do his part. She dug deep to dredge up the energy to do hers.

★ ★ ★

By the time she heard the Jeep's engine rumbling up the road, Mattie's legs were shaking and she felt she couldn't travel another step. She hunkered beside Robo, giving him love and hugs, while she waited for Hunter to get close enough for her to step into the road to signal to him. The sound of rain pattering on her hood was just about to drive her crazy.

She could hardly wait to get back to the mess tent and hoped there would be a warm meal. But even the thought of it filled her with guilt. Here she was worried about herself when a lost child was still out there in the rain without food of any kind, warm or cold. As the engine's growl drew near, she stood and straightened, groaning softly.

Hunter pulled up beside her and rolled down his window. "I take it you didn't get a hit."

"Nothing," she said, opening the back door to allow Robo to jump in before she hauled herself up into the seat behind him. The warmth from the heater combined with the ability to sit felt like heaven. "At least we know more about where the child isn't."

"Sometimes that's the best we can do, although it feels like a failure, doesn't it?"

"Yep." Mattie sank back against the seat with one arm around Robo. He yawned and settled with his head on her lap, making her wish she could just curl up around him and go to sleep too.

Hunter radioed incident command and gave a report, saving Mattie from having to do it when they reached their destination. Her stomach rumbled and gnawed at her backbone—she'd gone hours since her last energy bar. "Will there be dinner?"

"Yeah. Merc will cook something up. We'll have warm food tonight."

"That's good of him. Is he a volunteer?"

"The county pays him. He already has the grocery supplier and he helps out whenever we need him. His staff continues to run the store, so it doesn't interfere too much with how he makes a living. Hopefully it helps. It's a lot of work."

"I can imagine." Mattie sighed as the heater worked its magic, dulling enough of her chill that she could relax. She leaned her head against the headrest and closed her eyes. She reopened them when the Jeep hit a deep pothole and jostled her against her seat belt.

The headlights pierced the darkness as they drove downhill, rocking side to side, making her aches and pains from the day awaken to shout at her. She was relieved when the lights from the movie set began to peek through the dense forest, although several more minutes passed before they made it down to the mess tent.

Hunter slowed the Jeep and parked. "Shall we unload here or should I take you somewhere else?"

"Here is fine." When she opened the Jeep's door, the cold moist air hit her like an ocean wave. She unloaded Robo and grabbed her backpack. "Are you coming in for dinner?"

"Not yet," Hunter said. "I've checked in with canine SAR command and let Ken know our status, but I might touch base about plans for tomorrow."

"I guess I should do that."

"It's okay. I can take care of it. Anything you want me to pass on?"

Mattie thought for a moment. "It would be good for Drake to take the cadaver dog through Cecil's property and search upstream along the creek and other waterways that cross through there. Just to make sure . . . you know." Mattie didn't want to say, "just to make sure River isn't deceased and lying out there somewhere in the elements."

"Okay, I'll mention it to Ken. Then I might run home for the night. I'll see you in the morning."

"See you then. Thanks for the help today."

"Thank *you*. We appreciate you being here." Hunter revved the engine and pulled away.

Mattie hitched her backpack over one shoulder, picked up Robo's go bag, and turned wearily toward the mess tent. Once inside, she was immersed in the murmuring voices of volunteers who'd already grabbed meals and were seated at the table. She looked around for a familiar face and spotted Rena sitting by herself at the end of a table. With Robo at her side, Mattie made her way over, and when she approached, Rena looked up from her dinner and gave her a tired smile.

Mattie placed her backpack on one chair and sat in another closer to Rena. Robo pressed his way in between to stay near, and Mattie rested her hand on his head. "How is Dozer?"

Rena grimaced. "He's still alive if that's what you're wondering. The vet is supporting him tonight with IVs and is waiting on lab results to see what they turn up so she can treat him."

Mattie's heart went out to her as Rena looked away, obviously fighting back tears. "Geez, it's hard to wait, isn't it? I hope something definitive turns up. What does she think might be wrong?"

"She thinks that with the seizure, it's more likely to be epilepsy or something wrong in the brain rather than poison. I know that's what you were thinking."

*And I still am*, Mattie thought, *and Cole is too*. "I need to talk to you more about that. Did you hear about the possibility of poison pollution upstream from where we were searching this morning?"

Rena looked surprised. "No. What's that about?"

Mattie had dug through her backpack and served up a ration of kibble for Robo's dinner. He'd gobbled his food and was licking the bowl, so she gave him a bit more. "I'm starved. Let me go get some food and then I'll tell you all about it. Is that okay?"

"Sure. I'll be here for a while."

Since she didn't feel comfortable leaving Robo with a relative stranger, Mattie told him to come with her. Merc was serving heaping bowls of chili from large, steaming vats.

Looking cheerful, he greeted her as she approached. "How are you this evening, young lady?"

Not wanting to share her feeling of defeat from the long, arduous day, she tried to return his smile with a thin one of her own. "Hungry and tired. I'm grateful for the hot meal. Thanks so much for cooking."

"You are so welcome, my dear." His smile deepened as he handed her a bowl of what appeared to be beef and bean chili, which made her think of her foster mother, Teresa Lovato, or Mama T as everyone called her. Mama's chili could warm your heart and soul. Chili was one of Mattie's comfort foods, and she couldn't have been more pleased to see it on the menu tonight.

Merc gestured farther down the table. "Help yourself to as much cornbread as you want. There's fruit to choose from and cookies at the end down there. And if you want a refill on chili, there's more where that came from."

With Robo sticking close to her side, Mattie thanked him again and, moving down the table, she filled her tray. She snagged a cup of hot chocolate and a bottle of water and was turning to go back to her table when she spotted Drake entering the tent along with Banjo and Fritz. She angled their way to catch his eye, and then pointed out where she was sitting. Drake gave her a thumbs-up and, with both dogs at heel, carried his pack over to where Rena was waiting. She looked up in surprise.

Mattie arrived the same time Drake did. "The Colorado contingent wants to join you," she said to Rena. "Hope you don't mind."

Rena began to clear her things, wrapping her cookies in a napkin. "I'm about done here anyway. You can have the table."

"Don't go," Drake said as he put his pack down and opened it, taking out food and bowls for the dogs. "How's Dozer? I've been thinking of him and hoping he's okay."

Rena gave Drake a brief update. Mud spattered his face and clothing, and he looked to be in the same condition that Mattie was in.

"We'll keep Dozer in our thoughts and send up a little doggy prayer for his complete recovery," Drake said. He groaned softly as he leaned over to place the bowls on the ground. "Oy . . . I'm feelin' every step I made today. Especially after I had to put Fritz on a leash." He glanced at Mattie.

"That made for tough going, didn't it?" Mattie said.

Rena had stood but she hesitated before picking up her tray. "What are you talking about?"

Drake nodded at Mattie. "Mattie and Robo found dead animals that might indicate a polluted water source up to the west of here."

"That's what I wanted to tell you about," Mattie said. "It's something you should pass on to your vet."

Rena leaned forward. "Where? What's going on?"

"Do you know where Cecil Moore lives?" Mattie asked.

"No, I'm not totally familiar with this area even though I live just north of here."

"His place is to the west, up above where we searched this morning. He's the one who found dead deer on his place, and he and his guide dog led Hunter and me to them."

"His guide dog?"

"A seeing eye dog actually. Cecil is blind."

Drake looked surprised. "I didn't hear that part."

Mattie nodded and gave the others a brief description of how Cecil managed to hike on his own with Oscar's guidance.

"Hunter has reported the animals to Fish and Wildlife, and they'll pick them up in the morning for necropsy. There were three deer and a raccoon that we found, but it was getting dark so I finished up the search for River in that area with Robo on leash. Hunter stayed and took water samples from several streams that run through there. I think Fish and Wildlife will organize an investigation in the morning to see if they can find a source of contamination."

Rena slumped into a chair as an expression of dismay filled her face. "Is that what happened to Dozer?"

Mattie was surprised no one had told Rena yet, but maybe she'd just now returned to camp. "Maybe. Were you up in that area with him earlier?"

"Yeah." Rena squirmed in her seat, looking down at the table. "I decided to go farther uphill to search after I left you. I went up the road and then across toward the creek, working that area."

It was strange that Ken would then assign Mattie and Hunter to cover the same territory that he'd already sent Rena into, but then Mattie remembered that he had also assigned Mattie and Robo to cover the lower grid that Rena and Dozer had searched yesterday. "I guess Ken is having us double search toward the west then. He must believe that's where River would be most likely to go."

Rena blushed and she wouldn't meet Mattie's eyes. "I guess so."

It dawned on Mattie that maybe Rena had gone rogue to search on her own. Maybe Ken didn't know she'd left her field assistant assignment with Mattie and gone to search farther uphill.

Rena stood and picked up her tray. "I'd better go. I've got some things I need to do."

"Wait," Mattie said. "Do you think you could show Hunter or someone where you were with Dozer today? Maybe that could speed up the process of pinning down the water contamination site."

Rena shook her head. "I still don't think he was poisoned. And the vet thinks it's a seizure disorder."

"Yeah, but the vet doesn't know about the animals that were found this afternoon. You should call her and fill her in."

Rena nodded as she turned to leave.

"One more thing, Rena." Mattie stood to keep her from going. She believed this was important, and she would follow her if she had to. "Was Dozer on a leash? Did you see him drink water at a site that you could show us?"

Rena paused, shaking her head. "He was off leash doing an area search. Listen, I've got to go."

"Okay. See you tomorrow." Rena's answer had surprised Mattie, and she looked at Drake as she sat back down. "I don't think her dog has been trained for area searching. I think there's only one other dog in the SAR group here that air scents, and that's Ken's dog."

"That's right," Drake said. "I touched base with Ken at lunchtime, and he was heading back out to search another grid this afternoon. Do you know about Sarge?"

Mattie felt a jolt of alarm. "No, what about him?"

"He got sick shortly after lunch. Nausea, vomiting. He's been holed up in the trailer with Banjo, so Ken was short a team and planning to try to work a double. I took over Banjo's care when I got in this evening."

"Oh no. Sarge didn't drink contaminated water, did he?" She couldn't imagine that he would. They all carried their own clean water.

"No. Maybe it's a stomach bug, maybe the flu. I heard another one of the volunteers was sick this afternoon too. Hope we don't catch it."

"Geez. Hope Sarge feels better soon." Mattie shook her head as she settled down to eat her chili, which was already getting cold.

"He was doing better when I checked in on him."

"I sent a message to Ken to have you and Fritz work near that area where we found the dead animals. I hate to think of River drinking contaminated water."

Drake looked grim as he nodded. "I'll search there first thing tomorrow morning."

"Sorry . . . it's a dangerous assignment."

"It can be done." Drake sopped up sauce from the chili with his cornbread before standing to go get a refill.

"Have you heard where we're supposed to bunk tonight?" Mattie asked. "I'm headed for a shower and then bed."

"Piper said for us to stay where we are. He's going to put Cole in there too when he gets here."

"Oh, let me check and see when that will be." Mattie removed her phone from her inner coat pocket and found a text from Cole waiting for her. "He lands in Seattle at two o'clock this morning and will rent a car to drive around Puget Sound to get here. How long do you think that will take?"

"I don't know but probably at least a couple of hours. So he'll get here around four o'clock or so. We'll have time to get some good shuteye before he arrives," Drake said as he headed off for his second bowl of chili.

By the time she finished dinner, Mattie was dead on her feet and Robo had curled into a ball on the ground and fallen asleep. She leaned over him and placed a hand on his back, waking him gently. He opened one eye and as recognition filled his gaze, he heaved to his feet, shook himself from head to tail, and yawned.

"I need to go back to the camper to get some clean clothes and then I'll head for the shower," she told Drake. "I'll take Robo with me."

"Sure. I'll be there soon."

Mattie left the mess tent with Robo and went out into the drizzling rain, rushing to go check on Sarge. She was grateful that she could sleep among comrades that she knew, and Cole would be there before morning, bringing further comfort on a cold, rainy night.

# FOURTEEN

## Saturday, Early Morning

Cole steered carefully around a curve while his windshield wipers beat a steady rhythm, working hard to keep a small patch on the glass clear so he could peer out. Through a narrow strip of evergreens along the highway, his headlights lit a sharp drop beyond and then glinted off a body of water that he assumed must be Puget Sound. His tired eyes strained to see the road ahead to keep from plunging off the side of the hill into the deep abyss.

He'd been lucky to catch the redeye out of Denver, leaving around midnight Mountain Time and arriving in Seattle shortly before two AM Pacific. He'd been able to sleep about an hour on the plane, just enough to make him groggy by the time he disembarked in Seattle. But the cold damp air that hit him as he'd left the airport to wait for the shuttle to the car rental facility had awakened him as thoroughly as it chilled him.

How were Mattie and Robo doing after working outside all day in this soggy environment? He guessed he'd find out soon, although he hated to awaken them. The clock on the dash told him he'd been driving for over two hours, and he believed he'd be arriving at his destination soon. When he'd talked to Sheriff Piper earlier, he'd been given good directions as well as an address that he'd plugged into his navigation system.

Even as the thought entered his mind, the pleasant female voice from the Jeep Cherokee's sound system told him, "In half a mile, make a left turn," followed by a road with a string of numbers that evidently marked it instead of a name. With forest on both sides of the car, an incline on his left and the Sound on his right, he felt he was in the middle of nowhere. A quick glance in the rearview told him that no one was following, and he'd met very few cars on the road ahead, so slowing down to turn in this blinding rain shouldn't be a problem.

His navigation system spoke again and he spotted the road marked by a green sign bearing only numbers up ahead. He slowed and made the turn into a small clearing that contained several buildings—a gas station, grocery store, bar and grill, and a few other unmarked buildings that were probably people's homes. After driving on pavement for about fifty feet, his tires met the dirt and gravel surface that Piper had mentioned. He felt relief that he was on the correct route and only about three miles from the end of his journey.

The forest pressed in on both sides, reminding him of the Grimms' fairy tales that his ex-wife used to read to the girls. The Jeep pitched as he navigated the potholes in the muddy road. After entering the woods, the rain had eased, but as he climbed in elevation, a dense fog seeped in to cross the road in layers. He blinked to keep his bleary eyes from becoming mesmerized by the misty strands as they drifted across his vision.

It took the better part of a quarter hour to lumber uphill for three miles, but he finally reached the well-lit campsite that Piper had described. He turned into a short lane that led to illuminated structures beyond and had to thread his way between parked vans and media trucks crammed together so that there was barely room to pass. After coming out on the other side, a man dressed in full rain gear stepped into the road, his extended hand raised palm out to stop him.

Cole rolled down his window and the man came around from the front, bending to look inside. Rain drizzled in a rivulet from the front of his hood. "Hello," Cole said. "Terrible night to have to stand guard."

"Yes, sir." Looking stern, the guard shone a flashlight toward Cole, being careful to avoid directing it into his eyes. He flashed his name tag, which identified him as Deputy Gage Casey, Baker County Sheriff's Department. "What's your name, sir?"

"Cole Walker. I'm the veterinarian Sheriff Piper approved joining the K-9 SAR team."

"Yes, sir. I'm expecting you. Could you show your ID, please?"

"It's in my wallet in my back pocket. I'll get it for you." Cole unfastened his seat belt and twisted one hip upward as he reached to remove his wallet. He extracted his driver's license and handed it to the guard.

The guy shone his flashlight back and forth between the license and Cole's face and then handed it back to him. Only then did he crack a weary smile. "Okay, Dr. Walker, looks like you're who you say you are. Sorry about that, but we're being careful to limit visitors to the scene. And we have a strict no-media policy going on right now."

"Thus the vehicles parked out here, right?"

"Yeah, it's a nuisance. Did Sheriff Piper tell you where to go from here?"

"No, I had directions only to this spot. Does he expect me to check in with him?"

"No. He's had no sleep going on two days now, so he's checked out for the night. He told me to give you directions to the camper where you've been assigned. The other folks from Colorado are already in it."

"Sounds good. I appreciate it." Cole listened while the guard gave him directions, hoping he could follow them well enough not to awaken the others who were getting what he imagined was much-needed sleep.

He thanked the guard and waited while Casey stepped back from the window and turned away. Then he drove as quietly as the Jeep would allow through the narrow alleys that had been created for this movie set. Klieg lights and temporary floodlights made it easy to spot the landmarks the guard had given him, so he turned off his headlights to avoid swamping anyone's window with unwanted light. He found the camper he thought he was looking for and turned off the mud slick alleyway to pull to a stop beside its awning.

He knew he was in the right place when Mattie eased out of the partially open doorway with Robo trailing close behind. *Good golly, she's a sight for sore eyes.* As he turned off the engine, she darted around to the passenger side, first letting Robo into the back seat and then climbing into the front herself.

"Gosh, it's good to see you," she said as she leaned over the console into his embrace.

She was dressed in a heavy fleece sweatshirt and was carrying a wadded-up blanket that she laid in her lap. He held her close, taking in the scent of her hair while Robo nuzzled his ear and performed his happy dance in the back seat. "It's great to see you," he murmured into Mattie's hair as he pushed Robo back gently. "And you too, you big lug."

"I was worried about you driving here in all this rain," she said, pushing back to study him at arm's length. "Are you exhausted?"

"I didn't have any problems but the rain did slow me down. I got a little sleep on the plane."

She touched his cheek and his heart swelled. He turned his face into her palm and kissed it. Robo pushed his nose between the two of them, and Mattie ruffled his fur as she told him to lie down on the seat. After settling Robo, she said, "You look tired."

Cole smoothed her hair and tucked it behind her ear before brushing one of the scratches on her cheek. "You look tired too. And what's this?"

She shrugged as she clasped his hand in both of hers. "It was a long, hard day yesterday. In an hour and a half, we'll be reporting back to get organized before we start. Why don't you stay here at the camper and get some sleep until noon."

He looked around the interior of the Jeep. "I might be able to grab enough sleep right here to tide me over until I can get some coffee. Then I should be good to go."

"I'll stay out here with you," she said, lifting the edge of the blanket. "That's why I brought this. I was hoping we could keep from disturbing the others since the night is almost over."

"Sounds good." But he'd noticed that the damp cold had seeped into his vehicle since he'd turned off the Jeep's engine. Maybe he should turn on the heater again before the engine cooled completely. He switched the key to accessory power and turned up the temperature on the dual control. "Let's see if this will give us a little extra heat. I am bone chilled."

"I know," she said, giving him one of her smiles that warmed him more than the heater could. "No snow here, but this is a different kind of cold, isn't it?"

"Yeah, we're so used to the drought in Colorado. That dry cold isn't as chilling as this."

"Drake used to live here in Washington, and he said we'll get used to it. But I don't think we'll be here long enough for that."

"Yeah, maybe we'd need a year or so."

Mattie chuckled as she spread out the blanket over the two of them.

"Who's Drake?" Cole asked, figuring he might as well start matching names with new folks.

"He came with Sarge from Denver. He's paired with Fritz. Remember him? The bloodhound that does human remains detection?"

"Oh yeah, I wouldn't forget Fritz. Tell me about the dog that got sick. Did the vet decide what was wrong with it yet?"

Mattie filled him in on the details of what the vet was thinking as well as the evidence of dead wild animals that might indicate water pollution. "I told Rena to call her vet and let her know about the possibility that Dozer ingested something through the water, but she was acting all buttoned up about something, so I'm not sure she did. I hope the vet ordered screening for poisons on that sample I sent with her."

"She probably did, but seizure disorder is the more common cause for a first seizure. Poison would be an unusual diagnosis. If we can find out where Rena took the dog, I'll call in the morning just to check in. It'll be good for all of us to know what's going on."

"Yeah, we're protecting our dogs from drinking the water by keeping them on leash. It would be great to find out if we still need to do that or if we can let them run free to search the area."

"It could take a couple days for the labs to come in. We might even get necropsy results from the deer before that."

Mattie sighed. "There's nothing we can do about it tonight. Let's recline our seats and see if we can sleep."

With the engine off, the heater was already blowing cool air. "This isn't working, so I might as well switch it off," Cole said. He snuggled under the blanket, pulling the edge up to tuck around his shoulders, and then reached under it to clasp Mattie's hand. They both started reclining their seats using their free hands. "Darn this console. Makes me yearn for an old-fashioned bench seat instead of these buckets. Our ancestors knew where it was at when it came to cuddling in a car."

Mattie chuckled again, making his whole day. "Go to sleep, Cole."

Feeling satisfied now that he was with Mattie again, he closed his eyes and was out within minutes.

★ ★ ★

Mattie couldn't sleep. She'd been able to get almost eight hours before awakening to greet Cole. She'd slept the deep sleep of exhaustion, and years of insomnia had conditioned her to awaken in the early morning anyway. Back at home it would be approaching five o'clock, about the time she and Robo would get up to take their morning jog. The two of them needed to stay fit so they could handle their duties as Timber Creek's only K-9 team.

Cole had fallen asleep almost immediately, and now his head tilted back, his mouth dropped open, and he began to snore. She turned her head so she could watch him, remaining quiet while both Cole and Robo slept. These were her two cherished males, and she considered herself lucky to be confined in this chilly car with them while the windows misted over, shutting them off from the world. How could she hesitate to marry this man when he would drop everything to make sure that her dog was taken care of in this dangerous environment?

She thought of her other cherished people—Cole's daughters, Mrs. Gibbs, Mama T, and Mattie's own sister, mother, and grandmother out in California. They would all be together soon, in less than a week now, for her wedding. She'd been too busy to think of that. They would soon all be family. Cole's parents too.

Mild concern crossed her mind as she thought of the fact that she barely even knew her future parents-in-law. She'd met them once and that was it. Cole's dad had greeted her warmly, but his mother had been standoffish. Cole said not to take it personally, that his mother reacted to everyone that way. But it was hard not to when it was her new family they were talking about. Family meant everything to Mattie.

She pushed the unsettling thoughts from her mind. Listening to Cole and Robo take turns snoring, she closed her eyes and rested until she sensed it was six o'clock, the designated time for them to awaken. It was still dark when she checked her cell phone to see that it was indeed time to get ready for the day.

She heard the door to their camper open and swiped a circle free of fog to see Drake slip out with the two dogs. He waved at her and she waved back inside the clear circle on the windshield before he led the dogs away from the trailer to do their morning business. Robo raised his head and pricked his ears, alert to the happenings outside.

Cole still slept. She hated to awaken him but knew she needed to open the car door and get started. She touched his arm softly and he jerked awake. "I'm sorry to have to wake you, but it's time for me to meet the others at the mess tent. Drake is already up. Do you want to go sleep in the trailer?"

After rubbing his eyes, Cole drew his hand down his face. "No. No, I think I'll be good to go with you. I want to be able to see the area where you found the deer and back you up this morning."

"Are you sure?"

He looked at her with bleary eyes. "Of course. Can we get some coffee somewhere?"

"Yep, and a hot breakfast too, more than likely."

Cole stretched. "That'll do me."

Mattie knew he was still exhausted. "If you need to, you can always come back here any time today to sleep." The car seat hummed as she pushed the button to raise the back, and then she began folding up the blanket.

As Cole followed suit and raised his seat, the buzzing from the electronics seemed to excite Robo. That combined with sensing that the other dogs were up and about made him dance in place on the back seat. Mattie was glad to see that at least he appeared fully invigorated and would be ready to face another day of searching.

She pulled her hood up to cover her head and, with her hand on her door handle, she looked at Cole. "You brought a raincoat, right?"

"Sure did. It's in the back with my suitcase. I filled one side of it with clothes and the other with medical supplies and an emergency bag of equipment."

She gave him a smile and squeezed his hand. "Thanks again for doing this. Sounds like you're prepared."

He returned her smile with a warm but weary grin as he quirked one eyebrow. "Mattie, I would follow you to the end of the earth if I needed to."

She snorted a soft chuckle, gave him a quick peck on the cheek, and then opened her door to face the start of a new day.

# FIFTEEN

Things didn't go exactly as Cole had planned, but he guessed he hadn't really thought them through. He'd hoped to search the site where the deer had died with Mattie and then provide backup for her as she continued to search for the child. But time was running out for River and Mattie had been assigned elsewhere.

The boy had gone missing on Thursday and by this afternoon the first forty-eight hours would end. This search and rescue mission differed from criminal investigations in that the search window was tight, and each minute that ticked away could be the last for a child exposed to the elements.

Mattie and Robo were searching a new grid with Rena as their field assistant. And Cole had been assigned to Hunter to search the deer scene and surrounding area for possible pollutants. Sergeant Jim Madsen was feeling better this morning and had been assigned a new grid, and Drake would be going over territory around the deer site with his cadaver dog.

Now, Hunter was driving Cole, Rena, Mattie and Robo, and Drake and Fritz to their assignments, lurching up a narrow, muddy track choked with trees and underbrush that pressed in on both sides. The rain had stopped and while the morning held promise, they'd been advised that the forecast was for more rain that afternoon.

Cole had met Sheriff Piper and Rena at breakfast, where a hot meal and a stiff cup of coffee had chased the cobwebs from his brain. Rena had shared the name and phone number of the vet who was treating her dog, and Cole had managed a short conversation with the woman before getting into Hunter's Jeep to leave. The vet had been surprised to learn that dead wildlife had been found in the area where her patient had been and was planning to request a toxicology panel screen for the blood sample she'd sent to the lab yesterday.

Cole figured that if this dog had ingested poison, it would be hard to determine exactly what kind by doing a general panel screen. Not all poisons could be tested for in one panel, and the most likely identification would take place if the vet could screen for a specific chemical. He hoped to be able to provide further information regarding what that chemical might be after his search of the area today.

Drake and Fritz shared the front of the vehicle with Hunter while the rest of them sorted themselves out in the back. Robo had ended up in the rear compartment while Cole, Mattie, and Rena shared the back seat. Robo didn't act too happy about losing his place alongside Mattie, and it amused Cole that the big dog continued to press his head against her shoulder whenever he could.

Hunter pointed out the lane they would come back to after dropping off Mattie and Rena, and a couple of miles farther up the road, he found a pullout and stopped. Robo unloaded from the Jeep with a happy grin on his face, twirled a few times, and then at Mattie's gentle command, settled near her feet to have his search harness put in place. Obviously, he was excited to get back to work.

Cole wished he could stay and watch the two search together, but he climbed back in the Jeep so Hunter could turn around and go downhill, leaving Mattie and Rena at their assigned spot. Mattie lifted her hand in goodbye as Hunter squared the Jeep back into the trail and they lumbered off down the track.

When they reached the narrow lane they'd passed earlier, Hunter turned into it and drove to a cabin that had a front deck and looked freshly finished. Hunter parked out front, and before they could unload and approach the porch, a man and his German shepherd stepped outside.

At breakfast, Cole had been told about this pair, a blind man and his guide dog, and he was eager to meet them. Hunter introduced Cecil to Cole first, leaving Cole with the dilemma of not knowing how to respond. If he offered a handshake like he wanted to, Cecil wouldn't see it. But that awkward moment lasted only a split second, because Cecil extended his hand and Cole stepped up quickly to grasp it for a brief, firm shake before Hunter repeated the process to introduce Drake.

"I thought you were the Fish and Wildlife folks when I heard you drive up," Cecil said to Hunter. "When will they come?"

"They should be here sometime early this morning. They promised they'd get right on it. But we'll be going up there to finish searching the area for possible contamination now," Hunter said.

"All right. Do you want me to go up there with you this morning?"

"There's no need. We can find it on our own."

"Then I'll wait here in case the Fish and Wildlife people show up. I can show them the way."

"Sounds like a plan," Hunter said.

Cole was disappointed because he'd wanted to talk to Cecil, but he figured he might have a chance later in the morning. He decided to say as much. "I'm a veterinarian, and I'd love to talk to you about your dog sometime if we get a chance. Would that be okay with you?"

Cecil's face lit up as he placed his hand on his dog's head in a gesture of fondness and pride while the shepherd raised his face to be stroked. "Absolutely. I'd be glad to talk to you about Oscar anytime. He was trained at Guide Dogs for the Blind, and he's given me my independence back."

"I can see you're devoted to each other."

"No other bond like it. Stop in whenever you can."

Drake had gone back to the Jeep to put Fritz into his search harness, and he came back to them now. "We're ready to go."

"Thanks, Cecil," Hunter said. "Talk to you later."

Cecil raised his hand to wave them off before turning to go back into his cabin. Cole and Drake followed Hunter up a well-groomed pathway into the woods to a site where they could see the dead deer from the trail.

Once there, Hunter pointed off to the left. "I searched a little way up and down the creek to the south before it got too dark to continue last night. There's a gully over there," he said, waving his hand in the opposite direction, "where we found another deer and a raccoon. There's a stream that flows toward the creek that's part of the drainage on this property, but it looks like it doesn't always have water running through it. I think it might be dry in the summer when we don't have as much rain. I didn't have a chance to explore it yet."

"Did Mattie and Robo search this area right here?" Drake used his hand to sweep the area to both right and left.

"Yes, they searched a grid that went from the creek to the road and uphill to the spot where we dropped them off just now," explained Hunter.

"All right, I'll get started combing through here and then move on up into the territory she's searching today. We'll meet you back at the road farther up."

"And you're okay without a field assistant?" Hunter asked.

"Sure. I've got this area mapped out in my head and can radio if I need anything."

"Do that. We'll be close by, either following this drainage or going farther up the creek."

Cole listened to the plan, figuring he'd be with Hunter at least until noon and then maybe with Mattie later. Hunter struck off across the slick grassy slope, heading toward the gully he'd mentioned. Cole stayed close as they wound their way through pine and cedar that brushed the sides of his raincoat as he pressed through them. Moss grew everywhere, on live tree trunks and deadfall alike. The scent of pine and damp earth permeated the grove.

When they came to the gully, Cole spotted the dead deer. Hunter pointed to the left. "I searched this spot and below toward the creek but didn't make it upslope off to the right. We might as well start here."

"All right." Cole gestured to the other side of the gully. "I'll take that area so we can search both sides."

He crossed the narrow channel of water that ran slowly down the shallow slope. Soggy on both sides, the stream covered a space of about four feet. Grateful for his waterproof boots, Cole slogged through until he reached higher ground. He turned and headed upslope, keeping sight of Hunter as he zigzagged through the trees.

Eventually they came to the road they'd traveled on earlier, where a culvert had been laid underneath to manage the drainage.

Hunter stopped and waited for Cole to catch up to him. He indicated the expanse of forest on the other side of the road. "There isn't much beyond here, and the terrain becomes very rugged out there. We think that our lost child probably didn't cross this road because if he had, he would've used it to come back down."

"Yeah, I see what you mean. But you never know what a lost person will do. We searched for a ninety-year-old man once, assuming he wouldn't cross a barbed wire fence or a river, but turns out he crossed a river and two fences before he was found."

Hunter nodded, a half smile on his face. "You're right. And we do have folks searching this area too. They just haven't made it up this far yet."

"Let's see how far we can get following this stream. We'll stick to a narrow area on both sides so we don't disturb the scent trails."

"Actually, I'm afraid the rainfall has already done that. We'll go as far as we can until we have to turn around."

As they continued uphill, Cole understood Hunter's warning. Bushes and ferns clogged the gully, forcing them farther out from the water.

But they kept at it, bushwhacking through brambles that reached out to snag clothing and bite at their hands and legs. After an hour of torment, Cole came to an area that looked like it had been cleared years ago, where the underbrush had grown back but was not as ferocious. Hunter had reached it before him and together they entered the area to scout around.

Still headed upslope, Cole came upon an ancient tumbledown cabin, its roof caved in and only two of its walls still standing. "What's this?" he asked Hunter. "An old homestead?"

Hunter came closer to join him. "I'm not sure. Could be that or an old hunter's cabin. We're on state forest land here, not a private holding."

"It's remote." Cole continued uphill, searching as he went. Within thirty feet, he came upon an old corral, its rails down on the ground and overgrown with weeds and thorny bushes. Only a few fence posts were left standing.

He reached down with a gloved hand to push away the long grasses from a pile of corral poles and discovered some old boards that had probably been part of the fencing. They were tinted green.

"Hunter," he called. "Come take a look at this."

Hunter waded through knee-high brush to get there, peering down at the boards that Cole had revealed. He frowned as if puzzled. "Yeah, I see them. But I'm not sure why it's significant."

"See that green tint?"

"Yeah. They haven't been painted, though. Not sure what that is."

"These boards have been treated with arsenic," Cole said.

"What?"

"Arsenic was used as a wood preservative back in the day. Still is but to a lesser degree." Cole toed one of the boards. "We make sure people who have horses that crib on fences don't have this type of wood treatment on their place."

"Crib?"

"Yeah . . . bite and chew on their fence rails. There's enough arsenic here to make a horse sick or even kill it."

"But these boards look old. Could the arsenic still be in them?"

"Arsenic is an element. It never goes away."

Hunter straightened, looked around the area, and then pointed. "The drainage is right over there. Could this arsenic have gotten in the water?"

Cole started walking through the tall grass toward the bramble-choked gully. Within twenty yards he came upon a burned area only about ten feet upslope from the water. "Look at this," he said, pointing it out to Hunter. "Someone's been burning here."

Cole used his boot to move the ashes, stirring up chunks of unburned wood with edges that appeared to be remnants of the boards they'd just found. "Someone has burned these arsenic-treated boards here. The arsenic would still be in this ash."

Hunter squinted at the gully as if measuring the distance from the ash pile to the water. "Less than ten feet. The rain could've washed this ash into the drainage system."

"I think so too. I think we've found your source of contamination."

Hunter looked back at Cole. "What do we do? Bury it?"

Cole shook his head. "This ash is dangerous. We need to get someone in here to clean it up and haul it out. They might as well remove those boards too, to keep someone from accidentally burning them again. Even the gas in the smoke can be dangerous if inhaled."

"For Pete's sake. That's all we need. A public health issue."

Cole nodded, hoping River hadn't consumed water from the stream. "Tell the sheriff to notify Cecil that his well water could be polluted. Anyone else that lives nearby too."

Cole removed his glove and took his cell phone out of the inside pocket of his raincoat. No service. "I need to get down where I can call Rena's vet to tell her to test for arsenic."

Hunter reached for his radio. "I'll call it in to Sheriff Piper. He can relay a message to the vet. He might as well notify the hazmat team and get them up here as soon as possible. Let's flag this area with orange tape."

"All right. Have Piper notify all the volunteers, especially the K-9 teams and the people who've been assigned this area. I want to get back to where Drake and Fritz are working. They're in the most dangerous spot."

# SIXTEEN

When Mattie and Rena received word about the arsenic pollution, they had just finished searching their assigned grid. Rena's
face telegraphed her distress as she ended the radio transmission.

"I can't believe it. What are the odds that Dozer would drink
from a polluted stream?" Rena said under her breath, as if talking
to herself.

Mattie decided to answer anyway. "I guess it can happen, but
don't beat yourself up. It's a rare occurrence, especially when the
water flows as swiftly as it does here."

Rena scowled. "But you know better, don't you?"

Mattie figured Rena was taking out her frustration on her. "I
was coached to avoid standing water when I was assigned this gig.
In Colorado, that's often the case, so I was taught differently, that's
all. Things vary from place to place and in different jurisdictions."

Rena shrugged and made an attempt to wipe the scowl off her
face. She took her cell phone from her pocket and looked at it.
"No bars. Do you mind if I hike down to where I can call Dozer's
vet?"

"Didn't Piper say he'd already contacted her?"

"Yeah, but I want to talk to her too."

Mattie could understand that. "No problem. We're finished
here for the morning anyway. I'll radio Drake and see where he's
at and catch up with him. I want to make sure he gets Fritz to
sniff that area that Robo showed interest in."

Robo had spent extra time going over an area twice. Although
he'd hesitated, he didn't indicate that he'd found River's scent.
But experience had taught Mattie that when her dog showed that
much interest in an area, there might be something below the

surface that needed to be checked. She hoped it wasn't River's body. If that were the case, she would bet her next paycheck that Robo would hit on it anyway, even though he'd not been trained in human remains detection. She had marked the area with orange flagging tape on a short spike and notified Drake to look for it.

"I'll hike down on the road unless I can catch a ride." Rena turned and headed off in that direction.

Mattie pulled her radio from her pocket and pressed the mic on, calling for Drake. He answered within seconds.

"Drake here."

"This is Mattie. We're finished up here. Did you get the word about arsenic?"

"Affirmative."

"Where are you?"

"I'm coming up creekside in the state forest west of Cecil's place."

"I'm coming down to join you until you finish your grid."

"Sounds good. Over."

Mattie put away her radio and, keeping Robo on a leash, she headed downstream, staying close to the creek until she came upon Drake and Fritz. Drake raised his hand in greeting, but Fritz ignored them as he alternated his nose in the air and down on the ground, continuing to work the area.

Mattie kept Robo close to her and stayed out of the other team's way. Despite the morning's work, Fritz was still all business. "That place I told you about is just up ahead, closer to the road," she called to Drake, and he raised his hand in acknowledgment.

The bloodhound's burnished red coat and black nose provided a certain amount of camouflage against the trunks of the red cedars, which were almost the same color. But Drake's yellow raincoat was easy to spot, so Mattie kept him in sight as she and Robo fell in behind them and headed back uphill. Soon Drake veered off to the right, working his way toward the road.

When they came upon the orange flag that Mattie had posted earlier, Fritz put his nose to the ground and vacuumed up the scent, moving his head back and forth in rapid sweeps. Mattie's heart rate kicked up a notch and she moved in closer. Robo started

136 | Margaret Mizushima

to dance at the end of his leash, possibly sensing Mattie's dread as she wondered if Fritz would indicate a find.

Fritz buried his nose in the grasses and dirt and then sneezed. He lay down on the spot and looked up at his handler with his sad droopy eyes. Mattie's heart fluttered as Drake bent over his dog and fondled his ears.

"Did you find something, boy?" Drake asked. "What is it?"

Drake turned and made eye contact with Mattie. "You know what this might mean?"

"I can imagine." The search for River might have come to an end. Or . . . Mattie's mind whirled with possibilities. Could it be the body of someone else?

Others had gone missing in this area, but if Fritz discovered the body of a missing person, it wouldn't be buried underground. Unless that person was a victim of homicide. Could it be the body of someone who wasn't even on their radar?

Drake shrugged off his backpack to reach a folded metal probe bar strapped to the back. He straightened it into place before bending over Fritz again. "You're a good boy," he murmured, stroking the bloodhound's head and long ears. "Fritz, stand," he said, giving a gentle tug on the leash, and then, "Move over here, boy. That's right. Sit."

After moving Fritz out of the way, Drake approached the spot his dog had indicated.

Mattie put Robo in a sit-stay before removing her cell phone from her pocket. "I'll take pictures."

Even though the immediate area was covered in the usual moss and underbrush, the place that Fritz had indicated was rel-atively clear. Mattie had a bad feeling about the whole situation.

When she paused, Drake moved in with his probe bar. "I'll go slowly and see if there's anything close to the surface."

Mattie stood by, watching Drake as he probed below the sur-face with the bar, his face creased in a frown of concentration. Occasionally, she snapped a photo, just in case it would be needed later.

"This dirt is fairly loose," Drake said. He carefully pushed the bar lower and lower until he reached a level at least two feet deep. Suddenly the bar stalled as it struck something solid. He glanced up at Mattie in alarm. "I hit something."

Mattie leaned closer. "Maybe a tree root?"

"I don't think so." When Drake pulled the bar free, the odor of death seemed to seep out of the hole. He stepped back with his nose wrinkled in distaste. "You smell that?"

Robo pulled against his leash as he tried to surge forward. "Sit," Mattie said, reminding him of what he was supposed to be doing as she held Drake's gaze. "Smells like decomp."

"The indication from Fritz means it's human."

Mattie nodded, her heart in her throat. "I'll radio Piper," she said, taking her unit from her pocket and pressing on the mic.

When she relayed the bad news, Piper cursed. "Do you think it's our boy?"

"We can't tell, but there's an odor of decay," Mattie said.

"I'll be right up."

Mattie gave him the coordinates of their location and Piper ended the connection.

Drake had moved over beside Fritz during the transmission and was now hunkered down beside his dog, stroking his long ears and giving him loving pats. He rewarded Fritz with a toy, which he chewed on as he enjoyed an ear rub.

But then without prompting, Fritz dropped the toy and sniffed off to the side, moving slowly with his nose to the ground. He traveled about ten feet while Drake and Mattie fell still and silent, watching him. As her apprehension began to build, Mattie trailed her hand across Robo's head to his shoulder, keeping him in place. And then Fritz lay down again and stared at Drake.

"Oh no," Drake murmured under his breath as he and Mattie looked at each other. "Do you think he's found another grave?"

"Should we probe it now, or wait until Piper arrives?"

"Let's wait," Drake said, moving over to praise Fritz again. "This is more than we bargained for, and it's Piper's jurisdiction."

★ ★ ★

By the time Cole arrived at the scene, yellow tape blocked the volunteers who'd gathered to watch. Dread consumed him as he realized the lost boy might have been found.

Piper stood inside the taped-off area along with Mattie, Drake, and Sergeant Madsen. Deputy Casey had taken charge of onlooker control, telling everyone to step back to give the forensic team room to work.

Cole caught Mattie's eye as he and Hunter approached the crowd, and she moved to the edge of the taped-off area to join him. Robo greeted Cole as if he were a long-lost pal, prancing up to fawn at his legs. He leaned down to pet Robo as he studied Mattie to see how she was doing. She looked tired and worried, or maybe he was projecting his own feelings onto her.

"I hope it's not River," she said as she edged up to him, keeping her voice quiet so only he could hear. "Decomposition seems pretty far gone in these remains."

Piper raised his hands to shush the volunteers. "Okay, everybody, listen up. We're not going to uncover whatever we have here immediately. I've called in help from State Patrol Crime Lab to process this site just in case we have a crime scene. But from the looks of it, this is probably not our missing child. I need all of you to get back to your search grids and finish up. If you've already worked your area, go on back to camp for lunch and reassignment for this afternoon. We've got to keep looking."

Noise from another vehicle rumbled through the trees, and Cole turned to see who had arrived. Seemed awfully quick for the State Crime Lab team to reach this remote spot, but maybe they weren't coming from too far away. He dismissed that possibility as soon as a foursome materialized through the trees: a woman and three men.

He recognized the woman immediately. Chrystal Winter. Even though she looked drawn and pale, almost everyone would know that face from the big screen. She moved forward through the forest gracefully, flanked by two men who looked like body builders. The third man seemed to separate himself from the others as he hurried toward Piper.

Mattie whispered a private introduction near Cole's ear. "Chrystal and her two bodyguards. And River's dad, Roger Allen."

"What's going on, Sheriff? We heard someone found a body?" Roger asked.

Piper raised his hand to halt the foursome outside the crime scene tape. "Hold on, Mr. Allen—Ms. Winter. We're not sure what's been found yet, but we think it probably isn't River."

Chrystal released a soft moan and gripped the arm of one of her bodyguards. "Are you sure it's not him?" she whimpered.

"We'll know more once the State Crime Lab team can do their work here." Piper ducked under the crime scene tape to move closer to Chrystal. "I'm sorry, but we need for you to return to camp with the others."

Some of the volunteers had turned away to trudge downhill when the sheriff first directed everyone back to camp, but a few bystanders remained. Piper's gaze swept the remaining audience. "The volunteers are going back to camp now for lunch, but we'll resume the search for River as soon as possible. We're pretty sure we haven't found him here." He returned his gaze to River's parents. "Please go back to camp. I promise I'll find you and share more information as soon as I can."

Chrystal turned away, and Cole watched her stumble, gripping the arm of her bodyguard, as she started back toward their vehicle. Her movements were in direct opposition to the graceful way she'd glided through the forest when she first approached. It seemed odd, but perhaps learning that Piper didn't think her son had been buried at this site had left her limp with relief. Or was that what she wanted everyone to think?

Cole wasn't proud of himself for supposing the woman might be acting, but he couldn't help it. When he glanced back toward Mattie, she quirked one eyebrow, and he wondered if she was thinking the exact same thing.

"We should go," Mattie murmured.

"Sergeant Madsen, I need you and your crew to stay here," Piper said, projecting his voice. "Everyone else, please go on back to camp now."

Cole guessed he might be included in Madsen's crew and decided to stay with Mattie. Volunteers began moving away.

But Roger Allen also remained, his eyes filled with anguish. "Are you feeding us a line to get us to leave, or do you really think my son is *not* buried in this spot?"

Sympathy crossed Piper's tired face. "Mr. Allen," he said quietly. "I don't think this is your son's grave site. I believe the decomposition here is too far advanced. I'll let you know what we find as soon as possible."

Allen's apprehension appeared to ease slightly, but he leaned closer to Piper, his voice hard with intensity. "I tell you, Sheriff, my ex-wife knows more about this than she's saying. Don't take her show of grief at face value. Remember, she makes big bucks acting for a living. Have you questioned her?"

"I have. We're moving forward, Mr. Allen, and if we don't find River this afternoon, we'll be reevaluating our procedures for this search. But right now, please go back down with the others so we can continue our work."

Cole wondered what "reevaluating our procedures for this search" meant. Was it sheriff-speak for upgrading from searching for a lost child to something else, like maybe a kidnapping by a parent or a stranger? He'd once been on the parental side of a search like this, and it had been the most excruciating time of his life. His sympathy went out to this father.

Allen's face had fallen as he started to turn away, but then he stopped and pinned his gaze on Piper. "I'll go, but I need an update by two o'clock this afternoon. Time is wasting and another night is coming soon. We need a different plan."

"I understand your frustration," Piper said with an expression that looked like he really did. "I've got all the trained search and rescue folks I have available out here from sunrise to sunset, and we'll finish searching a five-mile radius by the end of the day. I'll give you an update as soon as I can, although I can't guarantee it will be exactly by two o'clock. I hear you, Mr. Allen, and I'll be in touch ASAP."

Allen wasn't pacified, but he turned and strode away through the forest, following Chrystal and her bodyguards. Cole hoped they'd waited for him.

After the father had gone, Piper swiped his hand down over his face. He gave Cole a speculative look and then turned to Sarge. "Dr. Walker isn't a cop, right?"

Sergeant Madsen turned a weary face toward Cole to study him, making him feel like a specimen. Cole felt Mattie move close enough to his side to brush against his arm, as if she were aligning herself with him.

"Dr. Walker is a sheriff's posse member in his county and has been trained as law enforcement backup. He knows how to handle himself," Sarge said, his voice sounding weaker than Cole was used to. The man looked sick, like he wasn't fully recovered from the stomach flu he'd suffered the day before. Or had he been exposed to the contaminated water?

Piper nodded at Cole before looking around at the group that was left: the Colorado contingent, a couple of crime scene techs, Hunter, and Deputy Casey. "This thing shows every sign of turning into a shit-storm, and I can already hear it rumbling. I've called in the state CID and we don't even know for sure yet that this site contains a human body."

Drake and Sarge looked offended.

"Oh, yes we do," Sarge said. He nodded at Fritz, who sat close to Drake's heel beside a short spike with orange flagging tape on it. "That dog has been trained to ignore the scent of animal remains and only hits on odor that comes from a human. He's the best in the business. You've got yourself not only one but two graves here."

"I admire your confidence," Piper said, "but I want to make sure we've got human remains here. Because if we don't, I can still call off the state crime scene investigators." He turned to the two crime scene investigators from his own department. "Hank, Julie, let's dig down deep enough to see what we've got."

The two set to work with a camera, shovel, and trowels, breaking up the soil carefully before scooping it out. They paused every few inches to take photos of their work.

As if tired, Sarge sank down to sit on the trunk of a felled tree nearby. "Mattie, could you take photos for me too?"

"Sure, Sarge," she said, lowering her backpack to the ground and pulling her cell phone from her pocket.

Cole figured Sarge would want photos of the process for future human remains handler training. Cole had seen Sarge and his dogs at work in a similar situation back home in Timber Creek and knew them to be invaluable resources at this type of crime scene. He had no doubt at all that these two CSIs would soon find two grave sites.

It didn't take long to dig a square hole two feet wide and two feet deep. Hank was down on his knees scooping out dirt with gloved hands when he looked up at Piper. "I've hit a sheet of plastic."

"Let's open it just enough to see what's there," Piper said.

Julie and Mattie took photos while Hank removed a tool from his kit to slit open the plastic. There was already enough odor seeping from the open hole that Cole felt sorry for the tech who had to do the dirty work.

Hank didn't linger after slitting the plastic bag. He arose with knife in hand. "Looks like fabric to me, although it's degraded. Does someone have a flashlight we can shine down in there?"

"I do," Mattie said, going to her pack to remove a flashlight. She offered it to Hank.

He shrugged, showing her his contaminated gloves. "Go ahead," he said, tilting his head toward the hole.

Mattie stepped up and shone the light downward. With a neutral expression that Cole had begun to think of as her cop face, she looked at Piper. "Do you want to take a look, Sheriff? I think it's probably clothing."

With a frown, Piper leaned over the hole. "I agree," he said, releasing a breath that bordered on a sigh. He stepped back and waved at the spike from which fluttered a short orange flag. "But we don't know for sure what's under there."

Sarge arose from where he'd been sitting. "Look, Pipe, this dog has had over a thousand hours of training, and he hasn't made a mistake in months. Unfortunately, you can count on two graves here."

"An older grave?" Piper asked, eyeing the plentiful grass that grew over the other site.

Sarge nodded, looking grim. "Yeah, I doubt that River Allen is buried in either of these two graves. You've probably got yourself at least two homicides here."

Piper's shoulders slumped. "Let's dig so we have an idea what we've got before our state team gets here."

# SEVENTEEN

Mattie hunkered down beside Robo, one arm hugging him close to her chest, while Hank and Julie carefully excavated the possible grave site. This situation was bringing back bad memories of a time when she'd found a child's grave near Redstone Ridge in the Colorado Rockies. Her empty stomach churned and she felt nauseous. Discovery of that grave site had unlocked memories she'd repressed as a two-year-old, a time when she'd actually seen the child shot and burned in the grave where he'd been buried.

The horror of it was close to the surface even now. Cole hovered nearby, and she knew he was remembering that day from about seven months ago. She took comfort in knowing she wasn't alone and Cole was there to share her burden.

Hank was down on his knees, removing dirt from the hole he'd dug through the grass and rich earth, using his gloved hands instead of a shovel. Deputy Casey had ended up taking Roger Allen back down to camp, his ex-wife having left without him. Drake and Fritz were combing the area, searching for sign of any other remains while Hunter followed along, doing a visual sweep. Mattie felt guilty about not going out to help, but Sarge had asked her to document with photos, so here she was at a grave site she didn't want to be at.

Hank leaned back on his heels. "I'm down to bone. Let's get a picture."

After Julie took her photo, Mattie centered her cell phone camera over the hole but could only glimpse the light brown curvature at the bottom that Hank must've referred to as bone. "I need more light," she said, reaching toward the flashlight that was now in Cole's hands.

"I'll shine it," he said, a bleak look on his face.

With more light, Mattie could tell that the tannish colored curve was indeed bone, dirty from years of being under the ground. Long enough for the flesh to decompose. "No plastic covering on this one," she said to Hank after taking the shot.

"Right. I'd say that this one was buried years earlier. I'm going to uncover a little more to see if we've got a skull here." Hank went back to work, leaning into the two-foot-deep hole.

"Okay," Piper said. "So we've got a skeleton and a body wrapped in plastic. Two different methods of burial at one site. The same doer or two different ones?"

Mattie didn't want to say, although she believed the same person or people had buried these two bodies side by side.

But evidently Sarge didn't share her hesitancy. "This is probably the work of the same perpetrator, although it could be a pair working together. The plastic might have been added to the more recent body because the doer cared more about the victim."

"Well, maybe," Piper said, leaning forward to watch Hank work. "I'm not so sure about the caring part, but you're probably right that we have one perpetrator here, maybe more but they're working together." He straightened and swept the area with his gaze, turning to cover a three-hundred-sixty-degree circle. "But these graves aren't necessarily tied in to the disappearance of River Allen."

Sarge grunted in a noncommittal way.

Hank continued to remove dirt one handful at a time, setting it aside in a pile that they would sort through later. After a few minutes he stopped and leaned back out of the way. "More photos," he said.

Cole shone the light, and Mattie could see the curve of a small skull, its empty sockets staring up at her. She quickly snapped a few pictures so she could then look away.

"Pipe," Sarge said. "This might have nothing to do with River Allen, but I'm afraid you've got yourself the bones of a child here. Seems a coincidence, don't it? And you know how we don't believe in coincidences."

"Crap," Piper said, taking the flashlight from Cole so he could see into the hole for himself. "State CID will send a detective to help with this site. They're going to have to work on identifying these bodies. I've collected dental records and DNA samples from the two kids who've gone missing since I've been in office, so we should know if we've got a match from those. I'm not sure about this set of older bones."

"How long we looking at for ID?" Sarge asked.

"Dental ID should be quick, maybe a couple of days. DNA could take weeks, depending on their backlog."

Sarge frowned. "What about River? Do you think the mom has something to do with his disappearance?"

Piper stepped back from the grave, shaking his head, and Mattie thought he looked like he'd aged in the two days since she'd met him. "I don't know. The dad is convinced of it, but I'm not. Yeah, she can't help but show some drama at times, but when I first interviewed her, she seemed genuinely distraught. I might be getting the wool pulled over my eyes, but I don't think she's involved. I'm more concerned about how this grave site could be related."

Mattie agreed with him. She didn't like the fact that a child was missing and they'd just turned up a hidden grave site containing the remains of another child. Even though she was outside her jurisdiction, she felt the need to push for upgrading the search for River from that of a lost child to a potential criminal investigation. "I agree we should be concerned, Sheriff," she said. "These area search dogs are finding nothing around the movie set except for that candy wrapper Robo found the first day."

A quick movement from Robo caught her eye as he jerked his head in her direction as if awaiting instruction.

"I keep wondering if someone used River's favorite candy to lure him away from the set," Mattie said.

Piper grimaced. "I heard back from my crime lab. They couldn't find any prints on that wrapper that were clear enough to lift. We plan to look further for touch DNA, but that could take weeks."

"That's disappointing," Mattie said, wishing they'd found some proof for her theory. "But I still wonder about it. River is old enough to know not to go with a stranger, which makes me think he might have gone with someone he knows."

"Like who? Got any suspects?" Piper asked.

"Not yet, but I think we need to direct an investigation into who River knows from the set and this community. Try to get a handle on who he might have trusted."

"I've already got that list." Piper looked frustrated. "I've been looking at that possibility since day one. I've talked to everyone on that list and gotten nowhere. The party line is that the boy walked away during the commotion from the fire. That's what they all seem to believe."

"Everyone except the dad," Cole said.

Mattie noted his grim face, and when he looked at her, she knew he was remembering the time when Sophie had been kidnapped. This must be bringing back those memories for him, and they had to be hard ones to reexamine.

Piper nodded at Cole but turned to Sarge. "Do you want to interview both parents, Jim? See if you get a different feel for the situation than I do?"

Sarge shook his head. "I'm no good at that. I'm a dog trainer and handler." He pointed at Mattie. "Mattie is too, but she helps with witness and suspect interviews in her jurisdiction all the time. I recommend you go with her."

Piper gave her a measuring look. "Why don't we talk to them together? See what you think?"

This wasn't at all what Mattie expected, but she couldn't wait to see what the parents had to say. "Let's do it as soon as possible. Then I think we need to take these dogs to every private holding and through every street in town to see if we can get a hit on our missing child in places where others might have hidden him."

Though deep inside she acknowledged her fear that someone had already taken River far, far away, she still gestured toward the open grave site. "If we have a child killer around here, we need to make sure River isn't in his hands at this very moment."

★  ★  ★

Mattie asked Cole to watch Robo while she went with Piper to the command center to conduct the interviews. She told Piper she wanted to talk to Roger Allen first. She'd already seen Chrystal in action, and she didn't trust her sincerity. The actress might be innocent of hiding her own child for media attention, but her emotional reactions were suspect in Mattie's opinion. She couldn't tell what was real and what was performance. On the other hand, she knew very little about the father. He might also be innocent of abducting his own child, but she didn't have any evidence to shift that possibility either way.

They met in a private room in Piper's incident command trailer, sitting around a small round table that had four chairs. Roger appeared eager to talk, despite his haggard appearance.

He focused his attention on the sheriff. "What's going on uphill?"

Piper met Roger's intense gaze. "We've found a grave site that needs to be excavated, but we can safely say that River is not buried there. Actually, this site probably has nothing to do with your son's disappearance."

Roger didn't show any relief. "How can you be sure of that?"

Piper shook his head. "I can't be, but we have no evidence at this point that links River to this grave site. Right now, I'm more interested in your theory that your ex-wife has something to do with River's disappearance. What makes you feel that way?"

Roger passed his hand down over his tired-looking face. "You've met her. She's a drama queen. She'd do anything for publicity."

Mattie wondered why Roger continued to take that stance. "What do you base that statement on? Do her past actions make you believe that?"

"Hell, yes. When we were on our honeymoon, she set up a huge press conference against my wishes. Trotted me out like a dog and pony show. Same thing when River was born. I asked her to keep our son's birth a private event, a blessing in our lives for only us to share. But she can't do anything without creating a media frenzy."

Mattie believed him. "Okay, but why now? What makes you think this is something she wants attention for now?"

Roger met her gaze. "Because she's slipping in the ratings. Her last movie got labeled a B-movie in the press, and she needs something to draw sympathy for her. This next movie comes out in a few months, so she's building up to promote it. Did you watch the news yesterday?"

"I was out in the woods all day looking for River," Mattie said, even as she heard Piper puff out an exasperated sigh.

Roger looked at Piper. "I know you're trying to keep the media out of this, but that reporter, Abby Day, seems to have jumped on the Chrystal Winter bandwagon. She interviewed Chrystal and it aired yesterday evening." Roger raised his pitch in a mockery of his ex-wife. "Oh, my poor baby. All these wonderful people are trying to help, but no one has been able to find him." He resumed his own voice. "No one can find him because she's hiding him somewhere. That's why!"

A quick glance at Piper told Mattie he seemed to be letting her take the lead, so she asked the obvious question. "If she's hiding him somewhere, where do you think that might be?"

"Maybe her home in Hollywood or her vacation home in Colorado. But those seem too obvious." Roger appeared increasingly vexed, and he looked back at Piper. "I don't know. She's got a sister that she's chummy with. Gail Franklin. She might know something, or she might even have River."

"Give me the names and contact information of anyone you think might give us information," Piper said. "We're expanding our investigative team."

The anger in Roger's expression turned to fear. "Does that mean you think this dead body you've found *is* related to River's disappearance?"

Finding the second set of remains had been kept from the child's parents, and Piper was quick to try to reassure the father. "We don't know that. But this discovery necessitates new resources, and we'll use them for investigating both River's disappearance and the new site."

Roger locked eyes with Piper. "So you'll have Chrystal investigated?"

"You as well," Piper said quietly.

"Me! You can't believe I had anything to do with this. I was hundreds of miles away."

"It's not unheard of for a parent to hire someone to kidnap their child," Piper said.

"It's routine to take a look at both parents when a child is missing," Mattie said, using the soothing tone she'd learned from working with Detective Stella LoSasso in the many interrogations she'd observed. "If you help us, we can clear you faster."

Roger looked annoyed. "Of course I'll help. Why do you think I came here?"

"Will you take a polygraph?" Piper asked.

Even though polygraphs weren't allowed as evidence in court, Mattie guessed Piper wanted to see if Roger would agree to it, which typically suggested innocence.

Roger's eyebrows raised. "Well, yeah, I guess so. But those things aren't very accurate, are they? I mean, I'd hate for it to be wrong. Then you'd think I'm guilty."

"We have an experienced guy who can do it," Piper said. "I'll arrange it."

Mattie remembered what the nanny, Sally Kessler, had told her. She decided to throw out a statement for Roger to react to. "Someone suggested that you weren't very engaged with River when you had him at your home for visitation."

Roger stared at her. "Who said that? River's nanny, who's probably in on this fiasco?" He wrung his hands and appeared to be trying to control his temper. "Look, I'm a working stiff. I'm not loaded like Chrystal is. I own my own advertising firm, and I can't always take time off when Chrystal allows me a chance to be with my own son. So the nanny comes, and when I have to work she has to work too, instead of having a vacation like she wants. She's probably pissed about that. Or . . ." His expression became speculative. "Maybe she's just trying to divert attention to me instead of Chrystal."

Mattie wondered if he could be right, although Sally had appeared sincere when Mattie had spoken to her. What would Roger Allen's motive be for taking his own child? "You said you get to see River when Chrystal allows you to. Is there a problem with her allowing court-ordered visitation rights?"

Roger drew a breath and exhaled, his cheeks puffed as if letting off steam. "Actually, no. It just irks me that she gets to have him more than I do, I guess."

Mattie nodded. "And sometimes your work schedule gets in the way."

"Exactly." Roger gripped his hands together again. "But I love my kid, and I try my damnedest to make sure we get quality time together when we can."

Mattie noticed that his eyelids had reddened, and she thought he'd grown teary. His emotions seemed to be all over the place, more those of a victim rather than a perpetrator. Or did he have a bit of the acting gene in him as well? "Do you wish he could be with you more often?" she asked.

Roger's shoulders slumped and he looked down at the table. "Truthfully, I'm happy the way things have been. I live alone and I'm always working. I can't afford a nanny, and Sally does a good job with River. She seems to care about him, and since he's not in school, she can handle his lessons. I can't afford that kind of thing."

Mattie believed it pained him to admit his ex-wife could take better care of his son than he could. "One more question from me then, Mr. Allen. If Ms. Winter is hiding River somewhere, do you believe he could be in danger?"

"Not really." Roger looked up to meet her eyes, a look of desperation on his face. "But I don't know what to believe. Maybe this is a ploy for publicity. Maybe he's lost in the woods. Maybe someone has taken him. I just want you guys to consider all options and to get to the bottom of it."

She didn't doubt his sincerity. "That's exactly what we plan to do."

# EIGHTEEN

After Roger left, Mattie and Piper sat at the table while Deputy Casey went to get Chrystal. Cole had dropped off sandwiches and coffee for both of them from the mess tent and, realizing she was starving, Mattie had grabbed this spare moment to dig in. Ham and cheese on rye tasted as good as anything she'd ever eaten.

"What do you think of what we learned from Roger Allen?" she asked Piper before taking another bite.

"I'm inclined to believe he's not involved and he's at as much of a loss as we are." Piper pushed about a fourth of his sandwich into his mouth in one bite.

Mattie nodded, chewing thoughtfully as she hurried to finish her meal. Were they at a loss? They'd cleared a large area, and they were now turning this case away from a search for a lost child and more toward a criminal investigation. She believed they might finally be on the right track.

Elements of what she knew flashed through her mind. Chrystal Winter was definitely filled with drama and seeking the spotlight, but her distress when they first met had appeared genuine. The circumstances surrounding River's disappearance—the nanny being sent away on an errand and a fire on the set as what might have been a distraction—seemed suspicious. The candy wrapper in the woods might have been handled by River or Robo might have been only identifying something outside the environmental norm. Again, she wished her dog could talk.

Back home, Stella would have lined the whiteboard with lists, so Mattie mentally created a list of her own as she finished her coffee. Potential Suspects: Chrystal Winter, Roger Allen, the nanny Sally Kessler, the bodyguards Buck and Gunner. She thought of the chainsaw carver, Edward Campbell, and decided to add him to that list as well, although she had no valid reason to do so other than his relatively close proximity to the crime scene and his reluctance to give permission to search his property. But of course, that could have been from pure prickliness.

Persons of Interest? Chrystal's sister Gail Franklin, all of the folks on the movie set, the residents of the town, and anyone living near the encampment. Well, at least they weren't at a loss for people to interview. There was plenty of work to do for the detective from the state CID, but Mattie planned to get started ASAP.

The sound of people climbing the steps at the main door had her setting down her coffee cup and standing to greet Chrystal. Buck angled his muscle-bound shoulders in through the door and swept his eyes around the room as if searching for danger.

Piper stepped over to the door and held it wide. "No reason for concern here, Buck. It's just Deputy Wray and me. You can wait outside."

"Mind if I check the other rooms?" Buck said as he passed by and headed down the short hallway that led toward what would normally be the sleeping quarters.

"Be my guest," Piper said to his retreating back before turning to offer a hand to Chrystal as she hovered on the platform by the open door.

"Wait," came a voice from behind Chrystal, which Mattie assumed came from Gunner.

Chrystal had reached for Piper's hand, but she dropped hers at Gunner's direction, shifting her eyes from Piper to Mattie and then back to Piper.

Buck came back from the rear of the trailer. "All clear. You can enter."

Mattie thought Piper looked strained at the drama, but evidently he didn't want to object to the team's safety concerns. She could understand in part since this woman's child was missing and who knew if she herself would become a target. But, after all, this was the incident command center and their show of protection seemed more like scripted theatre rather than necessary protocol.

Piper ushered Chrystal inside and gestured toward the table where Mattie was standing. But he stepped forward to block the door when Gunner tried to follow. "Go ahead and have a seat,

Ms. Winter. Gunner and Buck, I need you to wait outside. Our conversation with Ms. Winter is private."

Gunner lingered on the platform, looking at his partner for direction.

"Go ahead," Buck told him before looking back at Piper. "I need to stay."

"No, you don't. Ms. Winter is safe with us and you can wait just outside the door."

"It's okay, Buck," Chrystal said softly. "I'll be fine."

Buck gave her a possessive look as he headed for the door, and this combined with the way she'd gripped her bodyguard's arm while out at the grave site made Mattie wonder about the relationship between the two of them. If he was in love, what might he do at his employer's request?

Buck closed the door behind him, but since there was no sound of his feet going down the metal steps, Mattie assumed he'd taken up a post on the platform. Piper and Chrystal joined her and they all sat at the table.

Piper opened the conversation. "We can assure you that your son is not buried at the site that was found."

Chrystal nodded, her face pale. She'd tried to cover the ashen circles under her eyes with makeup, but they were still visible. Mattie thought she'd grown thinner in the two days since they'd met.

"That *is* a comfort, but I'm afraid of what this site might mean. It's horrible to know there's a body buried just a few miles from here, and my son is out there somewhere missing." Chrystal pressed her fingers against her lips as if holding back a sob.

"I agree that it's disturbing," Mattie said, wanting to establish rapport but not wanting to clarify that there were actually two bodies buried up above. "We're almost done with the area search around here, and we haven't found definite sign that your son is out in the woods. We'll be expanding our search this afternoon."

Mattie looked at Piper and he took over. "Because of the burial site that was found, I'm calling in the state crime investigation department. A detective and crime scene investigation team will be on site within the hour. At this point, I'll be asking for help with your son's disappearance as well. We might be looking at a crime instead of a lost child."

Chrystal burst into tears, sobbing as she covered her eyes. Piper and Mattie exchanged glances as they paused, letting Chrystal have a few moments to digest this information. After a long minute, Chrystal spoke between sobs. "As time has passed, I became afraid of that."

Mattie jumped at the opening. "Tell us what you've been thinking. Anything might help us find River."

Chrystal wiped her tears with her fingers and sniffled as she tried to compose herself. Piper stood and retrieved a box of tissues from a room down the hallway. Chrystal gave him a grateful look as she took one and delicately blew her nose.

"I really don't know what to think," Chrystal said, her voice husky. "But when no one found River the first day, I started to get scared. It feels like it's all my fault. I should've never sent Sally to town and left River alone."

"I understand you'd done that before and River was safe in his trailer here at the camp," Mattie said. "What was different about two days ago? Can you think of anything?"

"Nothing except the obvious. The fire." Chrystal gave her complete eye contact. "Nothing like that had ever happened before."

Mattie nodded. "Your two bodyguards. They stayed with you?"

Chrystal leaned forward, her arms at her stomach, and groaned as if in real pain. "Yes. I should've sent Gunner to check on River. I didn't think. What kind of mother doesn't think of her child during an emergency?"

Mattie didn't have an answer for that, or at least one the celebrity would want to hear, so she asked another question. "In hindsight, that fire could have been a diversion to get everyone away from River's trailer. We don't know that for a fact, but has anything like that ever happened before, either on a set or at your home?"

Chrystal met her gaze again. "No. Never."

"Is there anyone you can think of who might have wanted to target you or your son?"

"Not specifically, but there are always crazies out there. I hired Buck and Gunner a little over a year ago when I received death threats because of the role I played in my last movie. You know, the one where I played a character who tortured and murdered her husband and child."

Mattie hadn't seen the movie and, knowing the content, she wouldn't be watching it in the future. "You took these threats seriously then."

"Oh yeah, especially after someone left a dead squirrel at my gate. I mean, it was dead but not of natural causes, so it was disgusting."

"Did you have security cameras there?"

Chrystal shook her head. "Not then. We do now."

"Could this same person have targeted River?"

Chrystal threw up her hands before leaning forward to support her head with them, elbows on the table. "Who knows?"

"Did you report it to the police?" Mattie asked. "Was there an investigation done?"

"Yes, I reported it and they came out and took a look. They got some footage from other cameras in the area, but nothing definitive was found. They said to let them know if anything else happened. I hired Buck and Gunner and a security firm to fortify the house. Nothing has happened since then."

"Okay." Mattie decided to take another tack. "Think about River's dad. Do you have any concern that Mr. Allen might have taken River?"

Chrystal tightened her lips as she shook her head. "No. Roger isn't built that way. He's never protested our custody agreement, and he never asks for extra time with his son. He loves River, but he's too busy for him."

There seemed to be agreement on this point among nanny, father, and now mother. "Ms. Winter, have you—"

"Feel free to call me Chrystal."

Mattie started over again. "Chrystal, have you thought of anyone you employ or anyone on the set that might have taken River?"

Chrystal looked startled. "You mean my security team or Sally?"

Mattie nodded.

"No, of course not. Buck and Gunner were with me and I've had Sally for years. She loves River, and she's dedicated to him. She would never do anything to frighten or harm him."

"Okay, how about others from the set who don't know you and River as well?"

Chrystal paused as if thinking. Finally she said, "Not anyone I can think of. I mean, well, the props director has taken a special interest in River, but he seems truly nice. There's no reason why he would . . . I mean, surely he wouldn't . . ." Chrystal looked concerned as her words trailed off.

"What's his name?" Piper said.

"Uh . . . Bob Gibson. But don't tell him I mentioned him. He's probably just a nice man."

Piper got up from the table and went into the back area. Mattie could hear the now familiar sound of him connecting with someone on his radio.

"We have no reason to share that information with anyone you mention," Mattie said. Usually family members with missing children didn't hesitate in naming people who might know something, but Chrystal might be more sensitive to turning people against her because of her desire for popularity. "If you think of anyone we should talk to, please don't hesitate to tell Sheriff Piper."

"Okay." Chrystal lowered her gaze to the table while Mattie paused to give her time to think.

When Piper reentered the room, Chrystal looked back up but remained silent. Piper took his seat at the table, and Mattie decided to move on to the crux of what they needed to know. "There's been some speculation regarding whether or not you would orchestrate River's disappearance as a way to gain publicity."

Chrystal's eyes widened as if surprised before a frown lowered her eyebrows. "You can't be serious." Mattie held her gaze until Chrystal looked away toward Piper. "Who would say such a thing?"

Mattie replied before Piper could. "That's not as important as it is for us to know if it's a possibility."

"There is no truth to it whatsoever." Indignation consumed Chrystal's expression. "Is that what Roger thinks? Unbelievable!"

"That's not necessarily Mr. Allen's opinion, but it's something we heard, and I needed to ask the question. As you know, we need to explore all options," Mattie said.

Piper spoke up. "And just so you're aware . . . false reporting in this state is a crime punishable by a fine as well as jail time."

Chrystal pinned him with a stare. "I would never do such a thing."

"Is there anyone who might hold a grudge against you? Or who might want to hurt you by taking someone you love?" Mattie asked.

What little energy Chrystal's anger had given her seemed to vanish, and she looked deflated. "I can't say I've never made any enemies, but right now I can't think of anyone."

"Keep trying, okay? I know it's hard to believe that someone you know might have taken River, but it's more common than a child being kidnapped by a stranger." Mattie felt she needed to close this interview and move on. The urge to get back into the field pressed her. "Let us know if you think of anyone we should talk to," she said as she stood. "Sheriff Piper or his designee will be right here if you need us."

Chrystal became teary again as she took her leave. She leaned heavily on Buck's arm as he escorted her down the stairway and out into the muddy alleyway, with Gunner trailing behind. Deputy Casey was waiting right outside the door with a man Mattie hadn't met before.

Piper spoke in a quiet voice for Mattie's ears only. "I'm having background checks run on Buck, Gunner, and Sally Kessler. This man is Bob Gibson, the props guy. When I left the room earlier, I radioed Gage to bring him over so we could talk to him together before you go back out to search."

"All right," Mattie murmured, stepping back to let Piper take the lead.

Piper greeted Gibson and then led him over to the table, where he introduced Mattie and then invited him to sit. A rotund man of about fifty-something, Gibson tipped back the hood of his rain jacket to reveal long, brown hair shot liberally with gray, worn down past his shoulders. He swiped at the raindrops on his face with a broad hand and sausage-like fingers, his nails blunt cut and grimy.

"Mr. Gibson, thank you for coming over to talk to us." Piper leaned back in his chair as if relaxed and casual. "I understand you know River Allen and have spent some time with the boy?"

Gibson nodded, his face creased with concern. "I have. He's a good kid. Any news about him yet? I heard you discovered a body out there." He waved his hand in the direction of the door.

Mattie wondered how in the world that bit of information had been leaked already. If this man knew, the whole encampment probably did too.

Piper was frowning. "And how did you hear that?"

"Over at the mess tent. One of the camera guys told me. Is it true?"

Camera guys? Mattie instantly thought of Abby Day, who'd shown up with cameraman in tow.

"No information has been formally released. What I'm interested in is how well you know River," Piper said.

Gibson shrugged, looking puzzled, although Mattie wondered if his expression might not be genuine. "I just met the kid here on set a few weeks ago. He's interested in my work and his mom let him tour the props trailer. He liked the hand props the most, weapons like guns and knives and things like umbrellas and fake phones. He also wanted to see how the breakaway props worked, like the fake glass and furniture. Kids love that stuff."

Mattie didn't know why, but she felt a blip on her radar. The statement had been innocent enough, but she knew nothing about this man and his relationship with kids. And after all, this was a missing child investigation. "How so, Mr. Gibson? Tell me more about why you say kids love that stuff."

Gibson looked startled. "I don't know. I guess because every time we have kids on set they ask me all kinds of questions and they want to see my trailer."

"Like River did, I suppose. Did he seek you out or did you make an offer to show him your things?"

Gibson shifted his gaze from her to Piper and back. "I don't remember."

Piper leaned forward. "We can ask his mother and nanny that question if you don't recall."

Gibson lowered his gaze and studied the table. "I guess I offered. I thought Chrystal would be impressed if I showed the boy around. She's a huge star, you know. I thought . . . well, I just thought she'd like for her son to know more about the business."

"And you wanted to make an impression," Mattie said, thinking they needed to look into this man's background. He was acting dodgy. "What's your experience with children, Mr. Gibson?"

He glanced up at her before looking away. "Nothing special . . . you know, nieces and nephews. Occasionally kids tour the props trailer with their parents."

"No children of your own?"

"I'm not married." He looked flustered. "Look, I don't know what you're trying to imply here. Why all this interest in me and kids?"

Mattie decided to be honest. "I'm always interested in people's relationships with kids when it comes to a child's safety. And we *are* looking for a missing child here."

"Well, I don't know anything about that. I'm as clueless as you are, apparently. You can't pin anything on me."

Mattie leaned back in her chair and fixed him with her gaze. Piper remained quiet and the period of silence grew while Gibson squirmed in his chair.

Finally, Gibson pushed his chair back from the table. "I don't know anything about River Winter being missing. Now, if you'll excuse me, I've got work to do."

"Wait just a minute, Mr. Gibson," Mattie said. "No one's trying to pin anything on you, but I'm curious about why you think we might be. Is there anything you know about River Allen that you should tell us?"

Gibson's face had reddened. "No . . . he's just a kid that I showed the props to. That's all. We all know he'd wandered into the woods before, and that's what he's done again. I'm sorry you haven't been able to find him, but I don't have any idea where he might be."

"And is there anything about your past that you should share with us?" Piper added. Mattie was glad that he'd asked the question.

Gibson stared at him. "Nothing that's relevant, and I resent that question. Why are you treating me like a criminal?"

"Do you have a record that we should know about?" Piper asked.

Gibson stood. "There's nothing in my background that you need to know about, and I don't appreciate your insinuation. I know my rights. Unless I'm under arrest, this conversation is over."

"You're free to go whenever you wish," Piper said quietly. "Any help you can give us in determining why and how River has gone missing would be appreciated. If you're withholding information that could help us with our investigation, you need to know that would be considered obstruction."

"I don't know anything that would help you." Doing little to conceal his anger, Gibson turned and stormed out of the trailer.

Piper looked at Mattie. "I have a bad feeling that we're going to find something in this guy's background that we're not going to like."

"Like some crime directed at children?"

"Yeah, something like that. I'll add him to the list of people to check out."

Mattie agreed with Piper's assessment. Gibson had lit up like a Christmas tree at her line of questioning, even though it had started out gently enough. And she couldn't agree more about getting additional background info on the bodyguards and the nanny. River knew them all, and any of them might have lured him away.

But for now, the need to search private holdings in the area pressed at Mattie. She told Piper where she was headed next and left incident command to go find Cole and Robo.

# NINETEEN

Cole had waited for Mattie, and they were now jostling uphill in his rented SUV with Robo in the back seat. Piper had given her a map that not only showed the location of all private holdings but also the names of the owners. Piper wouldn't have had time that morning to do this type of research, which made Mattie think that he'd been planning all along to look into everyone in the surrounding area.

She looked up from studying the map to study Cole. He looked beat. "Are you sure you don't need some sleep? I could get another partner."

He glanced at her with raised eyebrows and a smile before focusing on the rough two-track. "I'm your partner, Mattie, and don't you forget it."

His statement warmed her heart. She reached out and squeezed his arm. "Partners for life."

Cole glanced at her with another smile. "Darn right."

Mattie turned back to the map. "Looks like the first holding is just a few miles past Cecil Moore's place. We'll be going by there in about half a mile. I want to stop and talk to him again." She told Cole about how Cecil had heard a cry for help many months ago. "Deputy Casey came up to investigate but didn't find anything. Thought it could be campers or tourists roughhousing or something like that. But I wonder . . ."

"If it could have been a shout for help from a person in one of those graves we found?"

"The more recent one . . . yes."

They fell silent as Mattie studied the map and Cole worked to avoid as many of the potholes on the road as he could. They both had experience navigating wilderness areas in Colorado using topo maps and GPS readings. She wasn't concerned that the two of them had been left to partner together while locals had teamed up.

They came to Cecil's driveway just as a heavy-duty pickup truck with four-wheel drive started to pull out into the road. Since the road was too narrow for both of them, Cole drove past and stopped long enough for the truck to head downhill. Full of energy from napping while Mattie was involved with interviews, Robo leaped to his feet to look out the rear window.

Straining to see around him, Mattie tried to look into the pickup bed, but it was covered with a tarp. A Washington Fish and Wildlife sign emblazoned the driver's side door.

"Looks like they've picked up the dead animals," she said.

"Yeah. Do you think we'll be privy to results of the necropsy?"

"I do. Piper wants our help, and Hunter would probably share info with us anyway."

Cole nodded as he backed down the hill so he could enter the lane. Cecil and Oscar were on the cabin's porch, pausing at the open door as if they'd been about to go inside. Cecil closed the door, gathered Oscar's harness and leash in his left hand, and turned to face them as they pulled in and parked. Robo whined and bounced around on the back seat, apparently excited to see Oscar again.

"You're going to stay here," Mattie told her dog as she hurried to get out of the vehicle. Once outside, she called, "Cecil, hello. It's Deputy Mattie Wray. I was here yesterday evening."

"Right," Cecil responded with a smile.

"And I have Dr. Cole Walker with me. I believe you met him this morning."

A nod and a larger smile for Cole. "Yes. Are you back for that talk about Oscar that you mentioned?"

Oscar's ears pricked when he heard his name.

"I wish we could take the time for that now," Cole said. "But I still have to come back later. We're on our way uphill to join the search for the missing child."

Cecil's face sobered. "How can I help?"

"You told us about the call for help that you heard a while back," Mattie said. "I want to find out more about it."

Cecil frowned and nodded. "What do you want to know?"

"Where were you when you heard it? Here or out farther on your property?"

"I was up on the northwest part of my loop, about dinner-time. I can give you the exact GPS coordinates if you want."

Mattie was surprised. "You have that?"

"Sure. I use GPS with voice feedback all the time when I'm out. It keeps me from having that moment when I feel absolutely lost. That's awful when it happens."

"The coordinates would help," Mattie said.

Cecil gave them to her from memory. "I memorized the coordinates when I heard them so I could report it to the sheriff's department. Not that it did any good."

"Because they didn't find anything?"

"No, because I don't think they really looked. I got the impression that Deputy Casey thought I was just a blind guy who didn't have any business being out here by myself. I wasn't happy when he was the one they sent. We have history together, and it hasn't been exactly good."

That lit up Mattie's radar. "What sort of history?"

Cecil rested his left hand on Oscar's head. "Over the past couple of years I've called in to report other concerns. People driving up the road in the middle of the night and stopping just outside my lane. It wakes up Oscar and makes him bark. And a year ago, I heard another call for help coming from the road. To be honest, the last time he warned me about false reporting to get attention. It pissed me off."

His expression said he was still angry about it.

"Let me make sure I understand this," Mattie said. "About a year ago, you heard a cry for help from the road during the night. Was it related to the vehicle stopping outside your lane?"

"No, that was separate, and it's happened more than once. I'm concerned that someone is scoping out my place, but Oscar warns me when it's happening."

"Good for Oscar. The biggest deterrent to burglary is a good dog with a big bark."

Cecil smiled. "He is that."

"Getting back to the cry for help you heard. You were on the northwest edge of your property. Which direction did the shout come from?"

"Farther northwest from there. I asked Hunter what was up that way the next time he stopped by. He said nothing but state forest, and there isn't even a road in there. The next holding west of my place is three miles farther up the road. There's not much else up that way except rough terrain and undeveloped forest land."

*And the grave sites of two unknown people, one definitely a child.* "Could you tell if the voice you heard was male or female?"

"Not really, but it was high-pitched. Sounded like a kid to me."

Mattie and Cole exchanged glances. She wondered if anyone had informed Cecil about the grave sites yet, but she didn't feel it was her place to do so. The decision to release information was Piper's. "Thanks for the info, Cecil. We'll be back when we have more time, but for now we need to get back to the search. It might be good for you to stick close to your cabin the next few days."

"Why is that?"

"Because of the water situation, I'm not sure it's safe in these woods. Cole or I will come back to let you know when we've cleared things nearby."

Cecil looked like he suspected there was more to it than what they were willing to share, which was true. "Okay . . . ," he said, drawing out the word. "But I can't stay cooped up forever. Stop in soon, okay?"

"Will do," Cole said. "I'll try to drop in by tomorrow at the latest."

They said their goodbyes and got back into the SUV with Robo. As Cole drove toward the road, he glanced at Mattie. "Apparently no one has told Cecil about the grave sites."

"Agreed. I didn't think I should do it either, although I hate to leave him without that information. I'm going to radio Piper and ask him to inform Cecil as soon as possible, or to give us permission to do it on our way back down today."

"What do you think about his feeling that Casey has dismissed his concerns and past reports?"

"I tend to give Cecil the benefit of the doubt that his reports are accurate. Casey might get frustrated finding nothing when he investigates, so he takes it out on the witness. It's common enough, I'm sorry to say."

Cole frowned and shook his head but didn't comment. The SUV lurched uphill on the rough track while Mattie radioed Piper. A female voice answered, saying Piper had stepped out for a few minutes to meet with the investigative team from the state. Mattie left a message for him about sharing info with Cecil Moore as soon as possible since his property was near the scene. She was told her message would be delivered within the hour.

"Things are moving along, and the state investigative team has arrived," she told Cole after signing off. She picked up her GPS unit and plugged in the coordinates Cecil had given. "It looks like Cecil was right on the edge of his property, and if the call for help came from farther northwest, it could possibly have come from across the road close to the grave site."

"Maybe closer to where we found the burned fencing?"

"Yeah, that's what it looks like."

"Hunter said that entire area has been assigned for searching this afternoon, so maybe Jim Madsen is on it."

"Either him or Ken and Knoxville," Mattie said.

"Can you radio the leader of the K-9 teams and tell them about Cecil reporting a call for help coming from that direction? Whoever goes in there should be extra alert for signs of human activity."

"That's Ken," Mattie said. "I'll let him know. And I'll notify Sarge just in case."

While Mattie handled the communications, Cole continued to drive uphill. They came to a private lane with a Bigfoot statue that might have been carved by Edward Campbell, the chainsaw guy down the road. Cole slowed to a stop when they encountered signs that read "PRIVATE—KEEP OUT" on both sides of the lane.

Mattie wanted to respect this person's privacy, but under the circumstances, they couldn't. With one child missing and at least one other child buried in the forest between Cecil's place and this one, the signage made Mattie even more eager to search the place. "We've got to go in and ask their permission to search."

"What about exigent circumstances?" Cole asked.

"I can only breach private property if I have probable cause to think our missing child is there. I don't have that in this case. Even though I'm acting outside of my jurisdiction, I have to respect those boundaries as a SAR member."

"I get it. Let's go on in."

After moving forward about fifty yards, they came up to another homemade sign with a rough drawing of a rifle aimed at a stick figure of a person. It was also labeled "KEEP OUT."

"Geez," Cole said. "Are you carrying your service weapon?"

"Yeah, but I hope I don't need it."

"Me too."

A roughly built cabin appeared through the trees and they soon broke into a small clearing. The sound of an axe against wood rang from somewhere beyond the cabin as they pulled up to park. They exited the Jeep, leaving Robo inside, and Mattie listened, trying to home in on the location of the noise.

"This way," she said, starting to go around the right side of the cabin.

"Hold on just one minute," a female voice called as the door to the cabin opened. A woman stepped out on the narrow plank step. She was dressed in a chambray shirt and too-large khaki pants that were hitched up by a belt. She looked to be about thirty-something, and her long, platinum blond hair was drawn back in a loose ponytail, straggly ends wafting around her face. She carried a rifle tucked neatly into the crook of her elbow and pointed down to the ground. "What are you doin' here? Can't you read? This is private property."

Mattie turned and approached the woman slowly while Cole remained farther back and to the side, as if providing another target if the woman decided to shoot. Mattie had no doubt that he would jump in to cover her if needed, but she planned for things not to come to that.

"Stay right where you are," the woman warned.

Mattie stopped. "I'm sorry to invade your privacy. I'm Deputy Mattie Wray, and I'm a member of a search and rescue team looking for a missing child."

A girl, small and thin, came out of the cabin to hide behind the woman, peeking around her legs but drawing back when Mattie made eye contact with her. Although it was impossible to tell exactly, Mattie guessed she might be about four or five years old. She was dressed in a long, sack-like cotton dress with leggings and worn tennis shoes. Her hair was identical to the woman's in color and style, and Mattie decided she could be the woman's daughter.

"There are no missing children around here, so you need to take your business somewhere else," the woman said.

"It looks like on our map that you own about ten acres here," Mattie said, smiling and hoping to still disarm the woman. "All the folks on private holdings up this road have given us permission to search to make sure this child isn't out in the woods somewhere. We hope you'll let us search your forest."

The chopping noise had stopped, and a man carrying an axe on his shoulder rounded the side of the cabin like a bear turning on a dog. "What's going on here?" he yelled as he approached.

Mattie turned to face him and felt Cole step in close beside her. She prepared to repeat her mission, but the man interrupted her as soon as she began to introduce herself.

"I don't care who you are. You need to get off my property now." He stopped about ten feet away, took a stand with his feet widespread, and balanced his axe in both hands out in front of him. He swung the axe head up a few inches and caught it back in his hand as if for emphasis.

Like his wife, he was dressed in a rather homespun-looking chambray shirt but with well-worn blue jeans. His face was streaked with dirt, and his gray-blond hair hung in greasy strands.

"And what's your name, sir?" she asked.

"None of your business."

Mattie explained they were looking for a missing child, but he cut her off again before she could finish.

"We know nothing about that, and there's no kid here that doesn't belong. You're not welcome to stay."

"This is a missing child we're talking about," Mattie said. "Everyone up to now has given permission for us to search. We'd appreciate if you'd let us check to make sure he's not in your woods somewhere."

He scoffed. "I don't care what 'everyone' around here does. No one goes out in my woods without me knowin' about it. Now you need to git."

The woman raised her rifle slightly. Cole stepped in between the woman and Mattie. Robo started barking from the back seat of the Jeep, his deep-throated growls muffled by the closed windows.

"We'll leave," Mattie said, hoping to defuse the situation. She started to turn away toward the Jeep but faced the man again as if having an afterthought. "Do you know Sheriff Piper or the forest ranger who covers this area, Hunter Bailey?"

The man lifted one eyebrow. "What's it matter if I do or don't?"

"Our search and rescue mission is under Sheriff Piper's command, fully authorized by his department. Hunter Bailey is part of our group. Please tell me your name so I can list you as a contact we made."

He screwed up his lips as if he had a bad taste in his mouth. "Frank Holt. And whoever you talk to makes no never-mind to me. If the sheriff wants to come onto my property, he has to get a warrant, which is something he won't be able to do. There's no reason why the police should invade our home."

The only reason Mattie could think of why these people were so adamantly opposed to her searching their property was that they had something to hide. She resisted the urge to tell them that and tried again to get their cooperation. "A lost child is an important reason to search these dense woods. Think how terrible it would be if your little girl got lost. You would probably want us to do everything we could to find her."

He scowled. "My girl isn't going to go wandering off and get lost. Now daylight's a-wasting. You need to go and let me get back to work."

"One last question. A while back, one of your neighbors heard a cry for help. Did either of you hear that too?" Mattie studied both of them, looking back and forth between the two.

"No, we did not," he said.

The woman glanced at him sharply but remained silent.

Mattie made eye contact with her. "Are you sure? It was in the early evening about dinnertime and it would have come from that direction." Mattie pointed toward the other side of the road.

She thought she detected the barest of nods from the woman before Frank Holt erupted.

"I said no! Now, you need to leave." He brandished his axe again by lifting the blade several inches.

Mattie studied the woman's face one last time, but she remained still and expressionless. "We'll leave now. If you hear or see anything that might help us find this child, please call the sheriff's department. We'll be in the area."

Cole stepped in close behind Mattie on their way back to the Jeep, covering her back. Robo bounced around inside the vehicle, eager to get out. She was sure he'd spied the gun, and his training would send him into full protection mode. She smoothed the fur on his head and praised him before asking him to settle down on the seat.

Once inside, Cole started the vehicle. "I'm glad that didn't blow up."

"I didn't think she would shoot. They were both more bark than bite."

Cole released a pent-up breath. "Maybe so. But why would they act that way unless they have something to hide?"

"My thought exactly." She reached for her radio. "I'll call it in to Piper and let him decide what he wants to do about it. In the meantime, we'll search all around the perimeter of this guy's property. If we find any evidence for probable cause, Piper can get that warrant."

"I think they heard the call for help too. Or at least the woman did."

Mattie nodded. "I agree. But she seemed unwilling to speak in front of her husband. I have to wonder what that means."

# TWENTY

Cole drove downhill until they reached the boundary of the Holt property. After finding a pull-off where they could park, Mattie unloaded Robo. He was already revved up after sensing the previous threat, and he trotted around the vehicle in excitement while Mattie retrieved his gear from the Jeep's rear compartment. The rain had let up, although the air was still thick with moisture. She zipped up her raincoat to protect her from the chill.

She called Robo and he came to sit at her feet, letting her put on his search harness. "Good boy," she murmured, stroking the fur on top of his head and gazing into the depths of his golden-brown eyes. "You're ready to go to work, aren't you?"

When she fastened the doggy goggles onto his face, Cole commented, "I see you've been able to use the goggles. What do you think of them?"

"They've been great to protect his eyes from all these thorns." She stroked Robo's velvety head, showing Cole the scratches left from his charging through the brambles. "I wish he had a helmet too."

"I bet we could find him one."

"They make SWAT helmets for dogs, but we haven't bought one for him yet."

"We should," Cole said.

"Yeah, I'll talk to Sheriff McCoy about that when I get home. But even a pet helmet for biking would help protect him from these brambles."

Mattie gave Robo his water, then she began patting his sides and using the chatter that he loved. In less than a minute she decided he was ready to go back into the forest to search, so she clipped on his leash and used the scent article to refresh his memory. "Let's go," she told him. "Search!"

Robo pushed his way through the roadside fern and brambles to get into the trees. Despite thorns snagging Mattie's pants and piercing the skin on her legs, she pressed her way through the bushes to follow him. Cole followed, and she could hear him mutter under his breath as he encountered the same thorny vines.

Once inside the barrier and under the forest canopy, the underbrush tamed and Robo started to weave his way through bushes and trees, sniffing along the ground and occasionally sampling the air. Mattie guided him back and forth along the boundary of the Holt property, working their way downhill until they had covered a border of about a hundred yards.

As they approached the road, Robo pressed his way back through the brambles with Mattie following. He poked his nose into some grassy underbrush at the road's edge, sneezed, and then sat and stared at the spot he'd touched.

Mattie's pulse quickened. "What did you find?"

She stroked the top of his head between the straps that held his goggles in place as she squatted beside him. He gave her a quick nudge with his nose before focusing back on the grass. Cole came up behind them.

Leaning forward, Mattie carefully parted the grass and spotted the glint of metal. "There's something here, Cole. Good boy, Robo. Good find," she said, giving him his toy. "Okay, move back a little so I can take a picture of it."

Cole took Robo's leash while Mattie pushed gently against him until he gave her some space. Cole continued to praise and pet him while Mattie took out her cell phone and snapped a picture. When she pushed the grass back further, she could identify the object—a fob with a set of two keys. With gloved hands, she picked it up to place in an evidence bag.

The silver fob had an inlaid pattern of a blue stream flowing through grassy hills made from small chips of colored ceramic tiles. The word "River" was etched in black below the pattern. During training, Robo might have missed the personal object the kids had planted that was supposed to help lead to the search target, but today, when the mission was real and more important than ever, her dog's performance had been spot on.

"Oh, my gosh!" Mattie showed the key fob to Cole. "This has to belong to our missing boy."

From the look on Cole's face, she guessed his excitement matched her own. He ruffled Robo's fur and hugged him close against his leg. "Good find, Robo. Good boy!" He looked at Mattie. "Is this close enough to the Holts to get that warrant?"

"Let's talk to Piper and see."

★　★　★

When she radioed Sheriff Piper, Mattie discovered he was at the grave site with the investigative team from the state. She and Cole drove downhill a couple of miles to find him there, and he met them by the road.

Mattie handed him the evidence bag. "Robo found this by the roadside about a hundred yards from the entry to the Holt property."

He looked at the fob and then back at her, his brows raised in surprise. "River Allen's?"

"Looks like it. Can we get a warrant to go onto their property?"

"I'll have one of River's parents confirm that it's his first and then see what I can do."

Mattie wanted things to move faster, especially since they'd already alerted the Holts that they were closing in on them. "We should post a guard by their road to make sure they don't leave and take River with them."

"I can post Gage Casey there right away. The state has taken over this site, so he's not needed here anymore."

"Do you know if it's a child in the more recent grave site yet?"

Piper looked grim. "We do. It is."

Mattie's heart sank. "Can you tell if it's male or female?"

"Clothing looks male. Remains are too decomposed for facial recognition, but hair color and clothing match the description of Jimmy Jordan, the nine-year-old that's been missing several years. Dental records might be able to identify him by the end of the day."

Mattie felt Cole's support as he moved near enough to press his arm up against hers. Her heart went out to this child's parents, who would soon learn that their son would never return to their home again.

"You should have the ME test those bodies for arsenic," Cole said.

Piper looked at him. "What are you thinking?"

"Maybe there was a reason that fencing was burned. The ash got into the drainage by accident, but maybe the ash was created on purpose to be used as a weapon."

Piper frowned. "But why? Why kill kids with arsenic?"

"I don't know the answer to that. I just think it's important to find out if the two are linked."

Mattie could see where Cole was coming from. "We've had some strange cases in Timber Creek where drugs and poisons were linked to controlling the victim. And then accidental overdose led to death. Now would be the time to test these bodies . . . just in case."

Piper paused to think it over. "All right. I'll suggest it to the ME."

"That makes two dead children in this vicinity," Mattie said. "Can we use exigent circumstances to search the Holt property?"

Piper looked wary. "You're moving too fast. This key fob might belong to River, but it wasn't on the Holts' property itself. I'll need to get a warrant."

Mattie felt an urgency to get things done. "How long will that take?"

"Once we identify this as River's, I can probably get a warrant within the hour. Now I'd best get back to camp and work on it." Piper turned and strode toward his Jeep.

"We'll finish searching around the property and be ready to enter as soon as we can," Mattie called after him.

Piper lifted a hand in acknowledgment as he got into his vehicle and drove downhill.

★   ★   ★

Mattie and Robo had cleared the perimeter of the Holts' property and gone back to Cole's Jeep to take a much-needed break. Thorny pricks and cuts on Mattie's legs stung and her muscles trembled from fatigue. Robo sagged into the back seat and groaned a heavy sigh before falling asleep.

Cole climbed into the passenger seat, his face gray with exhaustion. He ate the energy bar Mattie gave him in small bites as he laid his head back on the headrest.

"Here," she said, giving Cole a water bottle before circling the vehicle to settle into the driver's seat. "You need to get some sleep. I'll drive up closer to the Holt lane and park up there to wait for Piper."

He closed his eyes and reclined his seat to a forty-five-degree angle. "I just need a few minutes and then I'll be ready to go again."

Mattie thought it would take longer than that but started the engine and guided the Jeep slowly uphill, trying to avoid potholes as best she could. When Deputy Casey's vehicle came into view, she pulled over onto a wide spot on the two-track and stopped, leaving the engine on for warmth from the heater. She tipped her head back and rested her own eyes while they waited.

She dozed, but the growl from another vehicle's engine woke her as it rattled uphill and squeezed by. Sarge raised his hand in greeting from the passenger seat of Ranger Hunter Bailey's Jeep as their eyes met, with only inches between them. Mattie returned the greeting, even as she realized that Drake rode in the back seat with Banjo and Fritz. Piper's vehicle traveled close behind Hunter's. Piper was driving and a deputy Mattie hadn't seen before sat in the passenger seat, staring out at her without greeting.

Leaving the engine and heater running, Mattie slipped out of the Jeep, closing the door quietly behind her. Neither Cole nor Robo stirred.

She hurried up the two-track to join the officers, who were exiting their vehicles and gathering their gear. Both deputies, Casey and the one whose name tag read Dick Bockman, carried AR-15 rifles and wore firearms at their hips. Piper had his service weapon in its holster on his duty belt. All wore Kevlar vests. Hunter did a quick check on a rifle from his Jeep while Sarge and Drake stood by, leaving Banjo and Fritz in the vehicle.

As Mattie approached the group, Sarge handed her a Kevlar vest. "This is Piper's rodeo," he murmured, "but we're going to assist."

Piper focused on the Colorado contingent. "Consider yourselves deputized. Mattie, let's use your dog if we need him."

"Yes, sir." Mattie strapped on her vest while Piper briefed them. "We'll go in twos. Hunter, you ride with me. Dick, you go in with Gage. We'll drive in first and I'll serve the warrant." He pointed at his two deputies. "You two stay back about twenty feet and keep your eyes peeled. Shout if you see a gun and cover us if things head south. Jim, you come in through the trees with Drake, Mattie, and her dog for backup if needed. Once we've secured the property, we'll have you bring your bloodhounds in."

Mattie said to Piper, "I'll get Robo and wake up Cole so he knows what's going on."

Piper nodded. "But have Dr. Walker stay back in the Jeep."

"I will."

Mattie sprinted to Cole's Jeep. When she opened the door, he jerked awake, flinging his arm out to the side. Robo blinked his eyes and heaved himself up to his feet. Mattie quickly brought Cole up to speed while he rubbed the sleep from his eyes.

"Piper deputized Sarge, Drake, and me, but he wants you to stay here in the Jeep."

"I don't like that," he said, eyeing her.

Mattie gave him a thin smile before doing a quick check on her Glock. She knew exactly how much ammo she had in the gun, but she always checked it anyway. "Like Sarge says, this is Piper's rodeo. We have to follow his orders."

"Hmm . . ." Cole sounded disgruntled as he exited the vehicle. "I'll stay here, but as I said, I won't like it. How can I help you get ready?"

Mattie was headed to the back of the SUV, but Cole got there first and opened the hatch. Robo danced on the door's threshold, his eyes pinned on Mattie. She pulled Robo's go bag toward her and opened it, looking for his Kevlar vest. Within seconds she'd buckled the vest on him.

Sarge came up to the Jeep just as Mattie was ready to leave and handed Cole a snub-nosed revolver—evidently his backup weapon. "You're not licensed to carry in Washington, are you?" Sarge asked Cole.

"No."

"This is for your own protection only. If this thing heads south, you take cover and fire only in self-defense."

Cole agreed, making Mattie feel better that he wouldn't be helpless.

Mattie clasped Cole's hand briefly before leaving. With Robo in heel position, she and Sarge jogged back to where the others were waiting. Piper led the way in his vehicle, followed by the one driven by Casey.

Sarge waved his hand to the left. "Drake, you fan out that way. Mattie, you go right. I'll go up the road."

Mattie wanted to be in on the frontline action. At home, she and Robo would be out in front with Sheriff McCoy and Chief Deputy Ken Brody. Serving this type of warrant was common enough, and Robo was a valuable partner when it came to establishing cooperation. It seemed like a waste of his talent to assign him the role of backup.

Following Sarge's order, she pressed through the undergrowth and into the forest on the right. Once she reached the evergreen canopy, she hurried to position herself close to the cabin. Engine noise from the two Jeeps had stopped, and she figured Sheriff Piper was about to make his move.

A shot rang out. Mattie's adrenaline spiked as Robo charged to the end of his leash. To him, gunshots signaled "Attack!" But she held him back, seeking breaks in the underbrush as they charged through together. She spotted the cabin and hurried through the trees. She let Robo bark as they moved out into the open.

It felt like organized chaos. Frank Holt stood in front of his cabin, waving his rifle around. Robo barked and people shouted as everyone fanned out. There were seven officers against one, but Mattie feared for the safety of the woman and child who were probably still in the cabin.

Everyone yelled, "Put the gun down!"

But it was Robo that held Frank Holt's stare. Mattie shouted, "Put down the gun, or I'll send the dog."

Resignation filled Holt's face as he placed the gun on the ground and stepped back with his hands up, keeping his eyes pinned on Robo.

Deputies Casey and Bockman moved forward, shouting at Holt to lie down on the ground. Finally Holt went down on his knees and then lay spread-eagle face down. While Bockman covered Holt, Casey cuffed him. Piper stepped forward and picked up the rifle.

Mattie settled Robo with a command to guard. He quit barking and crouched, his eyes locked on Holt.

The wife and daughter were nowhere in sight. Mattie shouted to Piper, "The woman and child might still be in the cabin. Be careful—there could be another gun."

Sarge had already moved up onto the porch and was standing beside the door, his back to the heavy logs of the cabin wall, his firearm held ready. He called out, "Mrs. Holt, open this door. Come out slowly with your hands empty where I can see them."

No response. Mattie held her breath.

"This cabin is surrounded. Come outside where we can see you!" Sarge shouted.

Bockman had Frank Holt sitting up now, his hands cuffed behind his back. Mattie edged up closer where she could speak without shouting. "Mr. Holt, tell your wife to come outside unarmed. Protect your daughter from this thing going any further."

Frank Holt glared at her and Robo and then turned his head and spit on the ground. "Come outside, Emma!" he shouted. "Leave the gun on the floor."

The door creaked open and Emma Holt stepped outside with her hands up. Tears streamed down her face and she spoke between sobs. "Don't shoot. My little girl is here with me."

"Bring her out with you." Sarge motioned her forward. "Let me see her hands."

*Sarge probably doesn't know how young the child is,* Mattie thought. But still, it was good protocol to make sure the child wasn't armed. Children had been known to shoot both civilians and police officers.

"She doesn't have a gun! Don't shoot her!" Emma cried out. She struggled to control her sobs. "Come here, Betty. Come outside to Mama."

"Is there anyone else in the house?" Sarge asked.

"No. No one. It's just us." Emma sobbed as she bent and hugged her child against her legs.

Mattie's heart went out to both mother and daughter. It appeared the father had drawn them into this. As little Betty sidled out with her mother onto the porch, sobbing with fear and her hands to her mouth, Mattie felt thankful that these officers had handled this mess with professional integrity and all members of the family were safely secured. Mattie put Robo into a down-stay and moved toward the porch so she could take charge of patting down Emma before putting her in cuffs. The results of the property search would determine how the law enforcement team would move forward from here.

# TWENTY-ONE

With Robo at heel, Mattie jogged back to Cole's Jeep and found him standing outside of it holding Sarge's revolver down by his side. He broke into a relieved smile as soon as they made eye contact with each other. "Am I ever glad to see you."

"All's secure back there," she told him, waving her hand toward the cabin as she skirted to the back to load up Robo. "We can search the property now."

Drake and Sarge were right behind her. They climbed into Hunter's Jeep, where Banjo and Fritz waited, and Sarge fired up the engine to lead the way.

Mattie took the passenger seat and Cole drove down the lane. "When no more shots were fired, I hoped you were safe. Did anyone get hurt?" Cole asked.

"No one got hurt. Frank Holt came out threatening everyone with his rifle and telling them to get off his property. He fired a shot into the air, but they all held their fire, thank goodness. Holt looked like he was afraid of Robo, and he gave up. The woman— her name's Emma—and her daughter Betty are both all right and confined in the back of Casey's unit. We'll see if we can find anything."

"Seems like a heck of lot of trouble they went to if they're not hiding something."

"Yeah . . . let's hope it's something that leads to finding River alive and safe."

Once they arrived at the cabin, Mattie hurried to let Robo out of the vehicle. Within seconds she had him in front of a bowlful of water. When he finished drinking, she hustled over to Sarge and Drake to find out how Sarge wanted to split up the property for searching.

Banjo sat beside Sarge, his droopy face placid as ever while Robo danced at the end of his leash at Mattie's left heel. "Mattie, you take the cabin," Sarge said. "I'll cover the north side; and Drake, you go south. If the cabin clears, take Robo out to the south to follow up Drake."

"All right," Mattie said, leading Robo toward the plank porch at the front of the cabin. Cole followed behind, keeping his distance. She figured that even with Holt in cuffs and Emma in the squad car, Cole still felt he needed to watch her back. Since she wasn't sure if she should trust Holt's word that no one else was on the property, she decided it wasn't a bad idea. Anyone could be hiding out in that forest.

This time when Mattie refreshed Robo's memory with a whiff from the bagged scent article, he dipped his nose in briefly as if to say he didn't need it. Piper had already cleared the cabin, finding nobody inside, and was waiting in the main room for her to enter. A quick scan told her that the boxy log structure had been divided into three areas, a main room split into kitchen and living areas and two enclosed bedrooms. There was no bathroom; she'd spotted an outhouse in back earlier.

The kitchen contained a wood-burning stove similar to the one her foster mother, Teresa Lovato, used, a sink with a pump handle type faucet, and an old-fashioned ice chest for keeping things cool. Mattie led Robo into that area to sweep the room clockwise, keeping his leash in her left hand and indicating areas for him to sniff with her right. She even opened the ice chest and oven doors for him to search, wanting to cover every square inch of the cabin while they had a chance.

After clearing the kitchen she moved Robo into the space used as a living room. She guided Robo into areas with better airflow, systematically sweeping her right hand over the rustic wooden furniture that looked hand-carved. She directed him around the basket of yarns with what looked like part of a sweater lying on top still hooked to the needles, and into each corner and crevice of the log walls. Robo continued to work, his ears alternating between pointing forward and back, but he didn't indicate he'd picked up River's scent.

And since he'd been trained to pick up the scent of dozens of different drugs, she'd wondered if he would hit on any illegal substances. So far he hadn't.

She moved into the bedroom on the right first, a small one that must have been Betty's. A single bed with a sagging mattress sat on one side of the room, a makeshift closet partitioned off by a hanging sheet graced the opposite corner. Mattie guided Robo around the room, taking note of the simple toy box that contained only a few items: a ball, a stuffed bear, a homemade doll, and a set of crayons with a paper tablet. The bed's coverlet also looked homemade and a Raggedy Ann doll with a hand-stitched face sat in a place of honor on the pillow. Everything was neat and tidy, and Robo cleared the room quickly.

Mattie was beginning to feel defeated when she led Robo into the last room. Again, she found handmade wooden furniture, a tall chest of drawers, the bed's headboard made from what looked like woven tree branches that had been scraped and polished, a handsome quilt that took sewing talent to construct. Robo cleared this room as well, and she turned to find Piper watching from the doorway. "No indication of River Allen or illegal substances in this cabin," she told him.

His mouth tipped downward in a grimace. "Go ahead and follow up Drake in the forest," he told her. "Maybe you guys overreacted when you came here earlier."

His comment didn't sit well. "We didn't. You saw how suspicious Holt acted. And we found River's keys right there at the base of his property. We had to search here one way or another."

Piper held up a palm. "You're right. But some of these families just want to be left to themselves."

"That's fine until a SAR team needs to look for a lost child in their woods. Then it's a different matter," Mattie said.

"Okay. Go finish up. If we don't find anything illegal out here, I'll have to arrest Holt for resisting a warrant and endangering a law enforcement officer. But at least the woman and child can return to their cabin."

Mattie could tell Piper felt torn about the situation, but the fact remained that a citizen had threatened police officers with a dangerous weapon during a legal search of his property, and that was unnecessary no matter how much that citizen wanted to be left alone.

She led Robo toward the porch where Cole was waiting, so they could finish their hard-fought-for search in hopes of turning up evidence of River Allen's presence.

★   ★   ★

Scratched and bloody from ankle-grabbing brambles, Mattie, Robo, and Cole returned to the front of the cabin where the others had gathered with Piper. Mattie hadn't felt this low in a long time. Maybe Piper was right. Maybe she had overreacted when Holt refused access to his property.

But she couldn't deny the presence of River's key fob at the property boundary. That was still something, and she couldn't help but think the child was somewhere close. If only they could catch a break and Robo or one of the other dogs could catch a scent.

Drake had left the Holt property with Hunter to go search another grid, and Deputy Casey had taken Holt in to book him on charges of obstruction and endangerment. What little light that filtered through the clouds and the forest canopy had started to wane, and Mattie estimated they had only about an hour left before nightfall. She approached Sarge where he waited with Piper to see what next steps had been planned.

Sarge greeted her, his face gray with fatigue and apparent illness. "That was disappointing, but it had to be done. It could have been so much easier if only Holt had acted responsibly. Let's go across the road and finish up the day there. I'll ride along with you and Cole."

Piper had been standing with his arms crossed, but he dropped them to his sides and straightened, looking Mattie in the eye. "Jim's right. We had to do it. You're not to blame for things heading south when we arrived." He shrugged. "We're all tired, and it's been a long day. With the state here heading up the criminal investigation now, we'll be dismissing the SAR team tomorrow. Unfortunately, it looks like River's been taken and he's probably somewhere far away. We've done a lot of work in a short time, and we're grateful for your help. You might as well make arrangements to fly home."

It was an apology of sorts, and Mattie nodded her acceptance. Disappointment flooded her chest. Being sent home felt like failure.

She still couldn't shake the feeling, however, that River remained close by. The bodies of two dead children were proof that someone had kidnapped and held at least two other kids here until they died. She couldn't help but feel that River was suffering the same treatment and he faced the possibility of the same outcome. If only they could find him in time to prevent it.

She turned to Sarge. "I'll be ready to leave in just a few minutes, but first I have to speak to Mrs. Holt." She handed Robo's leash to Cole. "I'll be right back."

Emma Holt sat on the porch step holding her young daughter in her lap, her face drawn as if she felt pain at what had just transpired. If she'd been in charge instead of her husband, Mattie thought, things would have been different.

Emma watched Mattie approach, wariness taking over her countenance. She stood as if girding for battle.

Mattie paused about five feet away. "Mrs. Holt, I want to tell you I'm sorry for what just happened here. If your husband had reacted differently to a simple request to search for a lost child, this could have been avoided. We'll leave you in peace, but I felt earlier that you had something to tell me when I asked if you'd heard a shout for help a while back. Did you?"

Emma looked down at her daughter, who stood holding on to her mother's legs as if for dear life. "Actually, yes," she said looking up at Mattie. But then she stopped as if afraid to go on.

"Mrs. Holt, I won't press charges for obstruction in our search if you tell me now," Mattie said gently. "I would appreciate it if you could just let me know what you heard."

Her eyes downcast, she spoke so quietly that Mattie had to lean forward to hear her. "I heard something a few nights ago. A shout coming from downhill. Maybe near the road. It was just a shout, but it sounded like a child. I had no idea it might be a child in danger or I would have gone to look." She met Mattie's gaze. "Please believe me. I really thought it was nothing."

Mattie responded quickly. "I believe you. What night was this exactly?"

Emma paused as if thinking. "It would have been Thursday night."

The day River went missing. "Can you point out the direction you heard the shout come from?"

Emma pointed in the direction of the road and the downhill boundary of her property . . . the same direction as the spot where Robo found River's set of keys.

"Thank you, Mrs. Holt. I hope things work out okay for you and your husband."

Emma blinked back tears. "Frank is a hard man. Maybe he's paranoid about being around other people. He has his reasons for isolating himself, but sometimes he makes things harder on himself. And his family."

"Can you tell me why he isolates himself?" Mattie said quietly.

Emma lowered her head and spoke in a low tone. "He thinks people are after him. But I don't think his fears are real."

"Maybe you could see if you can get him help with that," Mattie suggested. "You could ask the sheriff if his county has mental health evaluations for prisoners who need them."

Emma shrugged. "Maybe."

Mattie felt the woman's helplessness, but they were running out of daylight and time, so she thanked Emma for her help and hurried back to where Cole waited for her.

"Sarge went on to the Jeep to load up Banjo," Cole told her as he handed Robo's leash back to her. "Why did Mrs. Holt point down the lane?"

Mattie told him what she'd learned while they hurried back to the Jeep. "That could be where River dropped the keys. This is pure speculation, but what if he was taken and somehow he escaped momentarily? There was a struggle and he dropped his keys. Or maybe he even dropped them on purpose. But then he was loaded into a vehicle and whisked away."

"That might not be too far from what actually happened."

"We need to go across the road and search that area where you found the burned fence poles. Did you see any type of structure when you were there?"

"Only a tumbledown cabin. Nothing with walls or a roof." Cole's eyes were sunken with fatigue.

"I know you're tired, but do you think you can show us exactly where you were?"

"Absolutely. I'm not that tired."

The Jeep came into sight and Mattie could see Sarge, backlit by the light inside the vehicle. "Sarge has the light on. Let's see what he's doing."

# TWENTY-TWO

Mattie rode in the back seat with the dogs while Cole found a wide place in the road to pull over near the spot where Robo had found River Allen's keys. "This should do," he said as he parked.

"It looks like that clearing will be due north from here," Sarge said. He'd been looking at a satellite image map while waiting in the Jeep for the few minutes Mattie needed to speak to Emma Holt. He'd found two clearings to check out: the one where Cole found the burn pile and another farther north.

Mattie stepped out from the relative warmth into the damp air. A breeze quickened from downhill, the direction of the water, bringing a moisture-laden mist that chilled her face as she pulled the drawstrings of her rain hood tight enough to at least protect the top of her head.

Sarge groaned as he stepped out of the front passenger seat to stand beside her.

"Are you okay to do this, Sarge?" Mattie asked, worried about his level of exertion. He looked like he still felt sick.

"Sure," he said, evidently more confident than Mattie. "Let's go back to work, Banjo."

When Robo heard the word "work," he pranced on the back seat and leaped out to join Banjo on the ground. The bloodhound, older by several years, gave Robo a stolid look as if to say "Kids." His face drooped more than usual and he looked worn out as he sat near Sarge's left heel. Mattie and Sarge both gave their dogs fresh water.

Mattie tried again to give Sarge an out if he needed one. "I can get in there and cover that area with Robo if Banjo needs a rest. He looks like he's just about had it."

Sarge studied his dog. "I agree that he's just about done, but I think he's got another hour left. Let's go together and split up the area. Then we'll have given it our all. It'll be dark soon and time for dinner and bed."

Mattie looked at Cole. "How about you? Need a break?"

"Nope, I'm doing fine." Cole checked his GPS unit and pointed into the woods. "This is the way Hunter and I went before. It should take only about ten minutes to find it."

Cole led the way into the woods, the dense canopy suppressing what little light remained. By now, Mattie was more familiar with the territory and even though her legs felt heavy with overuse, she scrambled over fallen trees and dodged around thorny vines, keeping up with Robo. He was in his element and looked as fresh as he had that morning. Sarge and Banjo fell behind and Mattie asked Cole to slow the pace.

When they entered a clearing, Cole turned and spoke over his shoulder. "This is it. Be more cautious than ever about the water through here."

His warning wasn't necessary. Mattie was already keeping a close eye on Robo and the cool, moist climate helped keep him hydrated.

Cole led them toward the tumbledown cabin he'd mentioned. As Mattie approached, she bent to peer under the fallen logs that crisscrossed the interior to see if furniture or anything that might be used as storage remained. Finding it too dark to see, she unearthed her headlamp from her backpack and put it on, directing its beam into the cabin's interior.

"See anything?" Sarge asked.

"Not much. The remnants of an old bed frame and what looks like a wooden trunk of some kind. I want to see what's inside it."

"It's not stable enough for you to go in there, Mattie," Cole said.

She reached out and gave one of the fallen crossbeams a shake and found it to be steady as it rested diagonally from an upper wall into the center of the cabin. "This site was possibly used to create a poisonous substance on purpose. Something tells me it's important. I'll go in only far enough to see that back wall. Robo, stay," she said, adding a hand gesture for emphasis.

She crouched and entered the front of the cabin before the men could protest. After ducking under the solid beam, she picked her way through the debris toward the back wall. She misjudged the depth of a log as she stooped under it, brushing her back against it. It groaned, making her flinch, but it held steady and she crept on, her headlight washing against the far wall as she swept its beam back and forth. Cobwebs stretched across the space between the fallen logs.

Then she spotted something on the wall beyond the bed frame. As she crawled closer, pulling down cobwebs as she went, she could make out a rusty eyebolt fixed into one of the logs. That's odd, she thought, wondering about its purpose. She turned to describe what she saw to Sarge, who was hunkered down just inside the cabin.

He raised his eyebrows in a startled look. "I saw something like that once in a basement that belonged to a serial kidnapper. He chained his victims to it."

A cold chill tickled Mattie's spine. Now she couldn't leave without opening that trunk. She lowered to her hands and knees to crawl forward, squeezing between logs that had fallen from the wall and ceiling. A dank odor radiated from the moss-infested logs and plank floor. She held her breath, imagining the rotten ceiling giving way and crushing her as she crept over the last few feet and reached the chest.

The latch on its front had rusted shut and she banged on it to rattle it loose. Wedging her gloved fingers beneath it, she tugged with all her might, finally levering it open. Rusty hinges creaked as she lifted the lid and a musty stench wafted out. Her headlamp lit the interior and she found it empty except for some yellowed, mildewed papers at the bottom.

She reached in and discovered they were stuck to the bottom of the trunk. Carefully peeling a corner of one the papers, she lifted it enough to tell that it looked like an old photo. It tore away as she tried to free it, leaving her with a three-inch fragment in her gloved hand. She turned the strip over and lit the image with her headlamp, but the photo was so degraded it was difficult to tell what she was looking at.

As her eyes adjusted to the mildew-eaten picture and the image assumed a shape she could recognize, it surprised her. The part of the photo she held showed half of the upper torso and face of a small child, possibly a girl, although the features on the half-face in the torn picture weren't clear enough for her to be sure. And she thought the girl appeared to be nude.

"What do you have there?" Sarge asked.

She looked at him. "It's a photo. It's in bad shape so I'm not sure . . . but I think it's a picture of a naked child."

"Huh . . ." Sarge seemed to be thinking. "We're in state forest, aren't we? Not a private holding."

"Hunter said it's state forest," Cole said. "He thought this cabin and corral were built decades ago and used by state forest service personnel at one time. It was more or less abandoned as far as upkeep when rangers and wildlife managers started using ATVs instead of horses to get around. Deer hunters used it for a while but not often, so it went unrepaired until it collapsed."

Mattie removed her glove and picked at the photo that was still stuck on the bottom of the chest, but to no avail. Not wanting to damage it further, she tried the corner of a different one, using her fingernail to pry up an edge. She worked at it carefully until she could lift most of the photo out whole.

She stared at the moisture-damaged picture until she could make out parts of it, and this picture had enough of the image left to stun her. It was a photo of a young boy in a lewd pose. She turned her head toward Sarge and Cole and her headlamp illuminated them as they sat hunkered down at the cabin opening.

"It's child pornography," she told them.

Cole's face registered surprise, but Sarge seemed to take it in stride.

"I was afraid of that," Sarge said. "I'm afraid of what this might mean. The missing boys, the kids buried in shallow graves, the possibility of arsenic poisoning . . . and of course River Allen gone missing." He shook his head. "Maybe we've uncovered evidence of a local kiddie porn ring."

"And River is a beautiful child." Mattie's mind turned over this possibility and leaped to next steps. "If child porn is what we're looking at, we need to make sure this doesn't get out to the media. Or even the locals involved with this search. Anyone could be a suspect. We don't want to alert the perpetrator and have him escape the area, taking River with him."

"Maybe he already has," Cole said, his face grim.

"We need to move fast," Sarge said. "Whoever left those photos abandoned this site years ago. If he's still in business, he's working from somewhere else, and I'd bet it's close by. We need to find that other clearing now before it gets fully dark."

Mattie placed the photos inside an evidence bag and tucked it inside her coat. She crawled toward the opening until she could duck-walk out from under the rest of the debris. Once out, she brushed cobwebs from her shoulder and head while Cole swept them off her back. After placing the photos safely into a zippered pocket inside her backpack, she gave Robo and Banjo some water, returned the bowl to her pack, and shrugged it on. "Should we search the area between here and the other clearing for River?"

"No," Sarge said. "Let's go there directly and see if we can find a structure. We'll come back and search the woods tomorrow morning."

Sarge and Banjo led the way, crossing the clearing to enter the forest on the other side. Twilight disappeared under the canopy, the dense woods absorbing what little light was left. The darkness forced them all to turn on their headlamps. Mattie's beam lit only the backside of Sarge as he struggled to make his way around trees and through underbrush. Branches snapped and cracked under their feet and a soft patter began overhead as raindrops thickened into a cold drizzle. She heard the wind start to blow through the canopy before she felt it on her face. The air grew thick with the sharp, clean scent of Douglas fir and western red cedar. As Cole began to fall behind, Mattie slowed to make sure that he could keep her in sight.

They trudged on until Sarge came to a halt. First Mattie and then Cole caught up to him.

"There's a faint trail here," Sarge said as he directed his headlamp beam and pointed. It ran diagonally across their route, coming from the southwest and heading northeast. "I don't know where this trail originated, but it might have come from the road. It's headed in the general direction of the clearing. I think we should take it."

"Sounds good," Mattie murmured, thinking it would make it so much easier, especially for Cole, whose energy seemed to be flagging. "Wait for just a minute."

She dug into her backpack again, this time to distribute energy bars all around. She hoped it would give Cole that extra boost he needed. Chewing as they went, they hiked on. But Mattie was soon disappointed as she found they still needed to climb over fallen timber and press through brambles on the almost imperceptible path. Evidently this was one that very few humans traveled.

Sarge paused frequently to check GPS readings with his map. During one of these stops, branches snapped in the distance and the sound of something crashing through deadfall filtered through the dense forest. "Wait," Mattie murmured. "What's that?"

"Lights off," Sarge said under his breath.

After switching off their headlamps, the darkness was complete. Anxiety prickled Mattie's neck as her eyes adjusted and the crackling sounds grew closer. A ghostly white flash floated chest high between the trees while the sound of snapping branches transformed into a rhythmic beat.

She strained to see, peering through the haze of icy drizzle, and the flash of white assumed the shape of a person's clothing. The pounding beat changed into the sound of a runner's footsteps. The runner's form took shape into someone small in stature. A child or teen? A small woman?

"Who goes there?" Sarge shouted.

The runner stopped briefly before charging off in a different direction. The white-clothed figure disappeared into the trees.

For a split second, Mattie considered sending Robo after the runner. He'd been trained to take down fugitives, but that would involve a bite and hold maneuver. This runner could very possibly be an innocent citizen, even a child, and she didn't want to subject someone to a dog bite except as a result of criminal action.

She decided to go after the runner herself. Robo was already straining against his leash, revved up from the noise, sight, and most likely the scent of the passing person. He would pick up the track with no problem.

"I'm going. Robo can track 'em." She let Robo pull her off the trail they'd been following. She didn't need to chat him up; he was ready to go. "Robo, track! Track 'em, boy!"

"Be careful, Mattie!" She sensed Cole fall in behind her.

"We'll come too," Sarge said.

Robo tugged on the leash, pulling her along as she flipped on her headlamp. She'd been working her dog on leash for hours, and that experience seemed to guide her footsteps as she hurried to keep pace with him. The headlamp's beam lit Robo's back and the ground between them as they rushed in the same direction the runner had taken.

Mattie followed Robo in a mad dash through the trees, struggling to stay on her feet and keep moving forward. At first, Cole and Sarge's headlamps helped light her way, but they gradually fell behind until she had to depend on only the light from her own.

She caught a glimpse of the runner's white clothing up ahead before the trees blocked her view. What was driving this person? Fear? Fear of something and the desire to escape? Or fear of being caught in a criminal act?

Mattie thought she'd take a chance and see if she could establish communication. Maybe a female voice would help establish trust. The runner was close enough that they were within shouting distance. "Wait!" she called. "Do you need help? We're from Search and Rescue."

A crash came from up ahead, and the sound of footsteps silenced. Robo continued to pull Mattie forward and her stride quickened. The thought of an ambush popped into her mind. A K-9 handler always had to worry about that when chasing fugitives. But the crashing sound spoke more of a fall than stepping aside to set up a trap.

Robo paused at the top of a ravine, and Mattie slipped off her headlamp to hold it away from her body as she directed its beam downhill. If this person was armed, there was no reason to provide a perfect target for a headshot.

A figure dressed in white lay crumpled at the base of the steep slope. Mattie could hear Sarge and Cole closing in behind her. Using caution, she continued to hold her light clear and slid slowly down the muddy pitch until she was within a few feet of the fallen runner.

Rising up on one arm, the person held up a hand as a shield against her headlamp's beam. Mattie glimpsed wild eyes within a pale face framed with long dark red hair that hung in wet strands. A young male. Probably a teen.

But it wasn't River Allen.

The kid collapsed back on the ground, sobbing.

"It's all right," she said in a soothing voice. Robo was reaching his nose forward to sniff, so she signaled him to lie down with a quiet command and a hand gesture. "You're safe. We won't hurt you."

The boy raised his head again before tucking himself into a human ball as if for protection. "Your dog," he said between sobs.

"My dog won't hurt you. We're part of a search and rescue team."

"Oh, God," the boy moaned. "I think I broke my ankle."

Mattie flicked her headlamp's beam to the boy's feet and saw he was wearing muddy sneakers. Both feet and ankles looked intact and angled in the right direction, so it was a relief to see that at least the boy hadn't suffered a compound fracture.

It looked like he had on thin, loose pants like pajamas and a dirty white sweatshirt. She'd kept her distance until the others could arrive, her training in police procedure dictating she move with caution. You never knew when someone bore a hidden weapon. Knives could be as dangerous as guns when an officer bent over a supposed victim.

"We're here, Mattie," Sarge said from behind her as they scrambled down the incline off to the side.

The boy whimpered and drew into a tighter ball.

"Don't be afraid," Mattie told him, moving closer. "We're all part of the search and rescue team. We've been looking for a lost child."

The kid raised his face again to look at her, but his eyes darted toward the men and he lowered his head quickly, covering it with his arms. His hands appeared to be empty, so Mattie told Robo to stay. She hovered near enough to see that he was shivering beneath his drenched clothing. "What are you doing out here without warm clothing?" she murmured.

He moaned again and stayed tucked into a tight fetal position.

# TWENTY-THREE

The sprint through the forest in the chilling rain got his blood pumping, and Cole felt reenergized. The sight of the fallen boy who seemed clearly terrified tugged at his heartstrings. He moved closer to stand by Mattie, where she'd leaned forward to place a hand on the kid's shoulder.

The kid shrank even further into himself at her touch. "Don't," he uttered between sobs.

Mattie shrugged off her backpack and handed it to Cole. "There's a space blanket inside the main compartment. Let's get him warm."

"What's your name, son?" Sarge said as he moved to kneel at the boy's back.

No answer—just the sound of quiet sobs.

Cole dug to the bottom of Mattie's pack, past her water supply and Robo's bowl and goggles, to a plastic bag holding a flat item. He opened the bag, removed a lightweight foil-backed covering, and shook it out to unfold it.

He hunkered down beside Mattie to spread the blanket over the shivering boy, tucking it in gently at his back and shoulders. He began talking to him in the quiet voice he used to soothe animals. "There now, that should warm you. You're drenched. This is a bad night to be out in the open like this. My name's Cole, and I'm a veterinarian. Let me take a look at your ankle. Which one is it that's hurt?"

The boy had calmed somewhat, although he remained shut down and didn't answer.

"I'll be gentle," Cole said, placing his hand lightly on one of the kid's knees. "Tell me if it hurts."

The boy allowed his touch, and Cole ran his hand down the boy's shin to his ankle, palpating gently. "Is this the one that hurts?"

"Huh-uh."

At least getting the kid to respond with a grunt was making some kind of progress. Cole rotated the foot gently, letting the boy feel the movement and pressure on his good ankle before he moved on to the one that was hurt. "There," he said in a quiet tone. "That's all I want to do with your other foot. I'll take it slow and careful."

The boy still shivered but his sobs had hushed. "Okay," he said, his voice barely audible.

*That's major progress*, Cole thought as he placed his hands on the boy's other knee. He palpated the shin and calf, moving to the ankle before pausing to hold the cold joint between his hands to warm it. "Is that okay?"

"Yeah."

Cole palpated the joint softly, and the kid sucked in his breath.

"It's pretty tender, isn't it?" Cole said as he continued to move his fingers around the anklebones and muscles beneath. He thought it might be sprained badly and not broken, but he couldn't tell for sure. He directed the beam of his headlamp downward and saw that the ankle was already starting to enlarge despite the cold temperature. "It looks like it's starting to swell, so I won't rotate your foot on this ankle. Let's just leave it alone." He raised his eyes to Mattie and Sarge. "Do either of you have a first aid kit?"

"Yes," they both answered at the same time.

"I've got it," Mattie said, removing a kit from her pack.

"I need the Ace bandage," Cole said, holding out his hand to receive it. He went on, speaking conversationally to the kid. "I'm glad you don't have on boots. It'll be easier to remove your shoe when we get you to a warm place."

"Don't take me back."

Cole had been careful to keep from shining his headlamp directly into the boy's eyes, but the glow at the edge of its beam showed them to be wide with fear. "Take you back where?" Cole asked.

Silence. Cole began to wrap the boy's ankle, securing the shoe to his foot to stabilize the joint. "We'll sacrifice this Ace bandage to the mud so we can leave your shoe on," he murmured, still keeping his voice low and soothing. "We're not going to take you back to the place you came from, if that's what you mean. Is that what you're afraid of?"

The boy nodded. "But . . ."

When the boy went silent, Cole continued to wrap. "You know, when I wrap a horse's foot, we leave his shoe on too. This will support your ankle and keep it from hurting so bad. Then we'll see if you can put any weight on it. We don't want to take you where you don't want to go, son. We want to keep you safe from harm. Can you tell me what you're afraid of?"

"I'm, uh . . ." The boy began to shiver again. "I'm Troy. Troy Alexander."

Mattie stirred beside Cole, and he noticed she wore a startled expression. "Troy, I'm Mattie. We're happy to meet you. I'm a sheriff's deputy from Colorado, and this other guy is Sergeant James Madsen of the Denver police. We know about you. There've been a lot of people out looking for you this past year."

"Year?" Troy looked up at Mattie.

She took off her headlamp, evidently so the boy could see her face. Robo was in a down position on the other side of Mattie, and he stretched his neck so he could lay his muzzle on Troy's arm. To Cole, it looked like a clear attempt at providing comfort.

*That dog is so smart.* At Mattie's command, he could take down a dangerous criminal, or on his own, he could sense a child's emotional distress. Either way, he was there for people.

"Yeah, you've been missing a little over a year," Mattie murmured as she stroked Robo's head. "This is Robo, by the way. He's trained to search for people."

Troy slowly reached his hand out from under the space blanket to touch Robo. The big lug licked his arm and edged forward to get closer. Cole realized the dog was working his magic.

"You found me," Troy said to Robo.

Mattie leaned back slightly, placing a hand on Robo's back while the boy continued to pet him. Cole finished the wrap, tearing the end so he could tie it securely. He could feel impatience coming off Jim Madsen in waves, but the sergeant seemed to trust Mattie's light touch with this interview and he stayed silent.

Mattie spoke again. "There's no way to tell you how happy we are to find you, Troy, but we weren't exactly out here looking for you. There's another boy who's been missing for a few days, and we've been searching for *him*."

Troy's eyes opened wide as he looked up at Mattie. "I think I know where he is," he said, barely above a whisper.

"You do?"

"Yeah." He uncovered his arm to point in the general direction from where he'd been running. "I think he's back there."

Mattie leaned forward. "At the place you don't want to go back to?"

Troy nodded.

Mattie looked up at Sarge and the two of them locked eyes for a moment. Cole remained still, resting his hands around the boy's swollen ankle to try to warm it. *There's no way this boy can lead them there*, Cole thought. *Not on this ankle.*

"I ran all this way," Troy said. "I just kept running downhill. I don't know how to get back there."

"That's all right," Mattie said. "You don't have to. Robo can find it."

Troy's eyebrows lifted. "How?"

"He can follow your scent trail and take us there. Tell me about this place so we know what we're looking for."

"It's like two places. One's like a shack . . ." Troy's voice trailed off before he continued. "The other place is more like a dugout. Or a cave in the side of the hill. It's got boards over the front. He chains us up in there."

Mattie shifted beside him, and Cole could feel her tension. "Is the cave near the shack?"

"Sort of. It's hidden back in the woods, but you can walk between the two places."

"Where is this boy you mentioned? In the shack or the cave?" Mattie asked.

Troy heaved a sigh that ended in a groan. "That's just it. We were together in the cave, but the guy came and got me hours ago."

Mattie continued. "What does the guy look like?"

"I don't know. He wears a mask. But he has long hair that he sometimes wears in a ponytail."

"Does he live in the shack?" Mattie asked.

"He just comes there." Troy lowered his face. "To take pictures," he added in a hoarse whisper.

Cole could feel this child's pain and couldn't keep silent. "It's all right, Troy. You're safe now."

It was as if a dam burst and Troy's words flowed. "He makes me do things. Nasty stuff. This new kid, his name's River. He looks kinda like a girl, with long blond hair. The guy wanted me to do stuff with him but I said no. He told me he'd make me sick if I didn't."

"He'd make you sick?" Cole asked.

"Yeah . . . he poisons me if I don't cooperate. Says it's arsenic. He thinks it's funny, but I think it could kill me."

"Right," Cole said. "Has he made River sick?"

"I don't think so, but I haven't seen him since this afternoon. The guy brought him back from the shack where he had him last night. River was crying and said the guy threatened to kill him if he didn't pose for the pictures. Then the guy came back to get me. He told me his plan, but I said no."

"Did he make you take arsenic?"

"No. He said I needed to think about it and he'd come back later. He left me in the shack tied to a bed, but I wiggled my hands free and got away. I . . ." He sobbed and covered his face with his hands.

Cole had a hunch the kid felt guilty. "It's okay, Troy. It's good that you got away."

"I left River," Troy said, fighting to control his sobs. "I didn't think I could get away with him slowing me down. I never should've left him."

Mattie placed her hand on Troy's shoulder and this time he didn't shrug it off. "You did the right thing, Troy. Sometimes you've got to act on your own. You got to us. Now we'll go find River."

Cole could hear the wind sigh through the tree branches up above, although he couldn't feel it down here in the ravine. Rain pattered the ground, finding its way through the evergreen canopy.

Mattie looked at Sarge. "Robo and I need to go before the rain washes away the scent."

Fear for her safety tightened Cole's chest. "One of us needs to go with her," he said.

"Robo's good, but we might need Banjo too," Sarge said.

Cole figured that would be the decision. It felt right for him to stay with the kid. He was the one with more medical training, and they seemed to have a rapport. "I'll stay with Troy. We'll see if we can get closer to the road."

"I think we should keep him a secret," Mattie said. "I can think of a bunch of people who could match this guy's description—homesteaders, volunteers, people on the movie set. We don't want to tip him off that we've got one of his kids."

Sarge's face puckered with distaste. "I agree, but we need medical help and backup. I'll radio Piper on a secure channel and I'll also relay our concerns. Cole, can you try to keep the kid warm?"

"I'll see what I can do."

Mattie dug into her backpack. "I've got a ferrocerium rod and a packet of dried tumbleweed here that should help you start a fire. Although everything is pretty wet." She looked worried as she handed the items to Cole.

"I can use this," he told her. "I'll scout around for wood covered in pitch."

"Let's try to move you to a more sheltered spot," Sarge said to Troy.

Troy groaned as he sat up. "I'll be okay," he said. "If Dr. Cole can help me, I can make it. Go find River before the rain messes things up."

"Good lad," Cole said, nodding at Troy before making eye contact with Mattie. "Good luck, and be careful."

# TWENTY-FOUR

Mattie felt elated they'd found Troy alive. But she feared that the kidnapper would return to his hideout and, after finding Troy missing, he'd kill River. She had to keep her hopes up. If they could find River and bring him home, *then* they could work on catching this pedophile scumbag.

Robo's patrol dog training had included backtracking a captured fugitive primarily to recover stolen goods or items the perp had hidden along the way during a chase. Once during training he'd recovered two different stashes of stolen jewelry and cash. In reality, in rural Timber Creek, they didn't have jewelry stores or robbers who escaped on foot to hide their stash like those in cities, but he'd made outstanding discoveries of evidence by using this skill.

*Tracking is tracking,* Mattie thought, and now she intended to ask Robo to backtrack Troy's scent trail on a search and rescue mission.

Robo was still crouched beside Troy. Mattie gave him a ration of fresh water while Sarge did the same for Banjo. Then she knelt and indicated Troy's arm with a hand gesture. "Robo, scent this."

It was the same command she used for scenting a captured fugitive or the beginning of a known scent trail in the absence of a target scent article. She had all the confidence in the world that her dog would know what she wanted. As a SAR dog, Banjo had been trained to always move forward toward the missing subject, but she felt certain the bloodhound would catch onto backtracking as soon as the two dogs got started.

Robo sniffed Troy's arm, and when the kid ran his hand up to fondle Robo's ears, her dog licked it several times. The mucous membranes in a dog's mouth and nose captured scent from human skin rafts, and Mattie knew that now Robo had catalogued Troy's scent in his brain. He would most likely remember this kid's unique odor forever. But just to make sure, she asked if she could snip a small piece of fabric from the tail of Troy's sweatshirt to keep as a scent article. She could use it to redirect Robo if he lost the track.

After bagging the scrap, Mattie stood and stroked Robo's head to get his attention. "Good boy," she murmured. "Good dog. Come."

She walked a few paces away with Robo at heel, dancing along with his eyes lifted to hers. Smiling down at him before bending to hug him against her leg and pat his sides, she felt grateful that she could always count on Robo to be ready to work. It might be raining or snowing or hot as hell, but her dog would be there to search out a track no matter what conditions were thrown at him.

Guessing at the spot where Troy had fallen and rolled downhill, Mattie used a sweeping gesture to indicate the ground, Robo took a moment to drop his nose and explore, but before long he raised his head and trotted uphill, checking the ground now and then.

"Good boy," Mattie cooed, making sure she reinforced his choices to let him know he understood what she wanted. "Let's go. Track."

She could hear Sarge directing Banjo the same way once Robo identified which way to go. They kept both dogs on lead while the two of them struck out between the trees in the dark forest. Mattie adjusted her headlamp as she hurried to keep up while Robo pulled hard at the end of the leash.

The aroma of wet forest surrounded her—the citrusy antiseptic scent from Douglas fir, the musky odor of mossy vegetation, the intense piney fragrance from lodgepole and cedar. Robo and Banjo would smell all these layers and more, including passing animals that they had been taught to ignore when on track.

Despite the soggy conditions, branches still snapped underfoot. The surge of adrenaline Mattie had felt when she learned that River was near subsided as they trudged through the forest, clambering over huge fallen trees, constantly moving uphill. The steep incline sapped her energy as the track went on and on into the night.

Banjo lagged, and Mattie figured the dog had almost reached his limit. She knew Sarge kept him well conditioned but he was older than Robo and he'd been working hard over long hours during the past few days. Gradually Sarge fell behind, but she didn't want to stop Robo's momentum, and she let him continue to pull her forward even though her arm and her legs ached with fatigue.

Raindrops splattered down through the canopy and fell with such intensity that it created a veil her headlamp couldn't penetrate. The forest seemed to close in on her, triggering her claustrophobia and taking her breath away. Keeping her eyes on Robo's back, she focused on smoothing her respirations. *Inhale, exhale. Everything's all right*, she told herself, although fear that Troy's scent trail would be washed away niggled at the back of her mind.

The incline eased and Mattie regained her breath. With the rain threatening their scent track she felt compelled to hurry. Robo showed no sign of stopping, although his pace had slowed and he seemed to be checking the ground more often, sometimes sweeping off to sniff foliage at the side of what Mattie guessed would be the path Troy had taken during his flight.

Nerves tickled her insecurities. Would Robo be able to stay on track after all? Where were Sarge and Banjo? She used a secure radio channel and her earpiece to check on him.

"I'm right behind you," he responded. "Banjo's still on track."

A wooden wall materialized at the edge of her headlamp's beam right in front of Robo, making her gasp. She reached out and touched the rough planks. Robo had led her right to a rough-cut door, to the exact spot where Troy had exited the ramshackle building.

Would the man who'd held Troy and River captive be on the inside? If so, he'd probably already heard Robo and her approach. She switched off her headlamp.

Mattie wanted to radio Sarge again but hated to even speak softly lest she reveal their presence. She bent to ruffle the fur at Robo's neck, a brief reward for a phenomenal job, while quietly leading him to the corner of the building. Straining to listen for sound from the inside, she scanned the woods for light from Sarge's headlamp. It was impossible to see into the darkness of the deep woods. No sound came from inside the shack or outside from the direction of the scent trail.

The darkness was so complete that she couldn't even see Robo's back. She slipped off her glove and ran her hand as far as his Kevlar vest, checking for bristling hair that would indicate danger. Because K-9 partners led their handlers right up to the bad guys, Mattie had learned to watch Robo's body language closely, looking for the hair at his ruff to stand on end.

She felt nothing but drenched fur. Staring out at the forest, she wondered what to do. Search the shack or wait for Sarge?

Mattie had never been very good at waiting. Thoughts of River sent her around the corner of the shack, searching for a window. Trees growing close to the wall and lumpy ground hindered her progress. She sensed that the shack had been built right into the forest, not a clearing. It wouldn't have been visible from the air.

A secret hideaway for degenerate activity. She pressed on, clearing her mind of the sickening thought to focus on the wall and the ground beneath her feet. After about twenty feet, she reached a corner without finding a window. Robo turned the corner and moved down the back wall, leading her along as she groped her way in the darkness, feeling the wall for an opening or window glass.

Nothing. They turned another corner and cleared the wall that led back to the front of the building. A windowless cage meant to imprison kids. By now she felt certain that no one lay in wait inside. She wanted to take Robo in to search.

As a police officer, she needed a warrant to enter an enclosed building where there was some expectation of privacy. But exigent circumstances, believing that one boy had been held prisoner here and another was still being held captive, gave her some leeway. The options were not always black and white, and she was certainly operating in the gray area at this point. But she needed her backup.

Speaking softly, she radioed Sarge. "I'm at the shack."

"We're still on track."

Mattie strained to see and glimpsed the twinkling of a light in the darkness before it disappeared. "I think I see you. You're close."

Within seconds, light from Sarge's headlamp bobbed back into view.

She switched her headlamp on to signal him. "The shack is right here."

Sarge and Banjo drew up next to her but not before Mattie noticed the dog was limping.

"Banjo's done," Sarge said. "I think it's his shoulder."

Mattie hoped it was from overuse and not a permanent problem. "I've been around the building. No windows. No noise coming from inside."

"Let's go in."

She was glad Sarge felt the same way she did.

"Send Robo in to clear it," Sarge said.

Robo could determine if someone was on the premises in seconds. But Mattie wanted them to go in together. "I'll breach the door and we'll take lead," she said.

Sarge put Banjo into a down-stay. They both tightened pistol-mounted lights onto their service weapons and took positions on each side of the door. Stories of wire-rigged shotguns firing when police officers opened closed doors filled Mattie's mind as she ran her hand down the plank door searching for a knob. She unclipped Robo's leash, settled him behind her against the wall, and told him to stay.

She pushed open the door. It creaked as it swung inward. No shot. No sound. Robo pressed against the back of her knee, eager to get around her. Her adrenaline surged as she sent Robo in and followed close behind, Glock held up and ready. She used the light mounted on it to scan the space. Sarge came in behind her.

Mattie spotted the bed first. Built of rough-cut timber with an elaborate headboard and footboard made of log, it loomed larger than life in the narrow room. The bed filled the enclosure as if choking the air out of it. Rumpled blankets covered a thin mattress, and Mattie could see ropes tied to the frame from which Troy had escaped.

She lost hope that River had been moved to the shack. She flashed her light down at Robo's neck, saw that the hair remained smooth, and then swept her light around the room. "Clear," she said to Sarge.

A camera sat on a tripod off to the side of the bed. A small generator sat against the left wall, a wire running from it to what looked like a klieg light. Reflectors stood at each side of the bed as if they were voyeurs. A piece of equipment called a gimbal, which Mattie could identify only because she'd seen one in a photo, rested against the wall, its purpose being to strap a camera to a videographer's body so he could adjust angles and distances when filming. Bile rose in her throat as she imagined the equipment in use.

An old metal cabinet sat against the other wall. "Robo, heel," she said, moving toward the rusty doors of the unit. He stayed at her left side. With a gloved hand, she opened a door, willing River to be inside the boxy container, only to be disappointed to find shelves lined with videos, magazines, and cameras. An open cardboard box on the bottom shelf appeared to be filled with sex toys and drug paraphernalia. She repressed a shudder.

Sarge made a sound of disgust.

A clear plastic container filled with ash sat on the top shelf. Ash laced with arsenic, enough to kill hundreds of people—a kidnapper's weapon in a deadly game to win control.

"Come with me," Mattie said, leading Robo toward a door in the back wall beyond the bed. She hoped River would be on the other side.

Following the same protocol she'd used to breach the outside door, she made Robo stay back against the wall while she grasped the knob firmly between two gloved fingers. If there were any fingerprints left by this disgusting pedophile, she wanted to avoid smearing them.

The knob turned easily. While standing back against the wall, she pushed the door inward, swinging it wide. She sent Robo in ahead of her, using the beam from her Glock to sweep the room. Another bed . . . this one without the fancy headboard but with a thicker mattress piled high with pillows and blankets. A lone tripod sat at the foot, telling her that even though there was no attached camera, filming had occurred in this room as well. A little shack of horrors.

But no sign of River.

Sarge was on the other side of the room, looking discouraged. "Let's use the dogs to do an area search and find this cave Troy talked about. I hope we'll find our boy there."

Mattie called Robo to her and clipped on his leash.

Sarge turned to leave. "I'll get Banjo and see if he's got a few more minutes left in him."

Mattie hated for the bloodhound to have to go back to work, but it couldn't be helped. They needed him. She shrugged off her backpack and began the process of giving Robo water.

A shot rang out. Two more shots followed from close by.

Robo surged against his leash. Taken by surprise, Mattie struggled to hold him. *Sarge! Is he all right?*

"Robo, out," she said firmly, giving him the command to stand down. He whined and backed off from tugging against his leash. "Stay with me."

She pressed on her radio. "Sarge. What's your status?"

Without waiting for a reply, she told Robo to heel and rushed across the room to the outside door. She held Robo by the handle on his vest as he danced beside her, eager for the command to attack.

She strained to see what was going on without stepping out from the shelter of the building. In the dead silence that followed the gunshots, she listened. She thought she heard the sound of someone running at a distance through the forest.

"Mattie." Sarge's voice, low but fierce, came through her earpiece.

Relief flooded through her. "I'm here," she said while she strained to see without leaving the cover of the wall. Even though it sounded as if the shooter had left, her training dictated that she shouldn't make an easy target of herself or Robo.

"I'm hit," he replied in a hoarse whisper.

*Officer down—this is different.* Without hesitation, she left the shelter to help her friend and mentor.

# TWENTY-FIVE

By providing a shoulder under Troy's arm, Cole had given the kid enough support for him to hobble up the incline and away from the ravine to escape any flash flooding that might occur. Finding shelter from the rain while staying hidden from the trail offered another challenge, but they'd picked their way through the trees until Cole found a tall fir that they could hole up under until help arrived. Sarge had radioed for a rescue party prior to leaving, but it would take them a while to get there.

Back home, there would be boulders, an overhang above a cliff face, or even a rocky cave to shelter in, but here things were different. A thick canopy was about the best that he could do for the kid.

After seating Troy with his back against the trunk and tucking the space blanket around his body, Cole dug out wet needles and cones until he hit dirt, clearing a space for a small fire. He'd found pitch-laden bark from the trunk of a nearby pine, and he'd harvested several peelings as well as some cones and dead branches still covered with brown needles. In Colorado that would be plenty to combine with Mattie's fire starter to achieve what they needed, but everything was so soggy here that he didn't know if a spark would catch and last. And he only had one, maybe two chances to create a source of warmth for this traumatized boy.

To keep the base of his fire from getting drowned out with accumulated water from rain, Cole scraped away dirt to create a moat-like effect around a slight mound inside a circle. This way, the moat would catch and siphon away rain while his blaze stayed high and dry in the middle.

"I'm going to gather some wood and see if I can find seed pods or other fluff to help get this fire started," he told Troy. "I'll be right back."

The boy looked up from where he sat huddled against the tree. "You won't go far?"

Naturally Troy was still afraid, and Cole tried to reassure him. "I'll stay within calling distance and won't be long."

Keeping to the range he'd promised, Cole had no trouble finding plenty of firewood among the deadfall, but his search for seedpods or milkweed fluff only ended in disappointment. He'd have to make do with the kindling he'd already found.

Troy looked relieved when he returned, and Cole thought the boy had probably been tracking his progress by watching for the light from his headlamp. He set down the wood he'd gathered before kneeling to start laying the fire. He was concerned that a fire might be spotted by Troy's captor but decided that providing warmth for the boy was worth the risk.

He worried about Mattie. No telling what they would find at the end of Robo's track. And he knew that dog well enough to be certain that he would find the shack that had become the boys' prison.

Cole took out his Leatherman tool, extracted a knife blade, and began peeling the bark from the sticks and twigs that he'd found. "If you peel the outside bark away, you can usually get down to drier wood," he said to Troy, just to make conversation to hopefully put him more at ease.

"Okay," Troy replied quietly. "Want me to help you?"

"No, not necessary. Just stay tucked in and try to warm up. I hope I can get this fire started, but there are no guarantees."

"It rains here all the time."

"Oh yeah? Did you grow up here?"

"No."

"Where you from, Troy?"

"Chicago."

That surprised Cole. Since Mattie and Jim had known this kid by name, it had been obvious that they'd been briefed about him being missing, but he'd thought the boy was local. Now Troy seemed less shut down and might be willing to talk. "How did you get out here then?"

"Camping trip."

"Oh gosh." A glance told Cole the boy was staring at him, watching him as he peeled sticks and stacked them in the middle of the fire mound. "How did you end up with the guy who held you captive?"

"Got up to use the outhouse in the middle of the night. Last thing I remember was something hit me on the head. I woke up when I was being carried and yelled for help, but the guy hit me again. Next time I woke up I was in the shack." He lowered his face against his bent knees as if to shield his feelings and thoughts.

Cole thought the kid had become overwhelmed with emotion. "I'm so sorry for what you've been through. Were your parents out here camping with you?"

Troy kept his face buried against his knees. "Huh-uh. Church camping trip."

"So there were other kids with you?"

"Yeah."

"All boys?"

"Yeah."

Cole sat back on his heels for a moment to think. Multiple boys at a campsite, chances of one of them going to the latrine during the night were high. Troy might not have been a target, just simply taken by being in the wrong place at the wrong time. Some guy with long hair, photographs in the ramshackle cabin . . . How long had this guy been in action?

Rage burned deep in his gut. Worry about Mattie running into the kidnapper was replaced by the hope that she and Jim *did* find him, so they could lock him up forever.

"Your parents are going to be overjoyed to know you've been found," Cole said.

"He told me they were dead."

"What?" Was this a form of cruelty or did the kidnapper know something that Cole didn't?

The boy wiped tears from his cheeks. "Yeah, that's what he said. But I don't know if I can trust the creep."

"I agree with that, Troy. Don't trust the creep. We'll see what's what when we get you back to safety and can talk to the sheriff. He'll know the truth."

Troy sniffed and leaned his forehead back onto his knees.

Cole talked to Troy while he laid the fire, hoping to keep his mind occupied. A wax-embedded hemp cord found inside the ferrocerium rod's bag provided the fluff Cole needed to add to the dried tumbleweed. After tucking a few slivers of magnesium from the rod into the pile, he built a teepee of kindling over the nest.

When all was in place, he struck the rod until a spark caught in the hemp cord. Both it and the magnesium flared, moving quickly into the tumbleweed.

Cole bent to blow gently on the dry material to help the flame move toward the wetter stuff he'd harvested from the forest. After adding peeled and splintered sticks carefully, he soon nurtured a plucky blaze that began to throw off enough heat to warm his hands.

"There," he said, leaning back on his heels and looking at Troy. "I think we've made it. I'll peel the moss off a couple of these small logs and get them ready to put on when it's a little bigger."

The kid sighed before tipping his head back against the tree trunk and closing his eyes. His thin face looked pinched with exhaustion and sadness. Cole wanted to question him more about his captor but decided it best to leave the kid alone. Maybe he could sleep and escape his haunting ordeal for a while.

Cole wished he could identify the kidnapper from Troy's description. As he went about building the fire, he thought of the men he'd met who had long hair. First came to mind Deputy Gage Casey . . . surely not him, but he knew from experience that law enforcement officers could be as crooked as civilians and even more wily.

Frank Holt, the family man who was now in police custody had long brown hair shot with gray. Maybe it could be him.

Then he thought of Bob Gibson, the prop manager Mattie had talked to earlier—that guy might even have a criminal history. And what about Chrystal's bodyguard, the one everybody called Gunner? His long hair had been pulled back in a man bun, but it could surely be let down into a ponytail. And being tied into Hollywood might make either of them more likely to know about filming home movies.

But it seemed like this guy was probably local. And there were scads of volunteers in the crowd who wore their hair long.

Troy's jaw had become slack and he was breathing evenly through his mouth. Cole was glad the boy had been able to find some respite in the oblivion of sleep. Overcome by his own exhaustion, Cole's eyelids began to droop. He stood, moving as quietly as possible, so that he wouldn't fall asleep and drop his guard. He needed to stay alert until this thing had ended.

# TWENTY-SIX

The darkness was complete, any light from the moon obliterated by the rain clouds. Mattie spoke quietly. "Sarge, where are you?"

"Here, behind this fallen tree."

Still holding her firearm in one hand and Robo's leash in the other, she let her dog pull her in the direction of Sarge's voice. She heard a rustle in front of her immediately before Robo stopped, but she couldn't see anything in the deep shadows.

"I'm right here," Sarge said in a hoarse whisper that came from the other side of a large tree trunk that she'd bumped up against. "I took cover."

Mattie slid one leg over the mossy barrier and crossed to the other side. She heard a soft whine and knew it was coming from Banjo. She went down on her knees and felt her way until she touched Sarge's boots. "How bad?"

"Bad enough. My leg." The rustling sound came again as Sarge struggled to move. "My first aid kit's in my pack."

"Here . . . hand it to me." Mattie took the backpack that Sarge thrust at her. Robo had hunkered down beside her, his nose reaching to sniff the pack, then back toward Sarge.

"Robo, leave it," she murmured, wanting him to back off from the injury. "Stay."

She dropped his leash and opened the pack to rummage through it blindly.

"It's in the inside pocket," Sarge said. "Front side."

Mattie found the zipper and was relieved when her fingers touched the familiar shape of the plastic case. "Got it."

Sarge was moving again, and she felt him struggle to sit. "I think I need a tourniquet," he said.

Mattie's heart tripped in alarm. "How bad's the bleeding?"

"I don't think it got an artery but . . . it's bad."

"I've got the kit, but we need some light. I heard the shooter run away after you returned fire. I'll keep the beam low and nestled behind this tree."

"All right."

Putting her headlamp down beside Sarge's legs, Mattie turned it on to low beam. Light glistened off the bright red blood on his left pant leg. There was a lot of it. Her gut squeezed as she positioned the first aid kit within the headlamp's beam.

She took out a small pair of scissors and reached for the bloody fabric. "Let me cut that away so I can see the wound."

Sarge sucked in a breath as she jostled his leg.

"Sorry," she whispered as she carefully cut a slit that included the hole where the bullet passed through the material.

"I'm okay," Sarge muttered.

With bloody fingers, Mattie picked up her headlamp and shone the light into the hole she'd created in his pants. Blood oozed from the gunshot wound, and much as she hated to see it, she was grateful that it wasn't spurting with each heartbeat, a sure sign of a torn artery. "Yeah," she murmured. "It's bleeding bad enough, but it doesn't look like an artery."

She slipped her hand through the hole to gently probe the backside of his leg. "Is there an exit wound?"

"I don't think so," Sarge said between gritted teeth. "I think it hit the bone. It felt like it broke when I went down."

It was all Mattie could do to keep from groaning. She tried to keep a positive front. "I'll use a QuikClot gauze pad and wrap it tightly. I think a pressure bandage is better than a tourniquet."

"Sounds good. We gotta hurry."

The urgency behind his words weren't for himself. It had taken only minutes to assess the wound, but every second gave the scumbag who shot Sarge a chance to get away. And what if he was headed toward River, planning to snatch the boy and disappear?

But Mattie couldn't leave Sarge until she knew he was stable. She applied the gauze pad to the open wound, wrapped it tightly with an Ace bandage to hold it in place, and then tied it off. She swept the headlamp beam upward to find Banjo huddled by Sarge's shoulder. "Is Banjo okay?"

"Yeah. He wasn't hurt. Just worn out." Sarge looked grim, his face gray with pain. "Mattie, I don't think I can stand. If you can find me a long stick that's not rotten, I'll try."

Keeping the headlamp low to the ground, Mattie scanned the immediate area. She found a branch by the tree trunk that looked to be about the length of a cane. "Try this."

Bracing one hand on the tree trunk and holding the branch with the other, Sarge got into position while Mattie circled to his back and grasped beneath his shoulders. "Now," he said, clutching the cane upright.

Mattie heaved while Sarge strained, gasping in pain as he tried to stand upright. It didn't work, but they managed to seat him on top of the tree trunk.

Sarge cursed. "I can't bear weight on it." He gripped her forearm. "Mattie, you've got to go on with Robo."

"I know."

"If you can get close, have Robo take the guy down. It's dark enough, he won't see him coming."

Mattie hoped he was right but figured the guy either had a headlamp or a flashlight, just like she did.

"You're going to have to let him off leash," Sarge said. "You can't take a chance of him getting hung up in the undergrowth during attack."

"Right." The thought of her dog getting injured or shot made her chest tighten. Her mind churned with what she knew: they were uphill from the polluted water, which lowered Robo's risk of being poisoned, but the guy had a gun and probably a light source—a possibility that terrified her, not for herself but for Robo.

It took only seconds to splash water into Robo's bowl to moisten his mouth and get him ready to track. Even as he lapped, Mattie started the chatter to let him know they were going back to work. "You wanna find a bad guy, Robo? You wanna find that shooter? Let's go, let's go get a bad guy."

It would be no problem for Robo to pick up this guy's track. Fugitives gave off a unique scent from stress or fear, which some handlers called endocrine sweat. It was her job to get him close to the place where the shots had come from, and he would do the rest. He'd search for the freshest human scent and lock onto the track. And she'd do her damnedest to keep up with him.

Sarge groaned again, cursing in frustration as he tried to shift his weight. "Mattie, I'm sorry I can't go."

"I know. You've got to stay here and stay alert in case he circles back. Do you have your radio?"

"Yeah. I'll radio Piper again and let him know I'm shot. Maybe they're close."

"Good. And Cole will keep Troy away from the trail, so he should be safe."

Sarge heaved a sigh. "Do you need anything else?"

"No. I'm ready"

"God go with you and keep you safe."

She could hear the fear in his tone and could only imagine what it would be like if she had to send one of her fellow officers into danger without covering his back. Comrades, they clasped each other's forearms one last time.

Robo was obviously ready, dancing at the end of his leash with boundless energy. Even though her own had flagged, the surge of adrenaline from the gunfire still buoyed her.

Mattie shrugged on her pack and secured the safety strap on her holster to assure she didn't lose her firearm while running. Robo was already tugging her in the direction she thought they should go, so she let him lead the way.

Maybe five minutes had passed, possibly enough time for the shooter to reach River's cave, if that's where he was headed. *Stay strong, kiddo*, she thought. If River hadn't been dosed with arsenic yet, she hoped he would fight. Anything to slow this guy down.

Sarge had lost a lot of blood, but she thrust her worry about him aside to focus on her dog. She wanted to keep Robo on leash until he'd established the track, but then she'd have to turn him loose. He was good about staying close if she asked him to, but without a light she'd be following him blind. She had to use her headlamp, much as she hated to.

Robo tugged her through the trees and undergrowth as she tried to follow as quietly as possible. Treading on the damp footing at this pace didn't create much noise. Using her free hand, she slipped her headlamp from her coat pocket and turned on its low beam. Holding it low and away from her body, she directed it downward to watch her footing, occasionally sweeping Robo's neck to see if his hackles were raised. He would be able to sense if the shooter were close and waiting in ambush. It was the best she could do.

When they reached a point where she thought the shots had come from, Mattie asked Robo to search for the bad guy. He was already doing exactly that, keeping his nose to the ground and sweeping his head back and forth as he quartered the foliage between the trees. He wove back and forth as he advanced until suddenly he stopped and stood at attention, his ears pricked.

His signal for a hit.

With a word of encouragement from Mattie, he put his nose to the ground again and moved forward. This time he didn't hesitate or sweep his head side to side. He'd clearly found the odor they were looking for, and he was on track. He shot straight ahead to the end of his leash.

Mattie said a prayer for her dog's safety as she bent and unclipped the only thing that tethered him to her. Stuffing his leash into her pocket, she hurried to keep up.

Unable to see beyond the beam of light at her feet, her other senses sharpened. Every snap of a twig and sound of a footfall signaled danger, both those coming from beneath her own feet as well as those coming from out in the forest. The rain had slackened, but the constant mist hung thick, forcing her to inhale it as her breath quickened. Piney aroma with undertones of musky vegetation filled her nostrils.

She stumbled on a slippery patch of moss but caught her balance and hurried on. Their many hours of training off-leash paid off as Robo reined in his energy to allow her to stay with him. When he went too fast, she murmured "Slow" for him to pause so she could catch up.

Minutes went by. Mattie tried to stay off to Robo's left, holding her headlamp out to her own left side, its low beam directed downward. If the shooter lay in ambush up ahead, she wanted Robo far away from her headlamp. She kept her right hand free in case she needed to draw her weapon.

Robo's pace quickened, telling her something was close. "Wait," Mattie whispered.

Robo paused. She snapped off her headlamp and stepped right to come up beside him. Reaching down, her cold fingers encountered the wet fur on his neck. Moving up to his head, she felt his hackles standing at attention. The hair at the nape of her own neck prickled, an ancient reflex buried deep in a human's reptilian brain that signaled danger.

*Bam!* The gunshot came within a split second. A bullet whizzed by her left side where she'd been standing when she turned off her headlamp.

She reached for Robo's vest, but it slipped beneath her fingers and he was gone. Her heartbeat tripped. She couldn't call him back; that would only increase his danger. He'd been trained to neutralize any threat to his handler, and that was exactly what he was doing.

One significant difference between search and rescue K-9s and patrol K-9s was apprehension training. Some SAR dogs might be trained in this specific technique, but most weren't. Mattie prayed that this shooter wouldn't expect a SAR dog to attack, and that Robo could take him by surprise.

There was just enough light for her to move through the trees, going after her dog to back him up.

"Aaahhh!" A scream of pain came from in front of her, followed by a gunshot.

Mattie's heart leaped and pounded in her chest. Was Robo okay? Then the sound of his fierce growl reached her, giving her something to home in on. She ran as fast as she could.

It was turmoil. Blind turmoil. But she'd experienced Robo's takedowns many times. The sound of a scuffle right in front of her told her she'd arrived. She flipped on her lamp that was still in her hand.

Robo held the guy by his right arm and was dragging him along the forest floor. Her dog's haunches were braced as he tugged his hardest, occasionally shaking his head in anger. During apprehension training with a guy in a bite suit, Robo's tail might be waving in play. But the gunshots had evidently revved up his prey drive. This attack was real. And it was serious.

She couldn't see the guy's hand. Where was the gun?

Mattie didn't hesitate. She ran and leaped toward the guy's back, tossing her headlamp to the side so she could reach for his left arm. The lamp fell with its beam shining upward into the sky, providing very little light to see by.

She landed on top of him with a thud.

"Umph."

Her weight knocked the air out of him. This was a fight to the death. She used her elbow to grind the guy's face into the ground while Robo continued to pull. He'd been trained to bite and hold, and he wouldn't let go until she told him to. But she couldn't see a gun. Was it still in the guy's right hand? Could he still shoot her dog?

"Good boy, Robo. Get 'im. Take 'im." If she had backup, she'd be telling Robo to let go at this point. But she wanted him to know she still needed his help. She encouraged him to hang on while she pinned the guy's chest down with her left forearm and reached beyond Robo's mighty teeth with her right hand to check for a gun. When she felt the guy's open fingers, relief washed through her.

*He must've dropped the gun.*

She reversed strategy, straddled his torso, and grabbed the guy's left arm. Twisting it up behind his back, she felt Robo give his right arm another powerful shake, not slackening a bit. The guy screamed in pain.

*We've got him, we've got him . . .*

She had to establish control. "Have you had enough?" she asked, her voice gruff with adrenaline.

"Gah . . ."

Mattie wrenched his arm up closer to his head. "Have you had enough?"

"Yes," he said in a strangled voice that she couldn't recognize.

"Stay still. Stop struggling, and I'll call off my dog. But if you move one little finger, he'll be right back on you."

Mattie stayed on top of the guy until she felt the fight go out of him. "Don't move," she warned him one more time before directing Robo. "Robo, out."

Her dog hesitated; she could tell he didn't want to let go.

"Out," she said again, and this time he dropped the guy's arm. "Guard."

In the diffuse light from the upright headlamp, she could see well enough to tell that Robo had taken a stance near the guy's right arm, which remained outstretched exactly where her dog had dropped it. "Good," she said to both her dog and the guy. "Stay still and he won't attack. You move that arm one inch, and he'll be all over you."

Robo bared his white teeth and they glistened against his black muzzle. But the guy didn't look up. As commanded, he didn't move a muscle and lay still with his face turned away.

Using a wrist flexion maneuver to maintain control of his left arm, Mattie reached for her zip tie cuffs on her duty belt with her free hand.

Suddenly the guy exploded beneath her. Raising his torso to knock her backward, he smashed her face with his head. She saw stars, but she gripped his left wrist with both hands and hung on.

With a deep rumbling growl, Robo attacked, going for the guy's right arm as he rose to his knees. Not needing a command, her dog had done what he was trained to do. Mattie held on tight and regained her senses and her footing as the guy struggled, spewing curses.

He shouted, "Robo, out!"

Robo paid no attention. He'd been trained to respond only to Mattie. His growl became even more ferocious as he backed up, tugging and shaking the man's arm until he screamed in pain.

*Fool*, Mattie thought, becoming confident that they had the guy back under control. "Good boy, Robo. Get 'im."

Though Robo was making progress in bringing the man down, he was still on his knees. Mattie used being on her feet to her advantage and wrenched his elbow up higher on his back. With a roar, the guy went down. This time Mattie pinned the small of his back with her knee, placing pressure on his kidneys.

He moaned. "Oh, gah!"

"That was stupid." She decided to let Robo continue to tug for a few seconds while she reached for her cuffs.

"Get him offa me!"

"He won't quit as long as you're struggling," she said, her breath heaving. The fight had winded her. Even with Robo tugging and growling, the guy tried to lie still. Mattie hurried and bound his left hand. "I'll call him off, but if you move, he'll be right back on you. Do you get it now?"

"Yeah! Just get him off!"

"Robo, out!" With her knee still in the guy's back, Mattie held his bound wrist in one hand as she reached for his right. It took another command to get Robo to release, but as soon as he did, she snatched the arm and bent it back to meet his left, making him bellow with pain. She didn't care.

"Robo, guard." The guy had his face turned away from her dog. "Look at him," she prompted until he turned to see Robo standing over him, white canines glistening.

A low growl rumbled in Robo's chest.

"If you're dumb enough to move again, you know what's going to happen." She finished cuffing his hands behind his back, pulling them tight.

"You're hurting me."

"Yeah? Well, I'd say you brought that on yourself."

"You have no right to sic your dog on me."

"I'd say shooting a law enforcement officer gives me the right. You didn't know what you were dealing with, did you? My dog's different from what you're used to." Mattie kept the man on his stomach while she patted him down. She felt an object in his front pants pocket. "Roll over."

"Not with that dog there."

"He's a trained police dog. He won't take you unless you try to hurt me." She nudged him in his side. "Now roll over."

Robo had stopped growling but he stayed in guard position while Mattie helped the guy roll.

"Do you have any needles in your pockets?" Mattie asked.

The guy muttered an oath. "See for yourself."

She doubted it. Arsenic seemed to be this guy's weapon of choice. She reached into his pocket and extracted a knife. After reminding Robo to guard, she finished the pat-down before standing to retrieve her headlamp. She placed it on high beam and swept the ground, locating a pistol about three feet from where his right arm had been. He must've been making a desperate attempt to reach it when he fought to get free that last time.

After securing the gun, she finally shone the light on the guy's face. He blinked and tried to turn away, but not before she got an ID.

Mercury Foster, the friendly grocer who'd been cooking for all the volunteers while inserting himself into the search and investigation. A respected member of his community. Pedophile, pornographer, kidnapper, and killer.

# TWENTY-SEVEN

"Where is River Allen?" Using some cord from her backpack, Mattie had trussed up Foster's legs, reinforced the bindings on his wrists, and tied him to a tree. She stood with Robo at her side a few feet away.

"How the hell should I know?" Foster growled, glaring up at her.

"Don't even try to pretend you don't know."

"You don't have anything against me. I was out here searching for the kid when you and your dog attacked me."

His words amazed her. "You won't be able to deny you shot a man when the bullet is matched to your gun."

He looked away from the glow of her headlamp. Mist had settled all around, making a halo around the light beam.

"And there's a whole shack full of evidence back there that will land you in prison. Pedophiles aren't treated well there, you know. You'll be seen as the scum of the earth that you are. Admit defeat and try to do something good for a change." When he didn't reply, she went on. "It doesn't matter if you help or not. My dog will find River."

"Go to hell."

"Clever," she said. She hated to leave the guy unguarded, but just in case he had a partner, she needed to find River as soon as possible. She had to keep the goal in sight. "Before you start thinking you can get away, remember that Robo can track you down. There's no way you can get away from us."

Not wanting to waste any more time, Mattie gestured for Robo to come with her and strode away.

After going a short distance, she paused to give Robo water and retrieve River's scent article from her pack. She needed to rely on air scenting, even though the child might be locked away behind a barrier within a cave. Whatever skin cells he'd shed between the shack and the cave were probably now washed away by the rain.

As Robo lapped the water eagerly, Mattie pondered what to do. She didn't want to inhibit Robo's ability to quarter the area as he searched for a scent cone. The poisoned stream was well below them now, so she believed it safe to let him search off leash. Once he'd quenched his thirst, he rarely stopped during a search to drink unless she told him to.

While Robo drank, she pulled her radio out of her pack and noted her GPS coordinate. Then she pushed the transmit button to talk to Sarge directly on their channel. "Sarge, this is Mattie."

He answered immediately. "This is Jim."

"Robo got him, Sarge. Are you alone?"

"Affirmative. Help is on the way."

Mattie thought it was safe to give Sarge the information he needed in case something happened to her. "It's Merc Foster."

"Message received loud and clear."

"He's hog-tied to a tree. Do you want the coordinates?"

"Will you be there?"

"We're going on to find the target."

"I'll take the coordinates."

Mattie gave them to him. "How are you doing?"

"I'll make it. Do you have directions to the target?"

"Negative. We're looking for scent."

There was a pause, and when Sarge came back on through the receiver, she heard the end of what might have been a string of curses. Clearly her mentor was frustrated. "When backup gets here, I'll send Piper to retrieve Foster."

"I'll let you know when we've succeeded."

"Stay in touch. Over."

She thought of Cole and wondered how he and Troy were doing. She hoped they were hidden someplace away from the elements.

Robo looked up at her and moved away from his collapsible dish, so she emptied it and stuffed it away in her pack. She knelt so she could stroke his head and hug him close to her chest. He'd gone above and beyond the call of duty today. *He's got to be feeling it as much as I am.*

She buried her nose in the fur at his neck, ignoring the twinge of soreness from Foster's reverse headbutt, and inhaled Robo's wet doggy scent. "Okay, buddy. We've gotta go to work and find River," she murmured as she stroked and patted him from head to tail. He wasn't exactly doing his happy dance like usual to show her he was ready to work, but he nuzzled her neck and shifted in her embrace. When he reached toward the bag that held River's scent article, she let him sink his nose into it for a good whiff.

"Let's go, Robo," she said, standing and tucking the bag away in her pack. She shrugged it on quickly and adjusted her headlamp to shine out toward the forest. Waving her arm toward the left, she gave him his cue. "Search! Go find River."

Robo bounded off, and Mattie hurried to keep up. Her whole body ached. Her back and arms had stiffened from wrestling down Foster. Her legs felt heavy and tired, the day's exertion taking its toll. Her head pounded, but she stayed close enough to keep Robo in sight as he lifted his nose and inhaled the damp air.

Even though the rain had stopped, drops of moisture formed and clung to her jacket, her hood, and even her skin. Wind chilled her face, both a blessing and a curse. Wind provided means for scent to be blown toward a SAR dog from their target, but it could also be hell for the humans involved, especially in a humid climate like this. She shuddered to think how cold and scared River would be locked up in a damp cave.

Feeling disoriented and able to see only a short distance using the eerie glow through the fog from her headlamp, Mattie focused on spotting Robo. Where was this cliff or rocky wall that provided the shelter of a cave? Without her dog, she could search through the night and never find it. Even with him . . . she didn't want to think about it. There was always the possibility that they couldn't find the boy.

Robo became a shadow that flitted in and out of her sight. After traveling what she thought might be a hundred yards, she decided she'd have to call him to return. But just then, he darted back into the dim halo at the edge of her light, heading toward the right this time. She hurried to catch up with him.

When Robo changed directions again, veering left while still moving forward, Mattie began to hope. *Has he picked up River's scent? Is he homing in on the boy's location?*

Robo slowed to a trot, making it easier to keep up with him. Though he kept his nose in the air most of the time, sometimes he dipped his head to the ground to smell the foliage. When the distance between his directional shifts shortened, Mattie's heart rate kicked up higher and her excitement grew. She knew her dog well enough to know he'd begun to work a scent cone.

Fueled by a new surge of adrenaline, Mattie followed, keeping to the middle while Robo weaved back and forth. Layers of gathering mist swirled in and out of her circle of light like ghosts among the trees. She sensed a change in her footing at the edge of an incline. Quickening her pace even as it grew steeper, she climbed the rise, staying close behind her dog.

He stopped at a rough plank wall that appeared to be built up against the face of a cliff. He raised his paw to scratch at a wooden door.

"Ahh!" A high-pitched utterance shrieked from behind the door. "Go away! Get! Get out of here!"

Mattie could hear the terror in the child's voice. "River," she called. "Is that you?"

Silence.

A rusted hasp nailed into the plank door was secured with a padlock. Mattie rattled and tugged it, but it wouldn't budge. She leaned against the door and spoke into a sliver of an opening at its edge. "My name's Mattie. It's my dog that scratched on the door. Don't be afraid. We've been looking for you and we want to take you home to your parents."

A quivery voice answered. "It's a dog?"

"Yes!" Mattie placed a hand on the rough wooden door, wishing she could reach inside and embrace the frightened boy. "Yes, and his name's Robo. Are you River?"

"Yeah."

"Are you beside the door, River?"

"No. He put a collar and chain around my neck."

A pain stabbed Mattie's gut. "Okay. I'm gonna try to get this door open."

"I thought your dog was a wolf."

River sounded stronger already. It would be good to keep the boy talking while she examined the door for hinges. "Do you like dogs?"

Apparently the hinges were mounted on the inside so she couldn't take the door off from out here.

"Yeah," River said. "I used to have one but he died of old age. I wish I still had a dog."

"Me too. They make good friends." Using her headlamp to scan the immediate area, she searched for the right size rock she could use to break the old hasp. "This door has a padlock on it that I'm going to try to beat off with a rock. It could get pretty noisy, but don't be afraid."

"Mr. Foster locked me up in here."

"I know. My dog and I caught him out in the woods and tied him up. He won't bother you again."

"You tied him up?"

"Yeah. Gave him a taste of his own medicine." She spotted a stone that looked like it could act as a hammer and went to pick it up. "Tell me, River. Is Mr. Foster the only person you've seen since he brought you here?"

"Yeah."

"So as far as you know, he doesn't have a partner?"

"Yeah. Did your dog help you catch him?" The child's natural curiosity, which might have led him into wanting to explore the forest in the first place, was definitely helping restore his equilibrium.

"He sure did," Mattie said. "He's a K-9 police dog. I'm his handler and a deputy sheriff from Colorado. We came all the way out here to look for you."

"Cool. I can't wait to see your dog."

"Let's do this then. I'm going to start hitting the door now."

"Okay."

The metal clanged as Mattie struck the padlock and hasp repeatedly until her fingers ached from the pounding she was giving them. The hasp finally began to sag enough to wedge the tip of a smaller rock under it. When she pounded that one downward under the metal flap, the nails that held it finally gave and the hasp fell away from the door. She was in!

A few feet away, Robo had sat watching her the entire time, and he scrambled inside the cave as soon as Mattie opened the door. She started to stop him, but as soon as her headlamp lit the small space within the earthen walls, she saw River on his knees, kneeling on a sleeping bag on top of one of two crude wooden pallets. He was holding his arms out toward Robo.

She quickly gave her dog permission to do what she knew he wanted. "Make friends, Robo."

Robo jumped onto the sleeping bag and into River's embrace. A chain secured to the head of the pallet rattled as River leaned forward, its other end attached to a thick leather collar around his neck. It made Mattie's heart ache to see what this child had endured. His long blond hair had become straggly and matted, his thin face pinched with fatigue and fear. The rims around his blue eyes were reddened, and dark circles, like bruises, marred the skin beneath them.

The stench from a bucket behind the crude bed assailed her sense of smell. She crouched next to the pallet and placed her hand on the child's shoulder. She could feel him trembling. "You're cold. Let me see if I can get this chain off you."

He raised one hand from around Robo's neck and pointed with a shaky finger. "He hung the key right there on the door."

At the top of the plank door, a hook held a small key. It was cruel of Foster to leave it in plain sight. Mattie retrieved it and went to work on the clasp that held the leather collar in place. The lock opened without a problem, and she laid the collar carefully down on the bed. Even as she did it, she was aware that she was disturbing a crime scene, but she refused to use her cell phone to snap a picture of this child wearing the collar when he'd already been subjected to unspeakable photography. She wanted to free him as soon as possible.

When the collar came off, River burst into tears, burying his face on Robo's neck. Mattie placed her hand on the boy's narrow shoulder and then eased down on the pallet next to him, encircling both child and dog with her arms and holding them close. They smelled musty and damp.

River was wearing a coat that looked waterproof, probably the one he'd worn when he left his trailer, but it might not have been enough to keep him warm under these conditions. Did

Foster lure him away from his studies, or did he decide to wander away himself?

Answers would be discovered soon enough. She rocked the child gently back and forth, waiting for his sobs to dwindle so she could radio Sarge to report.

# TWENTY-EIGHT

As much as Mattie hated to wait any longer in the cave, she wanted even less to traipse around the forest's rugged terrain with a child in tow. She needed help, and according to Sarge, they wouldn't have long to wait. At least there was some small amount of shelter from the elements inside these earthen walls.

After asking Robo to get down for a minute, she rearranged the sleeping bag into a nest that covered most of River's small body, and then she invited Robo back up on the pallet to snuggle with him.

"There," she said as she sat down beside the two of them. "That should help warm you. The others will be here soon to help."

River sniffed and leaned back against her, warming Mattie inside. She felt that he must trust her enough to begin to relax his guard. She placed her arm around him while Robo lay down next to his legs. "Are you thirsty?"

"Yeah. And hungry too."

She leaned down to pick up her backpack to hunt through it. "Here's an energy bar. You'll have to share my water supply. Go ahead and bite on the valve and suck on it."

He leaned forward to drink his fill and then settled back, leaning against her as he unwrapped the bar. "Thank you. That's the best water I ever tasted."

*Nice kid*, she thought as she slipped her pack down to the floor. Her mind jumped to Sophie, also this age, and Cole's focus on manners. Despite the extreme difference in the two kids' environments, someone had done the same type of coaching with River.

"Mr. Foster gave me M&M's," River said as he took a bite from his energy bar and chewed.

"Oh?" Mattie waited, hoping for more.

"He gave it to me when he came to the trailer. He said he had a really cool tunnel in the forest to show me if I'd come with him. I thought he was my friend. He wasn't a stranger, you know." River craned his neck to peer up at her, as if checking to see if she would scold him. "I knew him from the store."

"I understand," she told him, holding his gaze. "You thought he was a nice man from the grocery store, and he turned out to be a bad guy. Sometimes that happens to people and we're surprised. I think he had everyone fooled."

River sighed and leaned back against her again.

"You know what? I think Robo found that M&M wrapper," Mattie said. "Did you drop it on purpose?"

"No, I wouldn't have littered the forest on purpose, but I think I lost it when I was crawling through the tunnel we made in the vines."

"Yeah, I can see how that could happen."

"But I did drop my keychain on purpose," he said before biting the end of the bar. "I hope I can find it again," he said as he chewed his mouthful.

"Oh my gosh," Mattie said as she gave him a tight hug. "That was smart of you. Robo found your keychain too, and that's why we came to look for you on this side of the road. Good job, River!"

He ducked his head and smiled before sobering again. "Is my mom worried about me?"

"Oh yes. She'll be so glad to see you. Your dad, too. He came here to help look for you."

"He did?"

"Yeah. They're both very worried about you."

River remained silent while he took another bite and chewed, the wrapper crackling as he folded it back. He'd quit shivering. "I bet they'll be mad at me."

Mattie thought she knew what he was thinking but had learned to not make assumptions when it came to children. "Why?"

"Because I went with a stranger."

"Well . . . like you said, he wasn't really a stranger to you. You'll be more careful and not go with someone like that ever again. Your parents won't be mad at you, although they might act that way at first. Sometimes adults do that when they're really relieved."

River nodded, nibbling at his bar. "Will you tell me a story?"

Mattie hadn't expected that, and she had to blink away tears at the simple request. She thought of a story she'd just finished reading to Sophie. "Sure. I have a little girl your age and I'll tell you a story from a book we read together."

And even though Sophie wasn't really "hers" yet, Mattie thrilled at the thought that she soon would be. Sophie and Angela would become her daughters. Her dream of having a life with family and children would soon come true. And now, after finding this child after long days of searching, she swore she would protect her daughters from harm with all her might.

Hesitation about moving from the quiet cocoon of her own home into Cole's busy household had vanished during the past few days while she focused on finding this precious child and putting him back into the arms of his parents. Adjustments to being married with the added responsibilities of raising children might be challenging, but she could hardly wait for her new life to begin. She hugged River close and started the story. "Once upon a time . . ."

★ ★ ★

Water droplets spattered Mattie as she turned to watch the chopper rev up. It had taken hours for teams of SAR volunteers, deputies from Piper's department, and Washington state troopers to find and evacuate all of them from the forest: the injured Sarge, Cole with Troy Alexander, and River and Mattie. She heard they'd marched Foster, still in cuffs and between two state troopers, out of the forest.

Piper's efforts to coordinate the three-pronged rescue had paid off, with him spearheading the team that went to bring out River. Drake had also been a part of that particular crew, and it had been a relief to see his familiar grin when he stepped through the door of the cave with the others.

Two different helicopters had been called, one to lift River and Troy over to a children's hospital in Seattle, the other to take Sarge. Once Mattie turned River over to his mother's care, she'd stayed with Sarge. He drifted in and out from pain medication the

EMTs had given him, but the two of them were able to debrief as they waited for medical personnel to load him into the chopper.

Sarge was lying on a gurney, his leg stabilized with a brace. "Tell me what happened," he said. "How did Robo do?"

"He's perfect, Sarge, just the way you trained him. It's a long story, and I'll tell you every detail over coffee someday, but for now I'll sum up. Robo didn't have any trouble tracking down Foster. He shot at us and before I could stop him, Robo took off."

"I heard the shot. Good K-9 officer . . . he did just what he was supposed to do. Don't try to stop 'em, Mattie, you'll just interfere with their safety." He reached his hand toward her, and Mattie clasped it in one of hers. "You done good, Deputy."

She knew Sarge was trying to soften the lesson he wanted her to learn, but it was growing harder and harder to let Robo do his job. She was afraid of losing him. "It was Robo who did the good job. He apprehended Foster, had to take the guy down twice before he gave up."

Sarge squeezed her hand.

"After I hog-tied Foster, Robo went into air-scent mode, found the scent cone straightaway, and led me right to the cave where River was locked up behind a framework that held a wooden door."

"You've trained Robo for that, Mattie. You should be proud."

"I am proud of him. He's the best."

Sarge's attention seemed to waver and he withdrew his hand from hers to rub it down over his face. "I guess I'm headed to the hospital. Would you take care of Banjo for me?"

"Of course. Don't worry about him at all. Cole checked his shoulder and thinks it's a muscle strain. He'll be good as new in a few weeks."

"If it works out, Drake can take him back to Denver with him. But if not, can you and Cole take him?"

"Absolutely."

An EMT came up to transfer Sarge to the helicopter. "Time to go, Sergeant."

Sarge reached his hand out again, this time for a handshake. "I'll see you at your wedding," he said. "Save a dance for me."

Mattie struggled to control the tears that wanted to flow. "You bet. See you in a few days," she replied, although she highly doubted that he would be able to travel from Seattle to Denver and then to Timber Creek that quickly, and he certainly wouldn't be dancing. *He'll be lucky to be released from the hospital by my wedding date*, she thought as they wheeled Sarge off toward the chopper.

Backwash from the helicopter's rotors made Mattie take a step backward as the bird lifted off into the dark sky, its taillight flashing. Cole placed his arm around her shoulders to steady her, and Robo leaned against her leg as he raised his nose into the buffeting wind. Banjo whined a sad moan as if he missed his handler already.

Mattie bent to smooth the wet fur on top of Banjo's head. "It's okay, buddy. You'll see him again soon."

She turned to Cole. In the glow of the klieg lights they'd set up to light the helicopter pad, he looked utterly exhausted. "Let's go to the mess hall and see if anyone has brought food. Then we can get some sleep."

Cole rubbed his eyes. "Good idea."

Drake was still out at the crime scene, working the immediate area with Fritz to make sure there were no more dead bodies buried near the shack, so the camper would be quiet and have plenty of room. Dogs and humans were all in need of a good rest.

As they walked past incident command, Piper was coming out the door. "Do you two plan to leave in the morning?"

"We'll leave as soon as we can, sir," Mattie said. "If you no longer need us."

Piper reached to shake her hand and then Cole's. "You two made all the difference in the world to our rescue operation tonight. Words cannot express how grateful I am. I'll need you to make a statement before you go, but it can wait until morning." He made a sound of derision. "But I guess it's morning already. Get as much sleep as you need but plan to spend some time with me before you leave."

"Will do. I'm just glad that River and Troy have been found," Mattie said.

Piper sighed. "And at least we've found two of the ones who didn't make it. I hope to God there aren't more. I'm a fool for not seeing what was going on."

"I don't think anyone pegged the local grocer as a pedophile," Mattie said. "Will you let us know when the bodies are identified?"

"I'll contact you personally. After the job you and your dog did tonight, you deserve to be kept in the loop. Besides, unless Foster pleads guilty, you'll probably have to come back to testify in court." He looked at Cole. "And thank you, too, for taking care of Troy. You deserve some sleep. This has been a long, hard day."

"I'm glad it had a happy ending for River and his parents," Cole said. "Troy told me that Foster said his parents had died. There isn't any truth to that, is there?"

Piper looked disgusted. "Troy already told me about that. I assured him that they're both alive and tonight they're among the happiest folks on the planet. They'll arrive in Seattle on the first flight they can get."

Cole heaved a breath. "That's terrific. Have you heard anything about Rena Powell's SAR dog?"

"Dozer? I sure did. Rena called and said he's responding well. He tested positive for arsenic, of course, but it looks like he's going to be okay."

"More good news," Cole said.

Mattie thought Piper looked like he could use some sleep too, but he'd probably not get any the rest of the night. "We'll see you in a few hours then," she told him, giving him a short salute before turning away.

Cole took her arm as they slogged through the muddy alley that led to the mess tent. "If we can make time, I want to go back to Cecil Moore's cabin and talk to him about his seeing eye dog."

"Sounds great. We might as well end this trip with some fun."

Cole yawned as he gave her upper arm a gentle squeeze. "Well, Mattie, you've reinforced a lesson that you taught me before. I can't be with you all the time to try to keep you safe. I need to have faith that you can take care of yourself."

Mattie chuckled as she took hold of his hand. "Sounds exactly like what Sarge was trying to teach me about Robo."

Her dog pricked his ears and looked up at her. He did a little skip in the mud before settling in to match the slower pace of his friend Banjo.

As they approached the mess tent, Mattie was surprised to hear the hubbub of a rather large crowd inside. But when they stepped through the opening, she was even more surprised when people at the front began to stand and applaud. The applause swelled as the group of volunteers and local law enforcement officers seemed to spot them standing in the doorway. Soon the entire party had risen in a standing ovation, with folks whistling and shouting Robo's name.

Robo barked and danced with excitement as Mattie became overwhelmed with pride. With a grin, she saluted the crowd and held an open palm toward Robo, giving him all the credit. A successful mission had never felt so good.

# TWENTY-NINE

## Wedding Day

Wearing a fleece robe over new lingerie and a silky cream-colored slip, Mattie sat at the vanity in the master suite at Cole's house. She watched in the mirror while Rainbow arranged her hair in an upswept style that promised to be stunning. Or at least that's the promise Rainbow had made before she started.

Robo was sleeping on Bruno's dog bed in the corner of the room, completely oblivious to the commotion on the lower level of the house as people came and went, helping set up for the wedding that was now only an hour away.

Detective Stella LoSasso stood off to the side with her hands on her hips, as if supervising Rainbow's work. "We have to do something about those scratches on your face, Mattie. And that black eye! Geez. Do you have any concealer?"

Mattie didn't own much makeup. "Are you kidding?"

Stella gave her a smirk as their eyes met in the mirror. "No, I'm not kidding. You look like you fought through the brambles at the base of Rapunzel's tower."

"Actually, that's about what I did."

Rainbow fussed with a last curl. "I bought some new makeup for you since all of mine's too light. Hope I guessed the right shade."

"You didn't have to do that. I'll reimburse you for it."

"Don't worry about it. It's my gift."

"You two already gave me a gift by shopping for my wedding gown." Mattie glanced at the dress hanging in a clear plastic covering from the top of the closet door. "And I love it!"

While Mattie was away, Rainbow and Stella had teamed up, driven to Willow Springs, and bought several dresses, with the understanding that receipts would be kept and returns made after Mattie chose the dress that suited her best. And the choice had been easy when she saw the gown made from flowing, rich golden fabric, cut in a simple yet elegant style that fit like it was made explicitly for her.

"Good thing you'd already told me you didn't want a traditional wedding gown, so I had an idea of what you might want," Rainbow said. "We had so much fun. If you'd been there too, it would've been perfect."

"Oh gosh . . . I hate shopping. You did me a solid, and I'm glad you had fun."

"It was a blast," Stella said in a sarcastic tone.

Rainbow either didn't notice or chose to ignore the sarcasm as she stood back and studied her work. Mattie met Stella's eyes again in the mirror and mouthed "thank you."

Stella shrugged. "Her hair looks great, Rainbow. I think we better get started on the makeup. That'll be a challenge."

Mattie snorted, raising her hand to pat the back of her hair. "Thank you, Stella. That's what every bride wants to hear on her wedding day."

Stella reached for Rainbow's makeup tote, which was the size of a small suitcase, and plopped it on the vanity. "You know what I mean, Mattie. You've got natural beauty and don't need makeup, but you've done a number on your skin this past week. And look at those hands. What're we gonna do with those?"

Mattie spread both hands and inspected the collection of scratches, scabs, and bruises on them.

"Hmm . . . I've got a pair of white gloves at home I could run and go get," Rainbow said.

Mattie could only imagine it, looking like a debutante or a matron. Either way, it wasn't her style. "No gloves," she said firmly.

Stella snorted. "Are you sure? I've got a pair of purple nitrile gloves in my bag."

Mattie giggled, feeling lighter than she'd felt in weeks. "Lovely."

The three talked about makeup as Rainbow applied concealer and powder, trying to cover up the damage to Mattie's face. The conversation stayed light until, like most law enforcement officers that lived their jobs, Stella brought up Mattie's past mission.

"Is Sarge going to make it today?" Stella asked.

"No, but he called this morning. He's still in Seattle at a hotel near the hospital. His femur's been stabilized, but his doctors don't want him to travel for a few more days."

Stella looked sympathetic. "Poor guy. I bet he hates to miss your wedding."

Mattie nodded and suppressed a shudder as she remembered the blood seeping from the wound in Sarge's leg. "He's upset about it, but I told him to behave himself and do what the doctor says. We want him back in this game for the long run. He's also got to recover from the arsenic they found in his system."

"From the lunch that Foster handed him, right?"

"Right. It must've taken sheer willpower for Sarge to go out to search the day after he was so sick. He's one tough cop."

Stella grimaced. "True. And you could've been poisoned too."

Mattie thought back to how the meal that Foster had handed her had disappeared from the table when she'd been tied up helping Rena with Dozer. "Yeah, thank goodness that other volunteer took my meal, though the poor guy's been sick ever since. Foster would've knocked two dog teams out if he'd had his way."

Rainbow made a sound of distress as she gently dabbed concealer around Mattie's black eye.

"So, did Piper get back to you about the identity of those two bodies?" Stella asked.

Mattie used her fingertip to rub concealer over a scab on her cheek. "Yeah, he did. They found dental records that match both sets of teeth and they're waiting for DNA confirmation. One teen, Jimmy Jordan, died about a year ago, probably right before Foster kidnapped Troy. The other boy was about River's age, and he disappeared seven years ago. Arsenic was found in both of their hair samples."

"For the love of Pete," Stella muttered as she handed Rainbow a container of eye shadow.

"Go light on that," Mattie murmured to Rainbow. "I want Cole to be able to recognize me."

"And what about the shack?" Stella asked.

"Washington State Patrol Crime Lab has taken on that investigation. They've got fingerprints, DNA, videos, photos, you name it. They've even got a plastic container with Foster's fingerprints on it that's filled with arsenic-concentrated ash. He isn't going to get out of this one. They'll put him away for the rest of his life."

"Good!" Rainbow said emphatically. "Now, that's enough cop talk. Can we stick to the business at hand?"

A knock sounded at the door before Angela peeked in. "Mattie, your mom, sister, and grandma are here. Can I let them come up?"

Mattie's sister Julia and her family, their mother Ramona, and their *abuela* had driven in from California and were staying at the local motel. Mattie's heart swelled at the thought of her loved ones being here for her wedding. "Sure, Angie. And tell Sophie I'm about to put on my dress. She wanted to be here for that."

"She's *helping*," Angie said, grinning while she used finger quotes, "Mrs. Gibbs put the final touches on the table. I'll send her right up."

"Oh, and Angie . . ." Mattie turned to look at her soon-to-be stepdaughter. She was dressed in a pale blue sheath made of a soft jersey knit that set off her long, blond hair perfectly. "You look beautiful."

Angie blushed and said "Thank you" before ducking out the door.

"Okay, sit still and hold your eyes open," Rainbow said, brandishing a mascara wand. "We're down to a half hour before go time."

Mattie's heart skipped a beat as she swiveled back in her chair to face her friend with her eyes wide open, looking forward to her future.

★ ★ ★

Cole bent his knees to lower himself a few inches for Angie to pin on a boutonniere made with a single red rose, two white carnation buds, and a spray of white baby's breath. It matched Mattie's bouquet of red roses and white carnations that still rested on the top shelf of the refrigerator.

Angie straightened the shoulders of his new charcoal gray suit, cut in a western style, and stepped back to inspect him. "You look really handsome, Dad," she said with a smile that melted his heart.

"Why thank you, sweetheart. It means a lot to hear you say that." He and Angie had weathered a few tussles over the past year, some about Mattie and some about his ex-wife Olivia, but so far they'd always been able to see eye to eye or at least arrive at a compromise that suited them both.

"Yeah, your old dad has cleaned up pretty well," Garrett said, brushing invisible lint from Cole's sleeve. "I'm as happy as a calf in a milk barn, getting to see two of my favorite people in the world get hitched."

Cole grinned, something he couldn't stop doing today. "Me too. And having two of my favorite peeps stand up beside me is extra special." Unable to contain himself, he wrapped his two attendants, Garrett and Angie, in a bear hug.

Garrett pounded his back and Angie wriggled free after returning his hug for a brief second. "Peeps," she muttered, her tone telling Cole that he'd used a word that wasn't exactly in vogue anymore, at least not in her peer group.

"I'd better take Mattie her flowers," Angie said. "I'll be right back and make sure the music's ready."

"I think Ned has the music well in hand," Cole said.

Ned Dempsey, Rainbow's date, had brought his sound system over earlier and had set it up just inside the great room door. He would be in charge of running it, so no one in the family or wedding party needed to worry about it during the ceremony.

"I just want to make sure he has the playlist right," Angie said as she opened the refrigerator to retrieve the bouquet.

"Thanks, Angel," Cole said, truly grateful that his teenager seemed willing to embrace responsibility.

"She *is* an angel," Garrett murmured as Angie left the room.

Despite his happiness, a wave of grief for Garrett's lost daughter Grace swept through Cole, leaving him momentarily blindsided. He supposed his emotions were raw and right on the surface today. A good friend of Angie's, the girl had been murdered a little over a year ago, a tragic event that first brought Mattie and him together. He reached to squeeze his friend's forearm as their eyes met, both of them blinking back tears. "We'll always miss Grace," Cole said.

"Yes indeed," Garrett said quietly. "Especially during the good times."

The doorbell rang, and they both wiped their eyes as Cole said, "I better go see who's here. I'm expecting my parents, and I hope it will go well if I make sure Mom knows she's welcome."

"Anything I can do to help with that, bud?"

Cole smiled his gratitude for the offer. "Maybe keep an eye out and let me know if things start to head south? Be my wing-man if I need to intervene?"

Garrett chuckled softly. "You got it."

Cole made his way into the great room in time to see his dad help his mother remove her coat in the foyer. His dad looked striking in a brown western suit and his mother was beautiful in a royal blue, fitted dress. He strode up to embrace her, noticing the surprised look on her face as he drew her close. "You look gorgeous, Mom," he said softly in her ear before letting her go to step back.

"You look pretty good too," she said. "Cleaner than the last time I saw you."

Cole chuckled as he took her hand and tucked it into the crook of his arm. "Where's Jessie?"

"She's coming," his dad said. "She got a phone call and stayed in the car to take it. She said she'd be just a minute."

Cole's sister, Jessie, had driven from Denver the day before and stayed overnight at the ranch. He'd enlisted her to run interference with his mom in case it was needed.

Just then, the front door opened and Jessie stepped into the foyer, unbuttoning her coat as she came through the doorway. "Cole," she said, her eyebrows rising as their eyes met. "Oh my, you look handsome today."

"And you look as beautiful as always." Cole reached to give his sister a one-armed hug, his mother's hand still tucked in the elbow of his other arm. An attorney who lived in Denver, Jessie looked radiant in a dress the color of emeralds, her highlighted brunette hair in the latest style, gold jewelry at her throat and wrists. His kid sister always looked like she stepped out of a fashion magazine.

He gave his mother's hand a squeeze before releasing it, and then reached for Jessie's coat. "Let me take care of that for you."

His dad took over and escorted his mother into the great room to join the others waiting there while Jessie remained behind with Cole.

"Mom and I had a talk this morning about you being an adult who's old enough to handle your own mistakes," Jessie murmured as Cole hung her coat in the closet. She rolled her eyes. "Sorry, but that's the best I could do. I think she's taking the high ground and will be on her best behavior, though, so . . ."

Cole offered her his arm. "Sounds good. Hope for the best and plan for the worst. Garrett will help keep an eye on things too."

Jessie squeezed his elbow as she took his arm. "It'll all be okay. She loves us, Cole. She just has a hard time showing it."

"I know."

The door opened again, and Chief Deputy Ken Brody peered inside from the porch. "Knock, knock," he said when he saw Cole standing there. "Someone gettin' married here today?"

Cole gestured for him to come in. "You bet. Come in, Ken. Have you met my sister?"

Brody's eyes opened wide as he stared at Jessie, and Cole smiled as Jessie's eyebrows lifted while returning the deputy's gaze. Tall and dark, Ken's broad shoulders stretched the fabric on his suit jacket. He did look like he could catch a woman's eye.

"Pleased to meet you, Ken." Jessie extended her hand for a quick handshake while Ken mumbled something similar in return. Then she took his arm and tucked her hand into the crook at his elbow. "Shall we let Cole see to last minute details while we find a place in the living room?"

Cole couldn't help but chuckle as his sister led Brody away. The deputy looked as though he'd been gobsmacked . . . but in a good way.

★ ★ ★

Mattie paused at the top of the stairs, her gorgeous rose bouquet in hand. Pine bough garland made with red ribbon, bows, and pine cones graced the banister. She drew in a breath, allowing the aroma of pine forest to soothe her nerves. Sophie and Robo were a few treads below her, her special dog on a leash and hovering into a sit as he looked back over his shoulder to find her. "It's okay, Robo," she said in a stage whisper. "Go with Sophie."

Lyrical strains of Pachelbel's *Canon in D* performed by piano and cello wafted up the stairway and conversations hushed in the great room. Now Sophie looked back at Mattie, waiting for her cue. Mattie put up her hand in the stop signal and mouthed "Wait."

They smiled at each other, Sophie's brown eyes twinkling. She wore a forest green velvet dress, her brunette curls tied back with her signature red scarf that her Aunt Jessie had given her. Mattie thought she looked cute as a bug.

After a minute, Mattie gave Sophie a thumb's-up, and the child turned to walk slowly down the stairs, just as they'd practiced. Mattie stepped back to allow Stella and then Rainbow to walk ahead of her, both wearing the dresses of their choice: Stella's russet, which set off her auburn hair, and Rainbow's pale pink, giving her ivory skin a lustrous quality.

Ned Dempsey peeked around the archway from the great room, and his eyes opened wide as he apparently caught sight of Rainbow. Then he broke into a huge grin as the two appeared to be eyeing each other, making Mattie even more joyful than she'd been before. Ned was a great guy, and it pleased her that he made Rainbow happy.

Gold rings tied with red ribbon glinted at Robo's collar when he bobbed down the stairway at Sophie's heel. The two of them kept a slow pace while they crossed under the archway that led to the great room, where someone had hung mistletoe earlier. *Perfect*, Mattie thought, catching sight of it for the first time.

Stella and Rainbow entered before her, and then it was her turn. Never having been a fan of being in the spotlight, Mattie drew another steadying breath before crossing under the mistletoe. But she saw nothing but love and friendship on the faces of the people who awaited her in the great room.

She quickly sought out Cole, standing at the fireplace with Angela and Garrett. He was so handsome he snatched her breath away. His eyes set on hers, Cole conveyed messages of love and support; his smile told her his happiness matched her own. When she reached him, she handed her bouquet to Stella and then took his outstretched hand. He squeezed hers with a pressure that she returned, sending her own feelings of devotion and love through her touch and her gaze.

Sophie nestled in beside Angela, the older sister placing an arm around her, while Stella and Rainbow stood beside Mattie. Robo tugged at his leash as if wanting to come to Mattie, but she gave him a hand gesture to stay and then sit with Sophie so Angela could untie the rings that he carried. He sat, but his eyes never left her, as if hoping for a gesture to come.

As soon as the music stopped, Sheriff Abraham McCoy stepped up to join them, leaving his pretty wife to stand beside Garrett's wife, Leslie. Ned edged in close behind them.

Sheriff McCoy raised his hand in greeting to the group of wedding guests. "Welcome, everyone," he said in his deep baritone voice. "Today we gather to witness the marriage of two people we love and respect. You who are their family and their best friends will have the pleasure and the responsibility of supporting them as they venture into the next chapter of their lives together. This ceremony won't take long, so please stand and form a circle to show our love and fellowship with not only them but also with one another."

As everyone shuffled into position, Mattie took a moment to take in her guests, giving them a welcoming smile that she hoped wouldn't start to tremble. There was her grandmother, her mother, her sister Julia and her husband, and Julia's two sons, all beaming and happy. Cole's parents, Samuel and Nora. Samuel grinned and winked at her while Nora looked as if she might be in pain. Mattie hoped her soon-to-be mother-in-law was all right and wasn't getting sick.

Cole's sister, Jessie, gave her a radiant smile. And Brody, who was standing close to Jessie, gave her a sheepish sort of grin— Mattie wasn't sure why. What was he up to?

And there was her foster mother, Mama T, standing beside Mrs. Gibbs. The two women had linked arms and stood close together as if they couldn't contain their excitement, almost bringing Mattie to tears. These two women would always be mother figures to her . . . she wouldn't have survived without her Mama T, and she knew she could count on both of them, no matter what.

Off to the side, Belle and Bruno sat on their dog beds, and even as Mattie's gaze passed over them, Belle opened her lips in a wide yawn and settled down as if to nap. Bruno's sculpted ears pricked forward and he sat at attention, watching both Mattie and Cole as if expecting direction from one of them. Evidently Cole noticed too, because he gave Bruno a gesture to lie down, which he did immediately, although he kept his eyes pinned on Cole.

"Mattie and Cole, it's an honor to stand before you today to officiate your wedding. I'm usually a man of few words, but I want to tell you how much you both mean to me." The sheriff looked at Mattie. "I met Mattie when she was six years old, and I kept an eye on her as she grew up in this town."

Mattie was filled with emotion at all that had passed between them. As a young deputy, McCoy rescued her from an abusive relationship and later made sure she was placed in Mama T's foster home. He'd hired her to work for him at the sheriff's office and given her a chance to be Robo's handler.

McCoy continued. "We all know Mattie was a high school track star, and now she and Robo are known as superstars, not only in our community but in the whole western region of the United States. Mattie, we all respect you, we love you, and we're happier for you than words can express."

Mattie was glad when his gaze shifted to Cole, because his words were beginning to choke her up.

"And Cole. You also grew up in this town, not too many years behind me in school. We loved watching you on the football field during high school, and then we were excited to know you were headed off to vet school. We hoped you'd come back to fill the empty space for a veterinarian in our community, and you did. Not only that, but in spite of your busy practice, you've also served on the sheriff's posse to help keep this community safe. You're a man I respect and trust." McCoy paused and smiled. "And rest assured, we all love you too."

This brought a quiet chuckle from the audience.

"Now Mattie and Cole wish to exchange their vows and their rings. The wedding ring is a symbol of eternal love and commitment. But I'd like for all of you in this circle today to think of these rings also as our commitment to Mattie and Cole: to support them as they go forward with Angela and Sophie to form a family unit, and to support them as they do their good works in this community. Cole, please pledge your vow to Mattie as you give her this symbol of your love."

Cole took the ring that Angela handed him and turned to face Mattie, taking her left hand in his. "Mattie . . ." He paused, and through his gaze, she sensed how much he cherished her. "We've known each other over a year now, but we've been through more than most people go through in a lifetime. Every challenge along the way has shown me how much I admire and respect you, and my love for you has grown exponentially each month. I promise to be your loving and faithful husband and to stand beside you in good times and bad. I promise to share my life with you and give you all the support you need to achieve your goals and your dreams. I promise to listen to you and . . ."—he paused again to give her that quirky half-smile of his that she adored—". . . to give you space when you need it."

She suppressed a chuckle. He knew her so well.

Cole slipped her wedding band on her finger. "With this ring, I thee wed."

She'd seen the ring before. Even though she'd originally thought she wanted a plain gold band, Cole had insisted on one with a filigree pattern and several small diamonds, inset so they wouldn't get damaged in her line of work. She loved it. She twisted it around her finger, savoring the feel of it.

"Mattie, now it's your turn to pledge your vow to Cole and give him his ring," McCoy said.

Mattie's fingers trembled slightly as she took the ring from Angie. Angie grasped her hand for a brief moment, giving it a squeeze as their eyes met. The teen's smile was tremulous and her eyes brimmed with unshed tears. Mattie's heart swelled with love for this young woman whom she would soon be able to claim as her stepdaughter. She returned the squeeze and smile before turning back to take Cole's left hand.

"Cole," she said, clinging to his hand for support. "I've grown to trust you as well as love you this past year, and for me that's saying a lot. You've made me happy by offering to share your life, home, and family with me. You know I love your children as much as if they were my own flesh and blood, and I'm thrilled to become a part of the Walker family. I promise to be your loving and faithful wife and to stand beside you in good times and bad. I promise to protect you and our children to the best of my ability. And I promise to do my best to help you provide for and guide Angela and Sophie as they grow and make their own paths in the world. And . . ." She tried to show how much she cherished him also as she gazed into the depths of his brown eyes. "I'll try to always listen to you too, even when I don't agree with you."

She squeezed his hands and chuckled with the others, Cole included.

She placed the plain gold band on his finger. "With this ring, I thee wed."

McCoy's voice was full of joy. "With the power vested in me by the state of Colorado, I proclaim you wife and husband. Cole, you may kiss your bride."

At last Mattie was able to step into Cole's embrace, and their kiss was a promise of what was yet to come. Feeling shaky as she stepped back, she was immediately drawn into the arms of Stella and Rainbow while Cole shook hands with Garrett and hugged his two daughters. There were hugs all around the room and chatter enough to spur Belle and Bruno from their dog cushions. They joined Robo in the melee, circling everyone's legs, releasing a yip and a whine in celebration.

Cole's dad Samuel almost lifted Mattie off her feet as he gave her a tight hug. When he released her, he stepped back but continued to grasp her upper arms in his strong hands. "Welcome to our family, Mattie. I couldn't be more pleased to gain you as a daughter."

His words touched her and she smiled up at him, blinking to contain her happy tears, feeling grateful to have this kind man take the place of a father she'd never known. She glanced at Nora, who was hanging back behind her husband, as if hesitant to echo his sentiments. An awkward moment passed with Mattie not knowing what to do. Should she give her new mother-in-law a hug? Nora didn't look as if she wanted one.

Coming from behind Mattie, Angie moved in to stand beside her. The teen slipped an arm around Mattie's waist as she reached to squeeze her grandfather's outstretched hand. Then she released it quickly to give her grandmother a hug.

"Sophie and I are so happy you could come today, Grandma," Angie said. "It's great to have you and Grandpa help us welcome Mattie into the family. We'll have you over for dinner after Dad and Mattie get back from their honeymoon."

Suddenly, Cole was beside Mattie too, his arm encircling her shoulders. She glanced up at his face in time to catch the proud look he gave Angie. Sophie skipped up and nudged her way into the group.

"Mattie!" Sophie's brown eyes sparkled as she giggled. "That was so much fun!"

Mattie drew Sophie into her arms for a quick hug before the child turned around to hug her grandparents. Nora's face had filled with pleasure during the exchange with her granddaughters, and now she reached forward to squeeze Mattie's forearm.

"Welcome to the family, Mattie," Nora said, a thin smile softening her rather stern expression. "I appreciate you including the girls in your wedding vows."

Happiness consumed Mattie as she took Nora's hand in hers and squeezed her fingers. "I fell in love with the girls even before Cole. They mean the world to me."

"And it's apparent they return your fondness," Nora said.

Mattie felt herself flush as she glanced up at Cole. "And you raised such a great guy here, I couldn't help but fall in love with him too. He's a wonderful dad."

Embarrassed at having spilled out her feelings so blatantly, Mattie stopped talking and avoided eye contact with the others.

But Nora must have approved of her words, because she continued to clasp Mattie's hand and returned her finger squeeze. "I look forward to getting to know you better."

Mattie raised her eyes to meet her mother-in-law's gaze. "I look forward to that too. We'll be gone for only a few days, so we'll be in touch soon to schedule dinner." She tucked Nora's hand into the crook of her elbow. "Have you met my family from California yet? Let me introduce you to them."

# Acknowledgments

I want to express my heartfelt thanks to all who've supported this series and helped spread the word about each book, including readers, librarians, other writers, book reviewers and bloggers, and podcast and radio hosts.

I owe a hearty thank you to those who helped me with professional content in this book: Kathleen Donnelly, K-9 handler, co-owner of Sherlock Hounds, and author of the National Forest K-9 series; Charles Mizushima, DVM, retired; Anthony Corona and his guide dog Boaty; Cheryl McNeil Fisher and her retired golden retriever Sanka, who was the inspiration for Sammy the guide dog in her children's books; the Central Lakes Search and Rescue Unit; and friends and law enforcement officers who contributed information about terrain and procedures. Any inaccuracies or fictional enhancements of this content are mine alone.

Huge thanks to my publishing team: my agent, Terrie Wolf of AKA Literary Management; publisher Matthew Martz and the team at Crooked Lane Books, including Rebecca Nelson, Dulce Botello, Thaisheemarie Fatauzzi Perez, and Mikaela Bender; my editor, Martin Biro; my publicist, Maryglenn McCombs; and Madeline Rathle. It's been such a pleasure to work with these wonderful professionals.

Sincere appreciation goes to Scott Graham, author of the National Parks Mysteries; author Kathleen Donnelly; and to Bill Hazard for assistance with early drafts.

Hugs, love, and gratitude go to friends and family who've supported me throughout the years. It means the world to me. And unlike Mattie and Robo, we've encountered only friendly folks in our new neighborhood on the Olympic Peninsula.

Special thanks go to our new neighbors for their welcoming friendship, and to Sue Ohlson and Bill Curtsinger, owners of Sunrise CoffeeHouse, for hosting my very first author talk in the state of Washington.

And to my husband, Charlie; daughters, Sarah and Beth; and son-in-law, Adam: sending my love and deep gratitude for always being there.